ANOTHER

YEAR

WITH

UNDER

FIVES

Chris Sturgess

This is a work of fiction. Names and characters are the product of the author's imagination and any resemblance to actual persons, living or dead, is entirely coincidental.

The views expressed in this work are solely those of the author and do not necessarily reflect the views of the publisher, and the publisher hereby disclaims any responsibility for them.

ISBN: 9798651424450

PublishNation
www.publishnation.co.uk

Synopsis

Wendy is an older lady who works in a nursery school and when she started many years ago the emphasis was on fun and learning. She feels now that much of the fun has been taken away and the environment is now full of rules and regulations, not all of which she agrees with. So she grumbles and moans about them and she can't always keep her opinions to herself. She is often sarcastic and can be caustic at times but witty and warm too. Even if her working world was perfect with rosy cheeked, keen, polite children, she would still find something or someone to comment about.

As the year continues the reader gets to know the staff and children from Wendy's point of view, which is not always complimentary. There are the fun times and the ordinary times, although nothing is ever really ordinary when working with children. Working to a deadline can be stressful in any job; with children it is stressful plus unpredictable. Every day is different, taxing, diverse, exasperating and also fulfilling. But she has to let off steam somehow and Wendy's way is to say it as she sees it.

We meet Tanya, the highly qualified, straight out of college new member of staff. We have Brandon who joins the group doing his community service and also the unforgettable Fiona, the student from the local school doing some work experience.

We get a wonderful insight into the happenings at nursery school; the busy times and the special times; the visitors and the festive occasions; the madness of the carnival and the climax of Christmas.

The parents see a finished article, a painting or a card little realizing just what goes on behind the scenes. Have you ever wondered what goes on in the little under fives world? Here is a small insight to that world.

There is a lot of love and happiness in the whole nursery school and with Wendy too. She tries to hide it but it peeks through.

Author's Note

The views stated are 'Wendy's' views and not necessarily lawful or correct in their content.

All of the characters in this book are entirely fictional, even though some of them are loosely influenced by past colleagues. The author wishes to thank those wonderful people with whom she has worked over the years—you know who you are!

Chapter One

Tuesday 4th January

Why am I doing this? Why am I talking with myself in front of the hall mirror at eight-thirty on a cold and miserable January morning? I'm combing my hair and I'm talking to myself about the wisdom of what I'm about to do. I'm in my forties, my son is at senior school and my husband is at work and I could be having a lie-in, in my warm, cosy bed!

As it is, I've been rushing around filling a lunch-box for myself and my son, making the beds, sweeping the kitchen floor, taking the dog for a walk in the park, putting a load of washing into the machine and getting ready to go to nursery school again. Why? Yes why, that is another good question. Why do I do this to myself? At the end of last year and the year before that, I remember saying to all the staff in the school-room, "I won't be back. Wild horses won't drag me back, I've had enough. When the term finishes, so do I!" And yet here I am getting ready to face it all again. I really don't know how it happened. A persuasive phone conversation from the lady that runs the group and here I am getting ready to go to nursery school, again.

It took me many, many years to get around to having a child of my own and I love my son dearly, but I'm not really that keen on other people's children. Some women are overwhelmed with the 'motherly gene', but I don't seem to be. So why I do a job in which I look after other people's children is beyond me at times. Thank goodness I negotiated to only work there for two days a week this year.

Where's my scarf?

Maybe, as someone mentioned in the past, I must enjoy it. Enjoy it? You must be joking. My own son left nursery school ten years ago and I'm still there. It's not right. The other staff say I can't leave, they need me. It is fair to say they need someone to make up the required numbers, but why me? Honestly, why do they need *me*? I'm usually late; I moan; I grumble; I whinge on if things go wrong. I can't draw; I can't sing; I exaggerate if it helps my cause; I agree to things just to keep the peace—well, no, that's not really true, I agree to some things just to keep the peace and I have been known to fib sometimes, when I think it's necessary.

I don't have any original ideas, either, regarding... well, regarding anything really, and I know next to nothing about the running of the place. You would think that after twelve or so years I would know everything inside out, but no, I just about get my head round the rules and a new set are introduced, so now I just get on with things. If I see something needs doing, I do it, and if it's wrong, well, it's wrong.

Do I need my mackintosh or will my jacket do? I'll look out the window and see what the weather's up to. It was fine when I walked the dog earlier. Just my jacket will do.

There's a large group of people out there who like to make our lives awkward, as if childcare were not tough enough. Officials anywhere seem to be able to tell us what to do. I call them 'The Powers That Be', and that title covers just about anybody, including the bureaucrat sitting in an office, who has probably never had children, but is writing rules for us to abide by. Then there are the social services, the police, the local authorities, the local council, the government, the fire inspector, the nit nurse (or, should I say, the 'health visitor'), the insurance company, the road safety officer, and even the scout master, Ken, in charge of the hall which houses our nursery school. Ken likes to make himself look important by leaving us little notes telling us not to use his chairs or open his cupboards. Well Ken, if only you knew what we do when you're not around. They all know a great deal more about looking after children than we do, or so they would want us to believe, and they spend most of their time creating conflicting rules, regulations, procedures and requirements for us to try to make sense of.

Mind you, there's one rule that is broken day after day. The 'Don't Cuddle the Children' rule. Honestly, how can you see a little one crying and not want to give them a make-it-better hug. If cuddling an unhappy child makes me unsuitable, then I'm unsuitable. We're all parents ourselves at this nursery school and we have all been police-checked and if a cuddle is a criminal offence, then I'm guilty. I'm probably admitting too much here. Maybe I'll get the sack. Hmm, there's a thought.

Why aren't my gloves in my jacket pocket?

Oh well, at least it isn't raining, I'd better be off to school.

Where are my car keys?

I'm going to be late, again.

Our nursery school is about two miles away from my home and is in a building which we share with the local Scout group. As you go through the main entrance, you enter a corridor. At one end of the corridor, on the right, there are toilets and some storage rooms. When you turn left, you pass the kitchen door, and past the kitchen is the large main hall.

As you enter the main hall there's a serving hatch through to the kitchen on one side of the door and a large walk in cupboard on the other side. On the opposite wall is a huge picture window which looks out over a park and our enclosed garden area which we use when the weather is fine.

The main hall itself is light and spacious and there's even a basketball court painted on the floor, which the scouts must use.

When I arrive, only a few minutes late, the staff members are busy talking with some parents who are milling about. There are children old and new to our nursery school, some going off to play together, others clinging to mum. I throw off my coat and call out a cheery good morning to everyone.

The first day of term is always difficult with new mums hanging about, not sure whether they can leave 'little Johnny' or not, and other mums who just can't wait to get out of the door and have some free time at last. There are always new faces, new rules and new situations to deal with and, as I sign myself in the register, I can see that there are fourteen of our children from last year and eleven new ones.

I expect we will be spending most of the day repeating ourselves, saying again and again, "Say please" and "Say thank you", as we try to establish our way of doing things right from the start. We will be explaining why climbing on tables is not allowed and why we don't tolerate kicking or screeching or anything of that ilk. "Don't run" is another phrase that will be overworked in the first few days. There's bound to be at least one pair of wet knickers. Accidents do happen, so we will explain about asking to go to the toilet and how we would rather they ask us than have a little accident. We will also reassure them that we do have lots of nice spare clothes in our cupboard, so if a little accident does happen it won't matter too much.

We won't expect to get much work done today as we will have to have eyes in the back of our heads to be able to watch all that is going on, especially with the new children. I see that there is a table laid out with paper and crayons, so I make my way over there and sit down. I'm soon joined by some children and we introduce ourselves. They are happy to scribble away and I chat to them and doodle as I keep glancing around the room.

"Don't do that, I'll get you a tissue," I say, disapprovingly, as I jump up and head for the box of tissues. Why must children pick their noses? A quick wipe and that job's done, but I don't suppose it will be the only time I need to do that today.

The entire day seems to be filled with: "Say please", "Don't throw that", "Try saying please", "Don't run", "Can you remember to say thank you?", "Please try to sit still", "What is the magic word that makes things happen? Yes, it's please. Please try to remember. Please, please, please, please."

Another one of our other over used phrases is, "Look where you're going." Have you ever noticed how often children move in a forward direction, whether they're walking, driving or pushing something, and they're looking behind them!? The opportunity for accidents is great and we have to be in 'vigilant mode' all the time. It can be tedious and draining to constantly repeat ourselves, but hopefully the children will learn our ways quickly and then we will all benefit.

No time for much chit-chat or gossip with the rest of the staff because it is go, go, go. We are constantly looking around the room, jumping up from our chairs to attend to something and rushing here and there.

A few sniffles, a lot of runny noses, some spills, some minor breakages. Endless reminders to keep the noise down, sit still, don't run, say please, and say thank you. But don't be put off, it is a nursery school and, on the whole, a happy one.

The day has flown by in a continuing effort to keep order and at last it's time to welcome the parents who are here to collect their children. They have questions to ask, which we try to answer, and then it is with great relief that we can say our goodbyes, smile and wave as they leave.

I thought it would be a tough day and it was; still never mind, I'll soon be home. Home, that lovely, quiet place where I can have a cup of tea and a sit down, just what I need.

Thursday 6th January

Is it really Thursday today? That came round quickly! I notice there's quite a heavy frost outside when I pick the milk bottles off the front step, so I must remember to allow a few extra minutes to scrape the frost from the car windscreen. I think I'll just pop back upstairs and put on a thicker jumper.

I see my dog, Leo, has snuggled up on the bed and as I get closer to him his ears drop down. He has a beseeching look on his face as if to say, "Please don't lift me off the bed!" Okay, boy, you can stay there, I really don't have time to argue with you this morning.

The roads are slippery and everyone has to drive more slowly than usual, that's my excuse for being a bit late today. Hillary likes us to be in the hall and ready five minutes before the children come in at nine o'clock. I do my best but it is always a rush and a struggle. Once in the hall, Hillary asks me to be in charge of the register this morning, then to go and join Nicky at the colouring table.

All parents are supposed to enter their child's name in the register, along with the time the child is being collected and by whom. Simple, same as last year, I can cope with that. Obviously the old mums and dads know this routine, but I'll have to remember to explain it to any new parents I see. I'm asked a few questions about fees and other things and, as I don't commit myself to anything if I can help it, I direct all enquiries to our boss, Hillary.

I haven't introduced us yet, have I? We were so busy on Tuesday that I forgot. I'm Wendy. Aunty Wendy. We're all 'aunties' here as we feel it's friendlier for the children. Our boss is Aunty Hillary, a lady well known and highly respected in the town, as she has run private nursery schools here for thirty-odd years. She has even taught two generations of some of the local families! She's a slim lady with boundless energy and sense of fun, with a huge amount of the motherly gene and she also has an uncanny knack of getting the most out of children and adults alike.

Aunty Nicky is here today, a fairly new and valued addition to our staff. She dresses very fashionably and always wears make up and her hair is always neat and tidy. She is very much younger than the rest of us, at only twenty-one. She tolerates us 'slightly' older ladies very well. We often tease her for being 'the baby' but she just laughs it off.

I see Ro is also here, Aunty Rosemary, usually called Ro; she's a warm and friendly lady who has endless sympathy and compassion, and she's always taking extra courses to improve herself. Then there's Aunty Liz, a tall and elegant lady with lovely, large eyes and a wonderful complexion. She helps with the paperwork and the running of the group. Liz, like me, prefers quiet, tidy, clean children and as there are not many of those we often find we have a lot to moan about together.

There are eight or nine of us aunties altogether and we all rub along nicely. We work on different days and have known each other for a long time. They are all dedicated and caring with a vocation to childcare and, believe me, you do have to be someone really special to work day after day looking after twenty or more under five year olds.

And then there's me. I volunteered as a helper when my son was here and any extra pair of hands and eyes were appreciated. He is now sixteen and, as you can see, I'm still here.

I don't necessarily agree with the way we have to do things with all the rules and regulations, especially as they keep changing, so I find I'm often doing what comes naturally as opposed to what I'm supposed to be doing. I tend to go with common sense not dictates and luckily most of us are of the same mind. We're a happy bunch who get on well together and usually see the funny side of things. The one thing we all have in common is that the safety of the children is paramount. Even with my moaning and grumbling, I do love the children… well, most of them… well, the well-behaved ones… on good days.

Now, have all the staff signed in? Yes, except me. I'll sign in now, last as usual. I count heads and count names in the register, everyone is here and accounted for. I see Nicky has the crayons out ready at the colouring table and is looking at the sample of work we are going to be doing. It looks like we're colouring cats today, they shouldn't be too hard. I quickly name every piece of work using the register and now we can begin. Twenty-five names on worksheets, twenty-five children in the room, so far so good. Nicky and I usually sit with a child on either side of us so we are able to help them if necessary. Time for me to find the first four children and get started. The first four on the register today are Louise, Paul, Gemma, and Mavis. Mavis?

"Hey Nicky, we haven't had a Mavis before, do you know which child she is?"

"No, no I don't," she answers thoughtfully.

"I'll go and check in the book," I say.

Yes, there's usually one! The tired, frazzled mum who puts her own name in the register instead of her child's. She has too much to do and not enough time, and her mind is occupied with other things. I know how she feels. I've been known to post the shopping list and then have to struggle round the supermarket with nothing but an stamped addressed envelope in my hand. Yes, I understand you, Mavis. I'll have to have a quick word with you at lunchtime and in the meantime I'll just ask Hillary whose mum Mavis is. She tells me Jodie is the child's name and points her out to me. She's a pretty little girl with a long, blond hair tied into a pony-tail.

"Come and sit next to me, Sweetie. " I say to her and quickly alter the name on the paper and we begin the day's work.

Some people from The Powers That Be have sent us guidelines over the years about colouring. Some years we are to tell the children that cats, for example, are black, brown, tabby/orange, or a combination of those colours. Another year we're told to let the child use his or her imagination and that there is nothing wrong with green cats or purple cats.

Nicky asked me what we're supposed to be doing this term. I think she only asked as I'm the older of the two of us. I'm sure she's been here long enough to know I wouldn't actually know the answer! I forgot to ask Hillary what the guideline is for this year and, as she's now busy on the phone, I make a brave decision: I suggest we let the children do any colour they want.

I've probably made the wrong decision and once upon a time it would have worried me, but I can honestly say I won't be losing any sleep over it tonight.

We soon have cats of every colour and even a few rainbow ones as well and as they look so nice we tape them onto the walls for all to see.

Time for lunch already. Given the constant interruptions for trips to the loo, minor ownership disputes, finding tissues, milk-time, doing up shoes, and the odd cuddle, I think we've done quite well to finish all the work, especially considering we have so many new young ones to help.

We must get all the children to go to the toilet and wash their hands before we sit them down for lunch. That's an eye-opening experience, the trip to the loo. Over the years I have heard: "What's this tissue for?" "Why must we wash our hands?" "We don't have to wash our hands at nanny's house." "I need a poo."

All this just before we eat, it's no wonder we aunties don't eat too much.

Ten minutes to go until some of the morning children leave and the afternoon children arrive with their lunchboxes. Panic stations! Lots to do.

We like all the children who are going home to be seated and fairly quiet. Their cat pictures are taken off the walls and given to them along with cardigans, jumpers, sweatshirts, toys, cars, dolls, abandoned hair clips and all the other items that they deemed essential to bring with them but have completely forgotten about. At least one aunty is designated the job of keeping an eye on them at this time.

At the same time the morning children who are also staying for the afternoon session have to be seated at the tables at the other end of the room. An aunty or two is there to keep an eye on them and to help them with unpacking their lunchboxes and removing any film or foil and opening drinks flasks.

If all is as it should be we can open the doors and let in the parents. "Don't run" echoes round the room. Pandemonium for five minutes as excited children leave and more arrive. Luckily there are only a few extra children for the afternoon session today and they're quickly seated and their lunchboxes unpacked.

Lunch is a major event. The sights you see in the first few days! Horrendous! Things do improve slowly, but it is an uphill struggle. We try to encourage an eating order, i.e. sandwiches first, followed by crisps, then maybe their yoghurt or fruit, and lastly any chocolate or biscuit that has been included. Well, needless to say, the children want to eat their chocolate first. So a little discussion is tried, a lot of persuasion, and sometimes, in desperation, a little bribery or even confiscation until at least one sandwich has disappeared.

Some children prefer to play with their food rather than eat it and, to be fair, given the state of some of the offerings, I sometimes agree with them. To try to make sandwiches seem a little more appealing, we have been known to cut them into soldiers or teddy-bear shapes using a pastry-cutter kept just for that purpose.

We have seen sandwiches dunked in yoghurt. Sandwiches 'crumbed' so that the whole area around the plate looks like a winter snow scene. Also, crisps must taste better after a visit to the floor if the majority of children are to be believed. Even trying to get some of the children to sit still is an achievement, but we battle on because we're of the old school who happen to think table manners matter.

Those of us aunties who try to eat lunch risk chronic indigestion with all the getting up and sitting back down involved. Trying to stop little Johnny from stuffing a whole doughnut in his mouth, or seeing how far he can flick a bit of squashed sandwich, or threading Hula Hoops onto a girl's plaits, or balancing as much food as possible on his plate, or trying to drink from a cup without using his hands. All of this has to be attended to and explanations given.

Playing with food is not allowed and we try our best to discourage it, but at this point, I must admit to having used a banana as a telephone to try to defuse an awkward situations with humour. Pretending there is a person on the other end of the banana and talking about naughty table habits sometimes draws the children's attention away from what they're doing and can perhaps make them do what we want them to do instead. I see nothing wrong with that; let's face it, children must learn that this is a contradictory old world and sometimes it's a case of, 'do as we say, not as we do'.

As I look around the lunch tables today, I notice Jodie's not there, she's gone home. Bother! I forgot to have that word with Mavis; I'll try to remember to do it on Tuesday when I'm next in.

When everyone has finished eating we pack away all the lunchboxes and clear the tables. Cups and plates are put in the kitchen through the serving hatch, tables are wiped and re-positioned ready for the afternoon session. Usually one of us has a quick whiz round with the broom to pick up crumbs and rubbish, whilst another of us offers to wash up the dishes in the kitchen. The kitchen is sometimes referred to as 'the refuge' and used as a bolt hole whenever possible, especially by me.

The afternoon begins much as the morning did, with the register being checked to see all have signed in, and the outer doors double-checked to make sure they are locked, and then we start all over again. The afternoon children colour their cats and those morning children that are still here can just play and enjoy themselves. In one way it's a little more relaxed in the afternoons as there are not usually so many children, but in another way it's harder as we have to tidy away everything into the store cupboard and leave the hall clear for whoever is using it in the evening.

I'm pleased to say it's not too long before I notice a discreet clearing away of some toys and the unused tables being pushed quietly to the side of the room. Not long to go now, I think to myself.

We usually have one aunty entertain the children for the last ten minutes whilst the others of us rush about frantically clearing toys away. This entertainment can be singing, or a story, or a puppet show and it's intended to quieten the children and to get them used to sitting still. Ro is doing it today and is singing with them. She has one child on her lap, and the others are not too badly behaved considering this is still very new for some of them. I look at the clock and see it's just a few minutes to three, so I tap Ro on the shoulder to alert her and we hastily hand out the cat pictures.

So let's allow the mums in and let the children go home.

Now to quickly stack the chairs, sweep the floor, check the windows are closed and turn off the lights. At last, it's time for us to go home too.

Tuesday 11th January

Here we are again, the second week into the term. I'm a bit late again and, by the time I've removed my coat, spent a penny and done my hair, all the tables are set out and ready. Hillary asks me to work with Nicky again and I see we are going to colour a mother pig with some piglets today. The new children should be able to cope with this quite easy piece of work. We try to concentrate on getting the children to hold the crayons properly; it's amazing just how many can't. Most learn quickly enough once shown and the majority are keen to produce something nice to take home. There's still a lot of, "Don't do this" and "Don't do that", and I comment to Nicky that we sound just like Joyce Grenfell.

"Who's Joyce Grenfell?" she asks politely.

Who is Joyce Grenfell! What *does* she mean!? Everyone was bought up listening to her. Hearing excerpts from her books and records on the radio. I explain this to Nicky and I can see she hasn't a clue what I'm talking about. I try to recall one or two of Joyce Grenfell's stories and say to Nicky. "Joyce Grenfell had a slightly higher pitched voice than most and spoke with clear old fashioned BBC diction. Some of her sketches were about an imaginary school class and her one sided conversation with the children. One of them went something like this. 'We have a visitor this morning, Isn't that nice? Yes it is nice Sydney. Now what do we say to our visitor? Yes, that's right we all say hello. No Peggy she isn't wearing a funny hat its her hair. We have vivid imaginations today don't we? Don't do that George. Sydney take that paint brush out of you ear. George! Don't do that again.' And so the monologue would go on." I finish

"Was she old then?" continues Nicky.

Old! Old! Of course she's not old. Hold on. Listen to yourself, you're about to say she's not old, when in fact, she was old when you were young. She must be ancient! Oh my, where did those years go? I think I'll change the subject.

"How long is it till your wedding Nicky?"

"Only a few months now, we're getting married on the 3rd of April. I hope you can all come as I am going to invite you all," she answers happily.

"Thank you. Oh! How lovely. Where are you getting married?"

"At the old church at Lyminster."

"Ah, that's a lovely church." I say. "We had a family wedding there a year or two back and it was so nice."

"Yes, I agree," she says wistfully. "My Rob's parents were married there and when he took me to see it I couldn't believe how pretty it was. And afterwards we're going to the local pub in Lyminster for the reception. We can't afford a honeymoon, but hopefully we will have a holiday later in the year."

"I'll just go and make a note of that wedding date in my diary before I forget." I say.

We don't get much more chance to chatter on as we're asked to get ready for milk and biscuits, and of course tea or coffee for us aunties. We arrange the chairs in a horse-shoe shape for the children with our chairs across the gap. We choose a child, one who's been well-behaved and sitting still, to take round the biscuit tin. Taking round the biscuit tin is a prestigious and much sought-after job and as the term goes by you can see the eagerness in the children's faces, hoping to be picked to perform this task.

Most children cannot eat their biscuit until it's been waved at a friend or two, usually resulting in some biscuits being dropped on the floor. We have to be quick off our chairs to retrieve the biscuit, put it in the rubbish bin and explain that once it's been on the floor it cannot be eaten, and that they can have another one this time but they must be more careful in future.

Next, we choose another child to hand out the cold drinks. A child who has sat relatively still for the duration of eating their biscuit and managed not to drop it on the floor. Do we ask too much, I think to myself. At the beginning of each term we ask an older child to perform these tasks, so that the new youngsters will learn by watching. If the chosen child is showing off and a little exuberant in this task, then we sometimes get the odd splash of milk landing in someone's lap. Sometimes if the seated child is quiet, or shy, or not concentrating, we may even get the whole cupful on the floor, then the mop and bucket makes an appearance. And then we have some to explaining to do. Reminding the milk monitor to make sure the recipient has the cup before they let go of it

We are constantly watching and ready to act but this should be a relatively quiet time and we adults try to enjoy a cup of tea and a quick chat. It's also a time for a birthday to be shared with the group and then we all sing and make a fuss of the birthday person. Sometimes a kindly mum will send in fancy biscuits or fairy cakes. While this is very nice, it can cause so much trouble. If a mum sends in twenty cakes and we have twenty-three children that day... need I say more? Although, I will just say at this point, treats for the aunties are always most welcome!

Sitting here in the relative peace with my cup of tea, I've just had a thought: is Joyce Grenfell still alive?

When we're all finished I offer to wash up and rush into the kitchen before anyone else can, and in the quiet of the kitchen, I try to remember when I did actually hear anything about Joyce. I know it was a long time ago. Well, it doesn't really matter as I won't be bringing her name up in conversation again, as it's obviously too easy to give away one's age without realising it. I must try to think before speaking. How can I find out about her? It's niggling me now. I know, I'll call into the library on the way home.

Later that afternoon, I did just that and found that she had died quiet a few years ago in 1979, but I picked up one of her books, which will be a nice trip down memory lane for me later this evening.

Thursday 13th January

It's the thirteenth today. If I were superstitious I would see that as an excuse to spend all day in bed, out of harm's way. The warmth, the comfort, the quiet... ah, If only!

I arrive at school and have to remove my hat, coat, scarf and gloves before I can go for a much needed visit to the ladies'. Even after all that delay I still get in before Nicky, young, pretty Nicky. Am I jealous? Yes, probably.

I'm told she won't be in at all today, as she's down with a bad cold. I'm sorry to hear that but I expect she's tucked up in a warm and cosy bed, lucky thing.

That reminds me, when I first started here, if a child had a cold or something similar, we were able to administer cough medicine to the child, if the parent requested it. No problem, we're all mums and have done the same for our own children many times. But no, new regulations were introduced and that had to stop. The parent now has to come in and give the medicine themselves. No matter that they may be at work, or busy, or unavailable. We're not allowed to help. We, as the people who do this job, consider childcare to be a caring job, but with rules like that you do wonder at times. What the rule will be this term I haven't a clue, but I expect I'll be told if it's been changed again.

Back to today, who have we got here then? Julie. I can work well with her. She and I are more or less the same age. I know this for sure, as her sons have all finished university and she can't have sons that age and still be twenty-one!

"Hi, Julie, nice to see you, did you have a nice holiday?" I call across to her.

"Yes thanks." She answers quickly and I make my way over to Hillary to see what she wants me to do today.

"Hello, Wendy," says Hillary. "Can you be a general overseer today, please. No specific duties, just help out with playing, drawing, or whatever is needed. Ro has a problem with the toddler group and she and I need to sit together for a while to sort that out. Maybe help Julie with the painting if she needs it. I think we may need two on painting till the new ones get used to it. Is that okay with you?"

"Yes, that's fine." I reply. I turn and look at Julie, "Do you want me now?"

"No, maybe later," she says kindly.

I sit down at the puzzle table and I'm soon joined by one of our new boys who tells me his name is Simon. He's a chatty young fellow and he talks to me about what he had for Christmas, about his baby brother, how his toy train set can only be played with in his bedroom because his younger brother keeps touching it, and various other things that are obviously important to him.

He's a bright little button and as he's talking to me he's also completing the puzzles, and he soon has the table covered in finished jigsaws. He then astonishes me by casually asking, "Aunty Wendy, why do you call all the children 'sweetie'?"

I stare at him for a moment. It certainly hadn't taken him long to notice that! I wonder if he really wants to hear the truth, which is that I don't know who's who yet and probably won't until next Christmas! Or I could tell him that I say sweetie because they're all so lovely and sweet. I wonder which one he would believe.

Of course I do slowly start to remember the good ones and the memorable ones, memorable for whatever reason. The shy ones and the quiet ones, there are never enough of those. Then there are the designer label ones and the cheeky ones. The I'm-here-and-you-will-all-know-it ones. There are the thrown-together-in-a-hurry ones with shoes on the wrong feet. The I-want-my-mum one, who yells and cries and clings, and whose mother leaves with a heavy heart, guilty feelings and a sad face. Those children are usually playing happily in no time at all. And, last but not least, there is the smarty one. That's you, Simon! I've got you nicknamed in my mind already as 'Simon smarty pants'.

I think I need to change the subject so I ask him, "Do you want to do some more puzzles?" to which I get an enthusiastic, "Yes." So I fetch a pile of them from the cupboard and we're joined on and off by other children, but Simon spends most of the morning there completing puzzles. We find two puzzles with pieces missing and put them to one side ready to be thrown out. I have to leave Simon every now and again but he says he is happy to stay were he is. When Julie enquires if he wants to paint, he asks her if he can do it later as he is helping Aunty Wendy. Bless him!

I manage a quick chat with Julie at drinks time and I sit next to her at lunch time and have a longer chat. She has had such a busy Christmas and a holiday abroad and I want to know how it all went.

I'm glad to say lunch is a little more civilised today. It's amazing just how quickly children adapt when the rules are clearly explained to them. Mind you, there are always those who try their luck and see if they can get away with not eating their sandwiches but we are getting our message across to them slowly.

Simon eventually painted a very nice picture and was delighted when, after lunch, the train set was brought out of the cupboard. He played happily with it for most of the afternoon and did not mind at all when other children wanted to join in with him. I must just say, for a 'smarty pants', Simon is a really lovely and contented lad.

Julie has worked with Hillary for many, many years and she comes up with wonderful games and ideas to entertain the children. Julie and I are alike in a lot of ways, we are the same star sign and of a similar age and we do seem to understand each other very well. Also, we both like doing slightly unconventional things with the children, like playing with balloons or empty cardboard boxes, both of which can be great fun. It's probably not within the curriculum and probably not very educational, but it is fun and fun is the key word in Julie's book.

At the end of the session Julie is sitting singing with the children, having some fun with the 'Heads and Shoulders, Knees and Toes' song. She remembers the words to all the various songs and, unlike me, she can hold a tune. She never seems to get ruffled or ratty, and has amazing patience. She manages to show up all my faults without even trying. It's fortunate we're such good friends or I would feel completely inadequate in her company!

Whilst she is entertaining the children, the rest of us pack the toys away. We've had a few laughs, the odd tear or two and lots of soggy paintings, but on the whole a happy and productive day.

Tuesday 18th January

Another week begins. Time really does seem to fly by as you get older, as my mum was fond of saying. It is a dry, sunny day and I decide to cycle to school. As I cycle into the car park I don't see Nicky's car. It makes me wonder if she's feeling better or if she is still under the weather. I see no sign of her as I shout a general good morning to everyone else in the hall. It looks like it's Hillary, Mandy, Julie and me today.

"Hello Wendy." Comes a voice from the cupboard, and as I get closer I see Dawn is in there collecting paper.

"Hello Dawn, I don't get to see you too often. Are you here because Nicky is still ill?"

"Yes, I said I could do it if Nicky was still unwell today," she replies.

Dawn is another of our dedicated team, she is tall and slim and has short dark hair. Her two children are now at junior school but they both came here before that.

"Hello Wendy," calls Hillary. "Can you oversee again and do the loo runs today?"

Lucky, lucky me!

"And we have the Duplo bricks out, so will you please start off there?" Hillary adds.

Oh great! I always enjoy sitting on the cold, hard, dusty floor, being run into by no end of wheeled objects and having every construction I make reduced to rubble in seconds. This *is* going to be a fun day!

Simon comes over to join me and with him is a quiet little chap who has mumbled his name to me twice and I still can't grasp it. I dare not call him 'sweetie' as I'm sure Simon would have something to say about that.

We three decide to make a garage and soon have a building with room for many cars to fit inside. Simon is helping 'Sweetie' and the pair seem to be getting along swimmingly, so as soon as I get the chance I go over to the register to look up his name. Some of the names we have these days are amazing. We have a Traydon, that's a new name, I presume it's a boy's name and I certainly haven't heard it before. There's a Jazzier. Where have I heard that name? Wasn't there a Jazzier in those Space Wars films? We have a Topaz and a Dilly. Dilly, that's quite a nice name, unusual, but open to teasing I would think. Silly Dilly or Dilly Daydream pop into my mind.

I've noticed over the years that names seem to follow trends. Some years back we had a Kylie and a Jason or two, named after television personalities. The latest fad seems to be to name your child after the town or place it was conceived in. Hopefully people will see the wisdom of not doing this if the child was conceived locally here in Littlehampton. The nicknames would be inventive, I'm sure. I can see it now: "Here comes Little Hammy," or "Hammy Hampton," or "Titchy." And perhaps, as they

got older, the comments would get ruder, especially in football changing room or men only situations, given that 'Hampton' can refer to a part of the male anatomy, and having the prefix little would be asking for wise cracks! Still it would be worse if conceived in East Sussex. They have some real corkers. Upper Dicker; Lower Dicker; Pidding Hoe and Cocking to name but a few.

I remember reading somewhere that many, many years back the people from Littlehampton were called 'Hampton Shakers' due to the fact that it was a terribly marshy place and, with the dampness from the river, people caught the ague. A fever which left them with chills and fits of shivering. It's amazing what useless information I retain and yet anything remotely important goes straight out of my head!

Julie comes across to me and asks, "What're you doing? Can I help?"

I explain I need to know the name of the boy playing with Simon. She tells me his name is Mark.

"I'm pleased he has a normal name," I say to her. "He seems so shy and nervous. I don't think he would cope with an unusual name and the teasing that might go with it."

Julie and I exchange a few comments about the new names and remember some of the other unusual ones that we have had in the past.

"Do you remember Cattleya?" she asks me.

"Oh, yes I do."

Julie continues, " her father was an orchid buff and the 'Cattleya' was one of his favourites. I remember him saying it was a beautifully scented orchid."

"And Dorrinda-May, do you remember her?" I ask. "Dorrinda-May always sounded like an unfinished sentence to me. 'Dorrinda, may I sit next to you?' 'Dorrinda, may I have a biscuit?' Do you know what I mean?"

"Trust you to think like that," she says, amused. "What about Niamh? That's a pretty name. We've only ever had one of those that I know of."

"I could never spell that name." I admitted. "I always ended up spelling it phonetically and her mum used to get so cross with me, so much so that I used to tear the name off her piece of work before handing it to her, if I remembered to."

"Well, you should be able to spell Mark," she says as she goes off laughing to herself.

Milk time comes round quickly and Simon is chosen to hand out the biscuits. He's still fairly new but he's a confident young lad. He's rather tall and holds the biscuit tin so high that the seated children can't reach into it, and because the children are not taking any biscuits he decides to hand them out personally, one at a time. Not the right thing to do, but it amuses me.

After drinks Mark and Simon rush back to the Duplo bricks and Mark calls out, "Are you coming, Aunty Wendy?" How can I refuse? I make my way to the Duplo followed by a young boy called Steven. He's a serious little fellow but very likeable. We add an airport and a fire station to our garage. A bit later two girls, Gemma and Louise, come over and join us and we add a few houses and shops. Gemma has long, straight hair and a rather long, straight face to match, and she's a rather quiet little girl. Louise, on the other hand, has a mop of unruly curls, a sunny, round face and an inquisitive, talkative nature. They are like chalk and cheese to look at but are great friends and often play together.

These five children all play nicely as a group and we spend the rest of the morning crawling round the floor pushing cars into the garage and, on Steven's suggestion, we include a huge train track and stations. I find I'm quite enjoying myself too and it comes as a surprise when Hillary reminds us that we have to get the tables ready for lunch.

We always try to encourage the children to help tidy away some of the toys. When they've helped a little, an auntie reads to them whilst the rest of us move the tables into a horse-shoe shape, with the aunties' table across the top. We put the children's lunchboxes on the tables, so that when they've washed their hands they can find it and sit down. The ones going home are sat separately ready to be collected. The children are getting used to this procedure, but these switch-over times can be tricky as there's a lot of noise and activity. Things soon quieten down and some of us aunties as well as the children do manage to eat some food.

In the afternoons, we first try to finish off any outstanding work from the morning and as there are usually fewer children we often have more time to play with the children. We can engage in activities like simple board games and animal dominoes. There are often dolly tea parties to attend, and the dressing up box sometimes makes an appearance too. This is always popular but it rarely comes out in the morning sessions as it can be time consuming helping the children into and out of the clothes.

I'm sitting with three children playing animal pairs with large playing cards when Hillary comes over and tells me that on Thursday she wants us to do painting again, and would I mind taking home a couple of tabards and aprons to wash. She also indicates she wants me to start packing up as it is nearly time to go. I glance out of the window and I'm pleased to see it's not raining, as I came on my bicycle and I may get home without getting wet, which will make a nice change!

Thursday 20th January

I've remembered the tabards and aprons, including my own, and as much as I have rushed around at home to get here early, I'm only just on time. I don't know where the time goes!

No-one has started getting the painting equipment ready so I hurry to make a start. Painting is a fun activity but it seems to take forever to set up. Finding and laying out the plastic floor covering, manoeuvring easels out of the cupboard, finding the paint powder, brushes and containers, searching for suitable paper and naming it using the register, locating the aprons or small tabards for the children, and, finally, fetching a bowl of water and a towel from the kitchen for washing hands dotted with paint. Then to start mixing the paints, for some reason the red paint never mixes quickly and you end up stirring it for ages and you know it will still be lumpy no matter how hard you try or how long you take.

I just finish naming all the blank painting papers when Hillary comes past and says, "I'm a bit busy this morning, thanks for getting the painting under way. Are you happy to carry on?"

"Yes, I'm fine." I reply happily. I secure the top paper to one side of the easel and look for the first child, a girl called Lulu. I'm not sure which one she is yet so I ask Ro to point her out to me.

"She's over there with the dolls' pram." Ro tells me, pointing to a small girl with curly brown hair and a splash of freckles across her nose. She's happy to come and paint and follows me across the room pushing 'her' pram. Some of the new children have never worn aprons before and it can be a bit of a struggle to persuade them that it is necessary, but I have no such problems with Lulu. She quickly has one on and I think she must have painted before as she soon has the hang of things and is confidently applying paint to paper and seems to be enjoying herself.

Now I look round to find another child to work on the other side of the easel. Just at that moment little Mark comes over and says he would like to do a painting. I quickly find his paper and soon have an apron on him. I notice he is very precise and careful with each brush stroke. I do like to watch the children painting and also to see what they are creating. It always brightens my day when a child paints a big happy face, it makes me think they must be happy in themselves to do that.

Of course some of the work produced is unrecognisable and when the child asks, "Do you like what I've painted?" that's okay, because you always say yes. But when they ask, "Do you know what it is?" that's when things can get awkward as you don't want to upset them, and they expect you to know what it is as you're an aunty! I try to gather clues by asking, "Is it a person?" "Is it a toy?" "Is it always brown and purple with bits of orange, or can it be any colour?" and so on. However, you do get the odd stubborn child who insists that you guess it right first time—at which point I pretend that I'm needed elsewhere and hope, in my absence, that the artist goes off to play and forgets.

Some of their pieces of work are all one colour, perhaps like past famous artists the child is going through their blue period or their green period. Some children paint very nice pictures only to swipe the brush all over it, merging all the colours until a dull brown and green camouflage pattern is all you can see. Then they are happy and announce it's finished. I still don't fully understand that concept.

Occasionally a child doesn't want to paint, so I try to convince them that they do. I tell them that it's fun and it won't take long, and that they'll be upset at home-time if they're the only one without a painting. I offer to draw them a train or a doll so they can colour it. If none of that works, I resort to saying, "Oh don't then!", usually with a sigh of defeat. For some inexplicable reason that often works and a painting is produced.

As each painting is completed, I hang it on a wooden clothes horse to dry. When it fills up, I remove the earlier ones, which are a bit dryer, and pin them on to the walls hoping the paint is dry enough to not run. If I have some really wet paintings, I lay them on the floor and hope they will be dry before home-time. It can be quite busy and tiring but the time goes quickly.

I see Liz and Ro have started to clear away some toys to make space for lunchtime so I slide the easel over to one side, out of the way, but leave it ready to resume again after lunch. I notice I don't have too much paint on my tabard. I do have a blob of paint on my shoe and a smear on the elbow of my jumper but my tabard is comparatively clean.

I collect together the paintings for the children who are going home and carefully hand them out, some are still a bit tacky but, with care, should make it home in one piece.

After lunch today I see there's only seven afternoon children who will need to paint and they get finished fairly quickly. I take the brushes and containers into the kitchen to clean them and wash down the easel. There's still a lot of time left, so I ask if I can get the slide out. Hillary gives the go-ahead and Ro helps me. It's made of plastic and not too heavy, just bulky and awkward to manoeuvre and takes two of us to get it out of the cupboard.

The children love the slide and they rush over to us, eager to have a turn. We try to get them to form a queue and for safety's sake we have to be strict with them. We only allow them to slide down on their bottoms, not head-first or backwards. It usually takes two aunties to supervise, one at the steps and the other at the slide end to make sure there are no accidents.

Obviously we aunties help any of the little ones to climb up the steps and to steady them before they sit down to slide. They soon become confident and we're all pleased when this happens as our slide has attitude! Static electricity builds up and after a very short time we get small but sharp electric shocks from it. I seem to be very susceptible to it and it passes from me to whomever I happen to touch on the slide. The other aunties also get shocked, but not to such a degree. So a lot of my help is given verbally and if I do have to reach out to a child, the poor thing will get a short, sharp jab and give me a quizzical look. For me, one or two of these electric shocks are not too much of a problem, but after twenty or so it becomes very irritating. It's usually at this point that I find myself wondering why I ever suggest using the slide in the first place, especially as I know our slide and I do not get on well together!

The build up of static on the slide affects some of the children too. After a few goes, some of the girls come down the slide with their hair standing on end, fanned out around their heads. It looks bizarre and comical, and when this starts to happen other children like to stand at the foot of the slide to see whose hair is going to stand up. We do only use the slide for very short periods but it is fun for the children and always causes laughter amongst us all.

All too soon it's time to put the slide away. It's now fully 'charged', so as we shove it back into the cupboard, we all get shocked repeatedly. We dislike the cupboard, because there's never enough room for all the toys. Things are often put away in a rush at the end of the day, not necessarily in the right places. I feel sorry for Nora, who comes in early every morning to get a lot of the toys out of the cupboard for us. She must dread opening the cupboard door, wondering what will fall on her each day. Her two grand-daughters both came here a few years back and she used to enjoy popping in and helping when she could. I rarely see her these days but am grateful for what she does as I know we would all miss her early morning help.

Tuesday 25th January

The alarm didn't go off.
I've laddered my tights.

I've burnt the toast and now there's not enough bread for my sandwiches.

And who has had all the fruit?

Someone has moved my house keys.

The car won't start; I'll have to use my bike.

Oh no! The back tyre's flat, where's the pump?

It's raining!

I arrived late and I'm soaked to the skin.

I squelch into the hall and dump my bag and coat and grunt a reply to someone.

"You're soaked," says Hillary.

"Well, it *is* raining outside," is my curt reply. "I'll be all okay. I will soon dry off. I'm making myself a coffee, all right!"

I stick on a forced smile and say, "Just leave me alone and let me get through the next few hours."

Thursday 27th January

Maybe I did have a touch of PMT on Tuesday. Well, 'it' came in the middle of the night, like it does sometimes. So that meant stripping the bed, putting the sheets in the washing machine and re-making the bed. But we girls know all about that, don't we? We have the tummy pain, the inconvenience, the cost and the unfairness of it all. Why do women have all these things to put up with? I better not start on that, that's another bone of contention and I could keep moaning about it all day long.

I offer, yes offer, to do the loo runs, as I know I will need the loo a lot myself today. If you're in the right frame of mind the trips to the toilets can be quite revealing and quite funny sometimes. You get told all sorts of things when there are just two or three of you. The things some of you parents do! I've heard: "We don't have soft toilet paper at home, only at my aunty's house." "My dad picks his nose." "I can't go, my tummy's tired." (I like that one.) "My mum has boobies." "My granddad's teeth come out." "My mum and dad kiss." usually followed by a snigger or two. "My mum says my dad has two left feet." "Why must we wash our hands?" "My jumper's strangling my arms." (I like that one, too.) "For dinner I'm having spaghetti blobby nose." That one conjured up a picture I would rather not have visualised.

I sit down at the drawing-cum-colouring table, which is a table laden with colouring books and scrap paper so that the children can draw, colour, scribble, whenever they want to and they can come and go as they please.

It's not too long before I find I'm off to the toilets with two of our boys, Paul and Traydon. I deal with Paul quickly but then Traydon decides he needs a pooh. Nice. I sit him on the toilet seat and he innocently says. "Aunty Wendy, my dad farts,"

"Pardon!" I exclaim.

"I said my da…"

"No, no, don't repeat it." I interrupt, and he doesn't. Instead, he starts to sing a little song to himself. I ask him if he's okay for a minute and rush Paul back to the main hall. I quickly return to Traydon and wait while he finishes. As I help him to wash his hands he says, "Aunty Wendy, I fart in bed." I don't know what to say. I glance at his reflection in the mirror and he's innocently drying his hands. I'm not often at a loss for words, but I really don't know what to say, so I just hold his hand and we walk back to the hall. I smile to myself as I think now how innocently these things are said and to use *that word,* not even disguising it like my nanny used to. She used to say, "Pardon me, I've just popped a button." How times have changed!

On one later trip to the toilet, I only have little Sally to see to, so I decide to take my necessary items with me, thinking I could use the loo myself quickly, whilst she is using the other one. Never again! We only have two toilets in the ladies so we're in adjoining cubicles. I'm talking to her to reassure her I'm still nearby and at the same time I unwrap a tampon. A little voice asks, "Why are you eating sweets, Aunty Wendy?"

"I'm not eating a sweet, dear."

"Yes you are, I heard the paper!" Is her indignant reply.

How do I explain this one? I quickly finish what I'm doing and make a big fuss about washing our hands and even waste some time showing her how to blow bubbles with soap across her circled index finger and thumb, anything to take her mind of it. But all to no avail. As we walk back into the main room she runs over to Hillary and says, quite loudly, "Aunty Hillary, Aunty Hillary! Aunty Wendy ate a sweet in the toilet and didn't share!"

Why does the floor never open up and swallow you when you need it to?

Tuesday 1st February

It's the first of February today and it's Auntie Hillary's birthday. From the front seat of the car I pick up the card and potted plant that I have for her and go into the hall.

"Good morning all," I call out, "and Happy Birthday, Hillary!"

"Thank you," she replies happily.

"Morning, Wendy," calls Mandy, waving me towards her. "Come over here I want to ask you something. Would you mind making a birthday card with the children and they can give it to Hillary at break time?"

"Yes, that's okay, I can do that." I answer quietly. "I'll just get my coat off and give her this plant and card and then I'll go and see what I can find in the cupboard."

I'm not very artistic but I have the best of intentions. I find some pink card and tissue paper that I think I can use, then I go and sit at the colouring table. I fold the card in half and draw some rather odd-shaped flowers onto it and ask one or two of the kids to come over to colour them. Are we allowed to say kids? I doubt it, too late now. Whilst they're colouring, I cut some of the tissue paper into small pieces, scrunch them up and encourage some other children to stick them onto the flowers to give a 3-D effect. I try to involve as many of the children as possible to help so that everyone has done something on the card. The top of the card is coloured blue and a large yellow sunshine is added. Green is scribbled, ooops, 'coloured', around the stems of the flowers. A little ladybird appears, and a snail, and a smiling spider. We really have some fun with it and the finished card is bright and colourful, just what we need to cheer us up on this cold and windy day. I encourage all the children to sign the card and the aunties too. I just get it finished in time to present it to Aunty Hillary at milk time.

We all sit down in our circle ready and eager to hand the card over to Hillary, when she's called away to deal with a phone call. Obviously we can't continue without her.

Julie says, "We'll have to delay things a bit. We can't sing as it would be too noisy with Hillary on the phone, so any ideas?"

"We could have a general talk to the children, get to know them a bit better." I suggest.

"Okay, carry on," she says to me. I really didn't think I would actually have to do it myself, but I start. "Now children, as we have to wait a few minutes for Aunty Hillary to finish the phone call and come and join us, we are going to have a little talk about what work your daddies do."

That's an easy enough subject for them, or so I thought. There are a few who don't know, and a few responses so mumbled that I just have to say "That's nice" and move on. "My dad works in a shop." "My daddy drives a lorry." "My daddy sits on his bum all day and makes mummy cross." "My daddy sells toys." "My dad's a policeman." "My dad's got a taxi." "My daddy watches telly all day." "My daddy's a computer." (I don't think he meant that but I liked it.) "My daddy works at The Body Shop." "My dad works in an office."And then, "Which daddy do you mean?" Thank goodness I'm saved from answering that one as Aunty Hillary comes back to join us. Julie raises her eyebrows up on her forehead as if to say thank goodness for Hillary's timely arrival.

We all sing Happy Birthday to Hillary and give her the card which she opens and reads. She smiles and thanks the children.

On the way to work, I'd purchased some sticky buns for us aunties. I would have got some for the children too, but we're not allowed to give them cakes. Some children don't tolerate E numbers or additives, and others react to nuts or chocolate. Once you have taken all that lot into consideration, it hugely reduces your choices. But I did buy some jam biscuits for them which I put into the biscuit tin. Hillary reminds me to add in some bland ones just in case they are needed. As the biscuit tin is passed around, I notice most children opt for the jam ones. I just hope they'll be okay.

Aunty Hillary seems pleased with her card and thanks us all again before pinning it to the wall for all to see. I notice the sun has decided to peek through the clouds and that cheers up the day even more.

Whilst I've been making Hillary's card, Julie and Mandy have been working with the children colouring an umbrella and a pair of Wellington boots, some of which have also been tacked on to the walls. I offer my help and sit with them, and between us we soon get all that work finished.

We're in the middle of lunch when the doorbell rings. Hillary goes to answer the door and comes back into the room with a large, colourful bouquet of flowers. They're from her eldest son and she's delighted. The only container large enough to keep them fresh is a bucket and she positions it on the hatch, between the hall and the kitchen, so we can all share in the sight of them.

At the end of the day I'm asked to look after the children whilst the other aunties clear away. I dread doing this as I can't sing. I can never remember the words nor can I keep the tune going. Also, I don't seem to have quite the control the other aunties have in maintaining order and keeping the children's attention, but today I have a brain wave.

I notice the reflection of the sun off the face of my wrist watch has made a little bright area on the wall and by slowly moving my wrist I can make it move. I stare at this reflection and slowly the seated children quieten and wonder what I'm up to. I tell them to be quiet; I say they're very lucky as we have a 'fairy' visiting us. I make the little light-blob move along the floor closer to them. I move it onto one or two laps and if the children get too noisy or excited I quickly move my wrist and it disappears. I tell them they have frightened the fairy and if they want to see it again they will have to be quieter. The children are enthralled and we enjoy our time together watching the fairy go from lap to lap and floating across the floor. As I seem to be having so much success, for a change, even the aunties come over to see what I'm doing. I'm very pleased with myself. Well done me!

Thursday 3rd February

It's so cold and windy today, even my dog didn't seem to enjoy his quick walk around our local park this morning. We saw a few brave souls with heads down against the wind and walking more quickly than usual. Greetings and doggy sniffs were a lot quicker this morning.

When I get to school I see aunties, children and parents are bundled up with coats and hats and scarves and grumbling about the weather.

It doesn't feel warm in the main hall either and being such a large area we appreciate that it does take a little while to warm up. But this morning the hall feels cold as we enter and it just doesn't seem to be warming up.

The children are good to start with and just play and carry on as normal. But one by one they start to complain of being cold.

Hillary tells us that Nora had left a note for her saying how cold the hall was when she came in earlier to get the toys out and that she didn't think the boiler was on. None of us know anything about heating systems and Hillary adjusts the thermostat just in case it makes a difference. It doesn't. We look in our box of spare clothes and find plenty of jumpers and sweatshirts for the children but we are all getting colder.

Hillary phones the scout leader, Ken, to explain the situation. He offers to come straight round to investigate. He is as good as his word and arrives within minutes. He disappeared into the store cupboard where the boiler is housed.

As he comes out of the cupboard, Ken is shaking his head and declares, "there's no oil in the system and so it's shut itself down. The really cold weather we have been having lately must have used more oil than was expected. Somehow it's been overlooked and no one has noticed. I'm sorry there's nothing I can do right now except go and phone to see if I can get some oil delivered as quickly as possible."

"There's nothing we can do about this situation," Hillary announces to us all. "We have no heating and the room will just get colder and colder. So I'll have to phone the parents to come and collect their children."

We always insist on two or three contact numbers for each child and in this rare kind of situation they may all be needed. Just before Hillary starts phoning round to parents, grand parents, child minders, neighbours and work places, she asks Nicky and me to look after the children, and Liz and Ro to pack away the toys.

I explain to the children that we'll be having a different type of day today and encourage them to help tidy everything away in its rightful boxes and then we will have some fun.

"How about we have warm milk for the children today," suggests Ro. We all agree that's a good idea. Some of the children may not have had warm milk before but as we're all getting colder, not one of them commented or complained.

Whilst sipping my hot drink my mind wanders back to a similar situation that we had had many years before. On that occasion it was a dreadfully windy day and we could see bits of paper and plastic carrier bags being blown about in the park. Some gusts of wind were really strong and we could feel the building shudder at times. Fortunately we aunties had all managed to get in to school but now the wind was getting stronger and kept howling around our building. We knew it was extraordinary weather.

We had even drawn the curtains to shut out the sight of all the bending trees and rubbish being swept by. But you could still hear a clatter of a dustbin lid or some more heavy items being blown about. We could do nothing about the terrifying noise and it was getting worse as the morning progressed. One or two of the children began to get anxious and started to react badly and we knew we would have to call in the parents.

I remember Hillary went into the small hall and did the phoning around while another aunty and I were asked to sit the children down in a big circle and read to them. This we duly did. She read the story and I held an identical book and walked amongst the children showing them the pictures.

All of a sudden my son cried out and, I looked up, and I saw that a ceiling tile had come loose and had fallen onto the floor beside him. It had given him quite a shock. Luckily it was my son it had happened to, at least I was there for him and could give him a reassuring hug, although I don't suppose he saw it as lucky at the time. Poor little chap.

Anyway back to the present.

"What can we do with the children?" asks Nicky.

"We can do all sorts of games and jumping and skipping. In fact anything we can think of to keep them moving about," I reply. All the time thinking to myself, we can do all the noisy games we're never usually allowed to do. Ha-ha what fun! Julie would love to be here to join in. It sounds like her kind of mornings entertainment

When we have all finished our drinks I stand up and ask, "who wants to be a soldier?" A chorus of 'yes's' from the children is my answer.

"Okay, let's all be soldiers and stamp our feet and march around the room and make lots of noise for a change," I call out gleefully. No need to repeat myself as the children were up and off their chairs and soon became soldiers, not a neat and tidy platoon more a rabble, but it didn't matter as they were all moving about, swinging their arm and enjoying themselves and getting warmer.

We next hold hands in a circle and play 'Farmer's in His Den'. Then we all pretend to be wild animals and roar and growl and stalk around the room. Aunty Liz comes over to join us and we play 'Ring a Roses'. Then Liz says she wants to be a soldier, so we play soldiers again, marching and stomping. We pretend to be farm animals and then we play 'Hokey Cokey'. Then we're soldiers again. Next we all sit on the floor in pairs and sing and act 'Row, row, row your boat'. We try 'What's The Time Mr. Wolf?' and a little Keep Fit and then we become soldiers again and again and again. All the while the temperature is dropping and the room is getting colder but I can honestly say Nicky, Liz and I were as warm as toast.

One by one various adults arrived to collect the children and sign them out. Eventually all of them had gone. Peace and quiet descended. Nicky and I had probably strained our throats a bit and I had the beginnings of a headache, but at least we weren't cold.

Tuesday 8th February

As I walk into the hall one or two children come up to me to ask if they can be soldiers.

"Maybe later." I reply. "I'll have a word with Aunty Hillary and see what she says, okay?" This seems to satisfy them and off they go to play.

Hillary informs me that the scout leader sorted everything out and the oil arrived late on Thursday afternoon, so it was school as usual on Friday. "And," she adds theatrically, "your name was mud on Friday as the children all wanted to be noisy animals and even noisier soldiers! You may have some explaining to do to Dawn and Eve when you next see them. Anyway, I want you to help out with the loo runs today."

Is this some kind of punishment? I ask myself.

"And I want you to make a start on the scrapbooks for the children. I've drawn a couple of rainbows to start you off," she finishes.

We're called the Rainbow Nursery School and Playgroup, therefore we use the rainbow shape as a type of logo and put it onto any folders or scrapbooks for the children. We aunties are always on the look out for old magazines with nice pictures. Also calendars and Christmas cards and birthday cards for the children to cut out and stick into their scrap books.

I enjoy 'sticking' with the children but of course never admit it to anyone. When you have been in this job as long as I have, you learn never to admit to any preferences or skills. If you say you can draw, for example, you'll be inundated with requests for various animals or characters for the children to colour. You'll also be asked to make murals for the walls or create pictures for different events. The list goes on and on. So I try to keep quiet.

Even without admitting to any skills you're expected to help with the cutting-out of various items. It gets to be a bit of a chore after a while but we all do it so it spreads the work load a bit. Imagine cutting out seventy two penguins; seventy two motor cars or buses and seventy two mother elephants and their babies. You have to do that number so that there's one for every child on our register, a few spares to allow for the odd mistake and one for the main file to be kept as a reference. Remember too, that, that lot have to be drawn before cutting-out even begins! It is a wonderful way to spend a weekend! Oh, and I nearly forgot to say, all that lot would only be three days work! And it looks like I will be drawing and cutting out seventy rainbows by Thursday. I can see a joyous couple of evenings ahead for me.

I soon sort out a table and get together all the bits and bobs that I need and I find Dilly has sat a large doll in one chair and she is sat next to me expectantly.

"I'm making folders, Dilly. I don't have any work for you."

"Can I sit here and talk to you?" She asks sweetly. How can I refuse? I learn about her new baby sister, her many brothers, her favourite cartoons, her best dinners, a long story about 'granny' which is so long and confusing I lose the gist and just hope I'm saying yes and no in the right places. Then without a backward glance she grabs the doll and is off. She's goes over to the tea set and as I watch she collects a few more dolls and starts making tea for them all.

At milk time, I notice Dilly talking to a dolly who is sharing her chair and wonder if she has an underlying problem or anxiety. Then again at lunch time, I see she again has a dolly, this time under her chair.

Once we have eaten and cleared away Hillary has to go out for an hour or so and I ask Julie if we can play some circle games with the children and maybe be soldiers. She is more than happy to oblige and we have a noisy half an hour or so. It also means I've kept my word to those children who had asked about being soldiers earlier this morning.

I keep an eye on Dilly all afternoon and she plays happily with the dolls and the tea set. She appears contented and is happily singing little songs to them and telling them stories. I'm sure she's fine, but just for my own piece of mind, I mention my observations to Hillary when she returns. She tells me that there is no spare money in that family, and as Dilly is the only girl, except for the new baby. She probably has to play with the boys toys at home, so to have so many dolls to play with is probably the most precious part of Dilly's day. She also says she'll tell all the aunties to keep an eye on her just to be certain there is no problem.

Thursday 10th February

Before I'm allocated the dreaded loo run again, I try to look really busy gathering a few children to colour their rainbows and whilst they are doing that I clearly name each of the scrapbooks in bold felt-tip pen. I must look busy as I'm left to get on with it. There's quite a lot to do as I have to make a few more scrapbooks and I think it will be after half term before we'll progress to actually gluing the rainbows on.

Half term; dreaded by parents, loved by teachers and teacher helpers. A whole week off. Work to prepare and drawings to copy, and cutting out to do, but still a whole week away from here. Ahhh!

Our day passes without much incident. There is work; milk time; some more work; some play; lunch time. A bit more work and more play, so quite an ordinary day but, here's a little gem I want to share with you. I've just come back from a visit to the toilets, (the looking busy ploy only worked for so long) and this is what occurred. I had taken three boys down to the toilets. Michael had finished and was waiting nicely to have his hands washed. Traydon was in one cubicle and I was in the next cubicle with Mark struggling to pull up his trousers and untangle his braces, when a little voice said,

"You haven't got any paper. I'll get you some." That's Michael offering to help, how nice of him, I thought.

Then Traydon said, "it doesn't matter, I'm okay."

That is just what I would expect from you, Traydon. I think to myself.

Then Michael speaks again but very authoritatively this time. "Yes it does. You have to take some tissue, screw it up in your hand and drop it in the water, or you'll be told off."

Well, now we all know! I feel I will have some explaining to do on that subject.

HALF TERM WEEK

Chapter Two

Tuesday 23rd February

It's unusual for me to be in school at 8.45, I normally sneak in just on time or a little bit after nine. I suppose I'm refreshed and keen after the half term holiday. I would like you to think that but the truth is we had a staff meeting last night and punctuality was mentioned. I know my time keeping won't last and so does everyone else but today, I'm early.

These staff meetings are something else. We're the same staff, in the same building with the same age group of children but each year we have some new rules or regulations to add to our already long list. Or, even to override the old rules. Maybe it's to keep us on our toes I don't know, it just bewilders me.

Another item on the agenda last night, after punctuality, was the first aid box. It's compulsory that we have one and we can all appreciate that. Although we often ask ourselves why, as over the years it's been decreed, by someone in authority, that we're not allowed to apply bandages, we're not to use plasters, we're not to use 'magic' cream and nor can we administer medicine or give aspirins. So our compulsory medicine box has nothing in it for children. In fact, it has nothing in it period, as we're not to put any adult headache pills or pain killers or anything in there that may be given to or taken by a child. And now we have a new rule to follow which is, the first aid box must now be visible and available at all times. So instead of the useless thing sitting on a shelf in the cupboard, now it must be in the main hall for all to see. Is it me? Someone somewhere has been busy, haven't they? We do keep a couple of bags of frozen peas in the freezer in the kitchen, which we wrap up in a tea towel and use if two heads have bumped together. I wonder what the exact ruling on bumped heads is? Best not to ask, I think to myself. I've a lot of rainbows to stick onto scrapbooks, so had better get on.

Thursday 25th February

"I'm doing scrapbooks today, all right?" My tone of voice indicates no discussion or debate.

"I'm quite capable of finding the glue, thank you." I say tersely to Hillary as she comes out of the cupboard with one pot which she offers to me.

"I've got the spatulas and everything else I need, thank you."

"I know the children I want.

Is it drinks time yet?

I need, really need a coffee.

I'll tie your shoelace for you, just keep your foot still. Why all shoes don't have Velcro I'll never know." I say grumpily.

I moan my way through the rest of the day with the odd comments such as, "All right, all right, I'll stop all I'm doing and take you to the toilet. I can't work with you looking like that. I'll get a tissue for you, hold on. Is it lunch time? It must be lunch time soon as my stomach really aches."

I don't know why but I feel a little touchy today, perhaps it's that time of the month again. A nice cup of tea and a tuna and cress sandwich should help.

"Aunty Wendy, Aunty Wendy look. I've got boogies on my fingernail!! Cancel that sandwich, I'll just have a cup of coffee and a painkiller or two.

After a short while the painkillers kick in and I don't feel quite so grouchy and begin to enjoy helping the children glue their rainbows onto their folders. The afternoon chugs along nicely and as the sun has decided to come out, I offer, yes offer to look after the children whilst the hall is being cleared. I feel too rough to lug chairs and tables and heavy boxes of toys about and sitting having some 'fairy' fun is a lot easier and I'm pleased to say that, for me, the day ended a lot better than it started.

Tuesday 2nd March

I can't believe it's March already. My mum always commented on how time flew by as you got older, and I think she was right.

Aunty Hillary reminds us it's Mothering Sunday this month. This can be a sensitive area so we need to check first to make sure all the children have a mother in the household. In the past we have had grandparents bringing up the children or dads on their own, so we always clarify the situation now.

"If all the children have a mother this term," Hillary carries on, "I want you to come up with an new idea for a card. I've been looking through my file and I think we need something different."

'Don't ask me, I'm not good with ideas', I think to myself.

Mandy says, "I have an idea that might work."

I think, 'thank goodness for that because I haven't got a clue. I've not heard her idea but I know I'll like it, especially if it means I don't have to think of something.'

She continues,"If we cut out a teapot shaped card for the children to colour in, and when that is done we can attach a teabag-on-a-string, inside the card."

That's a nice idea, and definitely one I haven't done before. I knew I would like it.

Mandy is a very neat and tidy lady and has been known to be late on a few occasions just like me, well not quite like me, I think I hold the record on late arrivals. She has a quiet yet firm way with the children and patience by the bucketful, again just like me! Ha, who am I kidding?

Hillary likes the teapot idea and draws a couple of teapot shapes onto a piece of scrap paper and asks us which shape we prefer. We all agree that we like the fat, rounded old- fashioned shape and she goes into the cupboard to find some card. She draws a lovely fat teapot onto a folded A4 piece of card. Leaving room inside for a greeting and signature. We can't wait to either copy it or, in my case, draw round it. We're just like children ourselves at times, we enjoy doing something new and different, and as soon as a couple of teapots are cut out we start the children to work colouring them. Mothering Sunday falls on the fourteenth this year and it's the second today, so we don't have that much time.

"The children will have to have something to take home today," says Mandy. "The piece of work we had planned will take too long, any ideas?"

'Not asking for ideas again,' I think, 'that's twice in one day.'

"How about pop-up moles?" calls Julie quickly."Whenever we make pop-ups the children like them and they are fairly quick and easy. I can get some started and maybe one of you can help me later if I need it."

We're all so busy with the teapots and moles that the day flies by. The children's faces really light up when we explain just why they're making these cards for their mummies. They understand too, that they can't take them home today as it's a surprise for mummy to be given to mummy in a few days time.

I call across to Hillary to remind her to make a note to buy the tea bags with a string on and Nicky happens to mention that we will need envelopes for the cards. Hillary sends her into the store cupboard to see what paper she can find, and I truly don't know how it happened but somehow Nicky and I find ourselves sharing the job of taking home a load of paper to make seventy plus envelopes.

Thursday 4th March

We're getting on famously with our teapots. Some are multi-coloured, some striped, some have faces on them and a few are just one colour. We aunties write a greeting inside the card and the child signs his or her own name. Some of our new little ones need our help with writing their names, but the older ones who are leaving for big school, like to do their own names and kisses. We are busily working when Hillary announces,

"It looks like we are going to have a visitor join us at milk time."

She has seen the local police dog-handler walking his dog in the park and he has indicated he will call in. We arrange the chairs in the usual horseshoe-cum-circle shape and sit the children down. Most of them are really quite excited when John and his dog walk in but Jodie screams saying she does not like dogs. She is quickly scooped up into Aunty Liz's arms for reassurance, and they move away to the farthest chairs.

We know John, the dog handler quite well and when he exercises his dog on the park he always waves if he sees us looking. He tries to pop in every now and then and he usually has a short talk with the children, which is what he wants to do today. His subject this time is about some naughty boys and girls who have been spraying paint onto buildings and cars locally, and he asks if anyone in our group knows anything about this. He also asks if anyone here would do anything so naughty. The children reply with a chorus of "No's."

'Just give them a few years,' I think to myself.

John really is brilliant with the children. He's a tall man and well built and the children probably find him a bit formidable in his uniform and of course with his dog. He talks to them with authority and a little bit of humour and they sit quietly and listen. He really has their attention, you could hear a pin drop.

After his talk, he introduces Duke to all of us and explains Duke is an Alsatian dog and is three years old and that he and Duke have worked together for just over a year. He asks if any of the children would like to stroke Duke and if they would, they must put up their hands and not shout out, as Duke does not like shouting. (Fat chance.) But wait! Up go a lot of hands and hardly a murmur. Even little Jodie has put her fear aside and asks if she can pat him. Please can we keep that dog! Perhaps we could keep John too! Hillary suggests the children stay seated and that John walk Duke slowly past them and they can pat him as he goes by. This is enjoyed by all the children and when Duke licks Michael's hand and sits in front of him wagging his tail on the floor this causes great merriment.

We don't know if John signalled Duke to do it, and he never let on, but the children loved it.

Nicky has been making belated drinks for all of us, including John. Duke sits beautifully throughout and is rewarded with a biscuit and a bowl of water. Duke is very popular and all the children adore him by the end of the visit.

Once Duke has finished his drink, John stands up and says, "we have to go now. I'll try to come and see you all again soon. Goodbye and be good." The children chorus, 'goodbye' and we all wave as Hillary escorts John and Duke out.

Unbeknown to us Ro has been drawing an outline of an Alsatian dog on a piece of paper and Simon sees it and asks, "can I colour it, Aunty Ro?" Other children see it and want one too. Hillary is delighted and says if we can get a few ready, the children can have them. Ro draws some more and I trace a few whilst sipping the last of my coffee and the children just can't wait to have one to colour.

I find I'm using a little blackmail back at the 'teapot' table as I tell the children they have to complete some work on the pots, and whilst they are doing that I will trace a dog picture for them. I tell them that I can't trace a dog picture if they don't colour in their teapot. Quite a lot of pots get finished I'm happy to say.

The afternoon children are soon told all about the big policeman and his dog. John and Duke seem to have made a big impression. Nicky and Ro draw some more pictures of Duke over the lunch time and all the children have one to take home at the end of the day.

Hillary finds a book in the reading corner about a policeman and reads it to the children at home time whilst the rest of us clear away.

What a nice day.

Wednesday 10th March

Yes, Wednesday. I had a phone call last night to ask me if I could change my day from Thursday to today because Hillary has a staffing problem. Dawn is at home looking after her sick daughter; Eve has a hospital appointment and will be in later, and one of the local schools has a couple of inset days, so our staff with children at those schools can't come into nursery.

We used to be able to bring our children into the group with us if they had a school inset day. All of our children have been to this nursery school and know how to conduct themselves here and all are polite and well-behaved youngsters. They used to enjoy helping the little ones, showing off their reading skills and writing abilities and the little ones certainly liked having the older children here. 'They' could read, 'they' could draw, 'they' could write, 'they' could build wonderful things with the building bricks, 'they' could play great games and make monsters with the play dough. But, now 'they' are not welcome.

Some department somewhere amongst The Powers That Be have decided that our own children cannot possibly mix with the under fives. They can come into the building but have to spend the day in a separate room. Nice, really nice! So inset days are now a right pain in the bum and cause us a lot of problems, a lot like some of the other rules we have to abide by.

Anyway here I am. I'm feeling like a fish out of water as I know Wednesdays are very different to the other days as there's the young children's group. When I used to run it many years ago, we just called it mums and tots but that is not now politically correct. Now we have to encompass every parental combination and can't possibly call it mums and tots. Parents, guardians, aunties, uncles, grandparents and tots group is a bit of a mouthful, so young children's group, it is.

Hillary is here and Mandy, Rosemary and Liz. I know all of them, of course, but have not worked with some of them for ages. I know Rosemary and Eve run the young children's group but I don't know quite what is expected of me today.

Hillary calls me over and says, "will you help Rosemary get the room ready and work with her till Eve arrives."

"Hi, Wendy," says Rosemary. "Thanks for coming in. Let me explain what we need. There are the screens to get out of the cupboard, these are used to make a room within a room. Extra chairs and tables are needed and of course, extra toys. My toys are all in the green boxes and these have to be carried into the screened area along with just a few push along toys."

It's all quite hectic and physical and we have to be very careful to steer clear of the children but it soon takes shape. Ro asks me to position the push along toys in a certain place and then to arrange papers and wax crayons on one table and a few pots of paint, in non spill pots, on another. It is soon looking neat and tidy and inviting.

"That's all we can do for now, thanks for your help," she says. "I just have time to pop down to the loo before they start arriving at ten."

I expect by a quarter past ten it'll all be messed up. Did I say that out loud? Or did I just think it? I hope I only thought it.

I see Liz is working with the children making their teapot cards and I go and join her. I'm happy to be doing these with her as we work well together and we talk well together too. She enjoys a good moan and a grumble like I do and we both enjoy sarcasm and have a good laugh together. We have a lot in common and to my mind, today is turning out to be okay.

I'm glad to see Eve arrive just at ten o'clock which means I can stay this side of the screens chattering with Liz. The adults with their little ones arrive soon after Eve and I can see the corridor is filling up with prams and buggies. The noise level goes up quite considerably and it seems to be infectious. Rosemary's group make a noise, our group makes a noise, so Rosemary's group make more noise. Liz and I have a quick moan about the noise. It's lovely to have someone to really moan with.

We have to have our drinks promptly so that the cups are available for the tiny tots. It's a very hurried affair and we don't get chance to talk too much as we can hardly make ourselves heard above the noise next door. The cups are cleared away and washed quickly and Liz and I go back to the teapots.

We become very aware of male voices coming from over the screens. Any males who are able to come along are made welcome. It is not too often as many have work obligations and others may feel they will be the only male in a room full of females, which is often true, but if they can overcome that and visit we make them very welcome.

I have an opinion on it too. I feel they need to be dribbled on, painted on and have play-dough stuck to them like the rest of us. Why is it only us mums who have to have our clothes ruined and our hair messed up, but that is only my opinion.

We have had one or two very special dads, who, once they got over their initial shyness, really mixed in well with the group and I think they even enjoyed the experience. I suppose on reflection, it's a good thing we don't have too many men here or we would all be rushing down to the toilets, comb and compact in hand. And I would have to explain to Nicky what a compact is. If she didn't know who Joyce Grenfell was, then she certainly won't know what a compact is either. She's definitely too young that one.

A bit later on, we hear different sounds of activity from behind the screens, toys being moved and chairs too, then sweet singing led by Aunty Rosemary. The parents join in and the little ones participate too. We hear 'The Wheels on the Bus' and 'Bobbing Up and Down on the Big Red Tractor' and several nursery rhymes and simple songs. Then there is a noisy little number about monkeys on a bed which sounds like a favourite, as they sing it all over again. After this happy singing the parents begin to leave and eventually the noise level decreases. Rosemary and Eve move the screens and push their toys up against one wall. Liz explains to me that they put their stuff away when we have 'our' children safely sitting down for lunch.

I see both Ro and Eve in the kitchen having a well deserved hot drink whilst they wash up all the children's cups and paint brushes and containers. It's not too long before we in the main hall are rushing about getting the place ready for lunch and Ro puts the clean beakers on the hatch in readiness for us.

Once it's safe to do so, Ro and Eve begin moving all their gear back into the cupboard and they're still able to smile when they leave. How do they do it?

Hillary tells me I can leave now too if I want as there are only a few children in this afternoon. I don't need telling twice, I grab my coat and I'm off.

Tuesday 16th March

As we aunties' sign in, Hillary says, "we have had a couple of rather nice comments about the Mothers Day cards, so maybe all the hard work was worth it. Thank you, all. This week's going to be a lot quieter work wise and we should be able to play with the children a bit more."

I'm always wary when I hear Hillary say things like 'quieter week', in my experience it's asking for trouble saying things like that.

I sit down at the drawing table, goodness knows why, as about the only thing I can draw is a cat. And that's the type of cat made by drawing a circle for the body and a smaller circle on top for the head and little triangles on top of that for its ears and, when I do draw one, I make sure and tell each child it IS a cat, so there can be no confusion. I do try to draw other things and I'm quite relieved when they are crayoned over and no one can see the original out-lines.

Jodie comes over and sits with me and asks, "what are we doing today, Aunty Wendy?"

"It's going to be a relaxing day today, how about that?" I say. I'm not sure she fully understands what I meant but she smiles sweetly at me and starts to draw on a piece of paper.

"What are you drawing?" I enquire.

"A house."

"I think I'll draw a house, too." I say to her. I can manage a square shape with square windows, oblong door and triangle roof.

Simon and Mark come and sit with us and Simon asks, "can you draw me something to colour please?"

I dare not ask him what he'd like because in all likelihood it'll be something I can't draw, so I say, "here we go then." As I position a new piece of paper in front of me. "See if you'll like this." I don't tell him I'm attempting to draw a tractor in case it doesn't work out.

"It's a tractor!" He happily exclaims as I finish. I'm actually quite surprised with myself as it's a quite passable tractor and obviously recognisable. Mark asks if he can have one too.

Michael squeezes himself between Jodie and Mark and asks, "can you draw me a policeman and a dog?" I knew someone would ask for something I couldn't draw.

"I'm drawing tractors at the moment," I say to him pleasantly. "Would you like one?"

"No." He replies and off he goes. Oh well, you can't please everyone.

Whilst they're colouring their pictures, I glance across the room and see Dilly playing happily. She's a pretty little girl with long, straight, red/brown hair and big brown eyes and she is just so nice. She sometimes has that, 'I dressed myself' look about her. Jumper too big, possibly belonging to a brother, socks inside out, shoes on the wrong feet but none of it seems to matter to her. She's a happy and content little girl and at the moment she is in a little world of her own, and looking at her now is a joy. She's sitting with a doll on her lap, feeding it with a bottle, burping the doll on her shoulder every now and then, and singing a little song. Ah! It's scenes like that that make it all worth while. It seems my concerns over her were ill founded I'm glad to say.

"Oh no!" This comes from Hillary. "I've just noticed in the diary it'll be Easter soon. Did you know its Easter at the end of the month?" She asks everyone and no one in particular. "We must have Easter cards. Where's my Easter file. Didn't anyone realise? Why did no one say anything? We haven't got much time," she mutters away loudly to herself.

I knew it couldn't last, us having a quiet week.

"We'll need to start preparing work straight away. We'll need to make Easter cards. We'll need egg shapes cut out, and Easter baskets. We always have Easter baskets to put a few small sweet eggs in, and we must have rabbits and chicks, and lambs, and flowers for a collage for the wall. We always make a nice Easter picture and we always make chicken finger puppets, the children love those." Hillary is talking nineteen to the dozen and getting into a right old flap.

"Hold on a minute," calls Mandy as she walks over to Hillary. "Calm down. It's not our fault Easter falls early this year and none of us realised or mentioned it. Let's just talk this over and see what we can come up with."

Julie, Nicky, Mandy and I all have something to say too and all start talking at once and I find myself saying, "well if we can't do everything we usually do, we'll just have to cut down this year." That goes down like the proverbial lead Wellington boot if the look on Hillary's face is anything to go by.

"We can't cut down we always......" Hillary starts and Mandy interrupts her by saying, "lets talk this through."

Mandy sits herself next to Hillary and after some lengthy discussion Hillary calls us over and says, "I think I panicked a bit. I realise we don't have much time so we have tried to reduce the work load a bit. Mandy has suggested we incorporate the Easter basket and rabbit together as the card which could work. The rabbit can carry a little basket, into which we can put a few small chocolate eggs.

After more discussion we all agree we should make the chick finger puppets as the children, in the past, have so enjoyed doing them and Hillary insists we must have egg shapes, saying "It wouldn't be Easter without eggs, now would it?" We all have to agree with her on that point.

"I can trace some daffodils onto paper to make a nice picture." I offer, and hastily add. "Someone will have to draw a template of a daffodil for me first. Then we can use tissue paper on the trumpets to make them look a bit special and we can put those on the wall instead of a mural."

"Thank you, I think that would be good." Hillary says gratefully.

When she points out that we have just two weeks to draw, cut out, colour, stick, write on, and deliver everything we have decided on, we all feel like shrieking. And we know we'll all be going home with plenty of work to prepare.

But when Hillary says, "we always do singing for the parents at Easter." I think the looks on our faces, as we all glared at her, may have had something to do with the next sentence she uttered. "But maybe not this year."

Thursday 18th March

Going like the clappers. We're using nearly all our tables for working on. There's yellow, brown, white and cream, card and paper everywhere, also yellow tissue paper and green crepe paper. There are egg boxes, some whole and some already cut into 'baskets', crayons, glue and scissors and felt tip pens.

We have clean scrap paper on the floor ready to replenish the paper on the table tops when it gets too sticky and balls of gluey scrap paper pushed under the tables till we have time to clear it away properly. There are little dishes on the tables with orange beaks the size of your small finger nail, another dish with cotton wool balls and yet another dish with pink rabbit 'ears' in.

Felt pen and glue and whispers of cotton wool find their way onto nearly everything including clothing, hair, faces and fingers. The cotton wool even manages to get under your clothes and make you itch.

The poor children are sent from one table to another to stick this, draw that, colour this, sign here. Oh, what fun!

"We need to buy some very small edible eggs, Hillary. Shall I put them on a list before we forget?" calls Liz.

"We'll need to make envelopes and the paper for that is nearly all gone," adds Mandy. "We used most of it on the Mother's day cards."

"And more tissue paper is needed," I contribute. "So please can you add that to the list as well."

Pack up for lunch! Who said that? What do you mean pack up for lunch? Where's the morning gone?

The afternoon session is not quite so mad but it is a lot busier than it usually is.

Tuesday 23rd March

It's sunny but very cold as I cycle to school. I like to cycle when I can because not only do I feel it's healthier for me, but I see a lot more going at that slower pace. I can nosey into a few windows and gardens and today I'm rewarded with the sight of a few brave daffodils. They look cheerful and bright and must think spring is on its way even if the weather disagrees.

Once in school I'm asked to work with some of the older children today whilst they colour their Easter egg shapes, and I realise this is the last week or two for some of our older children. As they reach this stage we try to ensure that they really do know how to hold a pencil properly and not as a deadly weapon, and that they can write their names reasonably clearly. We also try to encourage their limited writing skills and colour and shape recognition. They tend to get more one-to-one attention for short periods of time during these last days with us. We also make games of putting on shoes and taking them off and doing up buttons and undoing them. This move to big school is such an important time for them and we try to bolster their confidence and tell them how clever they are to be going. Little do they know!

We had one lad who was reported to have said to his mum, 'I went to big school yesterday, now can I go back to nursery?' I hope that was true, it would mean we aren't too bad here after all.

We hear all kinds of comments from the children about their new uniforms, about their teachers visiting them at home and how they went to the big school for a look around. It's a major step and obviously some cope with it better than others.

I remember some years ago, two boys who were discussing their ages and their pending jump to "big school". The one lad was saying something along the lines of, 'I'm nearly five and I'm going to big school!' The other lad responded with, 'I'm nearly five too and I'm going to big school too.' And the rest of the day they seemed to have puffed out their chests and were telling everyone, with such glee in their voices, that they were going to big school. Such innocence.

Back to the present, each child now has a folder with his or her work in it and a list of contents written on the cover. Now we can all see at a glance just what is needed. I notice we seem to have got most of the Easter items started and some have a tick next to them indicating they are finished. We are getting on well, so let's crack on, colouring to do.

Thursday 25th March

It's so cold again.

I've no daffodils in my garden, no flowers at all.

It's raining on me now. Why does it always rain on me when I have to cycle?

Why is it the wind always blows against me and never pushes me along?

I'm late again. They're lucky I got here at all. The dog somehow managed to wriggle out of his harness and thought it was a great game when I was chasing him all around the park.

I should have stayed in bed today.

Boy, have I got a headache? And my stomach is so painful.

"Hillary, I'm going into the kitchen to take some of my pain relief pills then I'll do something sitting down," I say feeling very sorry for myself. "What is there to do?"

"I'll find you something," I hear her answer.

As I come back into the hall I see she has a table set up for me.

'What am I doing?' I mumble to myself. It looks like I'm colouring egg shapes again and sticking on bows.

I need a coffee.

`These plastic chairs are so hard.

It's much noisier in here than usual.

"Stick that there, you can do it," I say a touch crabbily.

"You want me to take you to the toilet? Again? All right.

Don't wave that spatula about.

"What now?" I grumble quietly at a poor unsuspecting child.

When is lunch?

More to the point when is home time?

P.M.T. Hormones. My age. Blame it on whatever you like. But it's here again.

Tuesday 30th March

Just this week to go, then two weeks off! Bliss.

Hillary asks, "are you feeling better today? You look better." Before I can reply she continues, "I want you to carry on with the Easter work and ensure every child has an Easter card."

I must say our rabbit Easter card is very nice this year and is shaping up to be a very novel card. It's a piece of card folded in half and cut into the shape of a sitting rabbit. In her paws she carries a coloured egg basket. (A bit of shaped egg box) To save time we have used white or brown card for the rabbit that needs no colouring but the children do have to colour the 'basket'. They then draw eyes and whiskers onto the rabbit and then stick on little pink ears and a fluffy cotton-wool tail. Then at the last moment we will count out small, wrapped, chocolate eggs to go into the baskets and they will be held in place with a small dot of glue.

When I think back, it's amazing how many different cards and keepsakes we have made. Rabbits, chicks, lambs, flowers and egg shapes have all been utilised to the full. Chick cards in an array of designs, chick collages, chick badges, chick pictures, chick masks, chick headbands, chick finger puppets. You name it and we've probably made it at some time or another.

We seem to be getting on fine with this year's selection and I notice this morning, that someone has slipped a few more, small, cardboard egg shapes into each folder. I bet that was Hillary.

"Hillary, what are these small egg shapes for?" As if I need to ask.

"I put them in there, just in case they were needed." I knew she had. She continues, "there are some children who are here for their last week, in fact it may well be the last day for some. So can you check they have all their work completed and ready to take home and also make sure they've finished their scrap books and their needlework."

It's exciting and sad to be working with these children for the last time. I settle down to check the folders and can see some of them are bulging with work. I discover these belong to the children who are leaving us and their needlework bags have been put into their folders.

Aunty Dawn usually does the needlework with these older children. They make a small bag by sewing wool onto open weave Binca fabric. They choose all their own colours and once shown what to do are amazingly adept. One or two are sometimes overly enthusiastic with the needles and we have to explain how dangerous that can be, but once that's corrected, it's a pastime the majority enjoy. When they've finished the wool stage, Dawn takes the bags home and lines them with cotton material and then a fastener is attached. It is then given back to its owner and a strap is easily fixed on. Then the bag is, proudly, paraded round the room for all to admire.

Considering the panic we were in at the beginning of the month, we have all calmed down noticeably now, and as we work we have time to chatter to the children and listen properly to them, instead of the distracted 'Mmmms' and 'Oh yes dear', of the last few weeks.

Off to the toilets again. Have I mentioned our wonderful toilets? They're a fair walk from the main hall and in the winter are freezing cold. The gents or boys, I should say, have two cubicles, two urinals, two wash-hand basins, a mirror and three windows, all three of which open to allow fresh air in, and it's lovely and light in there.

Our female toilets are cramped. We have two toilet cubicles and two wash hand basins, one of the hand basins is broken at the plug hole and water dribbles down onto the floor, so there's always an unpleasant mildewy smell in there. We have one light which flickers constantly even when a new florescent tube has been fitted. We have asked various electricians to check it and they all say it's safe. It may be safe but it's very, very irritating! We have a rubbish bin which is either squashed under the hand basin or is used to prop open the door so that at busy times we can gain an extra few inches of space. We have hung onto one mirror and we did have three windows but now two are blanked off as we had to part with some of our precious loo space to accommodate a disabled person's toilet.

We had been here in the scout hall for about two years when The Powers That Be decided we had to have facilities for a disabled person. Why they couldn't have thought of it earlier and told the planners and builders, we don't know. It would have been much easier and cheaper to incorporate it in the building stage. Not only did we have to find room for a disabled person's loo, we were even asked to contribute some money towards it. That came as no surprise, but it did annoy us. Anyway, a few feet were squeezed from the hallway and a few vital feet were squeezed from our loo space. Did I mention we also share our meagre space with the broom cupboard? So when I say it's not the most pleasant of places and gets quite squashed in there, I really mean it.

But we do have a very nice functional disabled person's toilet. The only thing is I don't think it has ever been used in all the years we've been here. We don't have any disabled children or parents, nor does the scout group as far as I know. I don't think the dance group who use the hall some evenings have any disabled people, but at least we have one should it ever be needed. It was probably all designed by a man because if a woman had had a say in it, she would have known that we girls need more toilets than the boys do. She would have known how vital mirrors are and that we would appreciate a bit of space. She would have known we would need lights that work and I would like to think she would have argued for an extra window or two, knowing the importance of fresh air. I'm sure a lady would have considered all of this and made sure we were left with a nice area. I also like to think a woman would have totally re-thought the positioning of the disabled toilet. We all wonder why they didn't pinch some space from the boys' area. Still, there's nothing we can do about it now - except moan and we do that frequently!

Thursday 1st April

Last day! Yippee! Well, last day for me. This morning when I was getting my bike from the shed I heard a scuffling noise coming from a cardboard box and knew my tortoise had awoken. I looked in the box and sure enough Ethal tortoise was awake. I checked in the other box and Henry tortoise looked up at me too. "You will have to wait in here a bit longer," I say to them. "I will get you out and bath you when I come home."

I peddled like crazy trying not to be too late to school and quickly shoved my bike against the wall and rushed into the hall. Once there I was asked to check all the Easter work again and I find nearly everyone has finished everything in their files so the morning was spent getting the last few items finished.

At milk time we found a few moments to talk about Nicky's forthcoming wedding and we all hoped the weather would be pleasant for her.

I mention all the Easter work is completed, so Hillary smiled and said, "Let's play. Pull the wooden playhouse out of the cupboard and today we will have it as a police station. We have those toy helmets that John dropped in for us and the children love wearing them."

The children have wonderful imaginations. This play house is painted with an outdoor scene, with trees, flowers, woodland animals and pixies, yet when we say it's a hospital or a post office or a house, they happily accept it as that. Today we make a sign saying 'Police station' and stick it over the doorway, and our forest abode is a police station.

Liz happily announces,"I'll make a bus; we haven't had one for ages." She starts arranging the chairs in pairs, one pair behind another, with a gap between for the aisle, and more pairs of chairs on the other side of the aisle. The children rush to sit on these seats and she nominates a conductor, although this age group have probably never seen a bus conductor. She shows the children how to issue imaginary tickets and off they go. Throughout the rest of the morning we can hear her saying that the bus is off to the zoo, or the swimming pool, or the park and they usually sing a song or two as they go.

On one of the tables we have set out a shop with different toys for sale and because we have the tills out, we need to make some money. Nicky and I soon find some card and start cutting out different sized circles which we get the children to colour, and a number is put on them in felt-tip pen to represent different coins. Then of course, some bright spark wants a purse to keep their money in. So we find more card and paper and purse making begins. This game is going well and is very popular so we keep alternating the shopkeeper as everyone wants a turn.

We hear someone is crying in the playhouse-cum-police station so I get up and go to investigate. Poor Brian is upset. I sit his slight frame on my lap and in between sobs he tells me he's been sent to prison. He didn't want to go to prison! He hadn't done anything wrong! Poor love. I can't help but chuckle to myself. We have a little hug and a talk. Then I wipe his face and his nose for him, and put his glasses back on. I take the police sign off the playhouse and we transfer the shop into there. As there are two windows in the playhouse and we can have two shopkeepers. I ask Brian if he wants to be one. That put a smile back on his face and ended another mini crisis.

We do have to dismantle Liz's bus at lunchtime as we need the chairs but we leave the other games out for the afternoon session and the bus reappears as soon as lunch is over.

We also make a game of who can take off their plimsolls and put their street shoes on. Who can put the shoes on the correct feet and who can tie laces. We also practice putting on coats and doing them up properly. We have a large dice shaped toy with different fastenings on each side. Laces, buckles, velcro, zips, buttons of different sizes and we make a game with that too by rolling it and whatever appears on top we choose a child to tackle that fastening. It is not played with very often which is a shame as it is educational and fun.

It all made a nice change and resulted in a very happy day. Hopefully when we come back next term, it will be warmer and bring an end to the constant green tramlines on every child's top lip! I won't miss them I can tell you. When you see a child with them, you grab a tissue and say 'Blow your nose.' Some children respond to that but I remember we had an interesting situation not so long back, I was asking this lad to 'blow his nose' and he was not responding at all. 'Blow, blow your nose, come on now.' I urged. Still nothing. Then a slightly older child interrupted and said to him, 'Sniff backwards.' It worked! Child's logic I suppose. Children never cease to amaze me.

The weather is warm and the cycle home is delightful, with spring flowers appearing in many gardens.

Home at last now to sort out the pets, two tortoise and a dog.

END OF TERM

Chapter Three

Tuesday 20th April

Here I am again all refreshed and raring to go, well, refreshed anyway. The sun is shining and it really is feeling milder. I have hung out a line of washing so I hope the weather holds out. It's a pleasure to ride my bike to school today and I'm quite warm when I arrive.

I've only been in the door a few minutes and I'm given a gift by Simon.

"Oh! Thank you, how nice. I'll put them in water." I walk into the kitchen and put water into a plastic cup and add the three squashed dandelions and a muddy daffodil and place them on the hatchway for everyone to see. Not a huge bouquet but the thought was there.

As I come back into the hall I see Nicky and Hillary talking together near the register. I join them to see what Hillary wants me to do today. They're talking about Nicky's wedding and I join in and politely ask, "who did your wedding cake? It was wonderful."

"Thank you, one or two people have asked," Nicky beams. "The local baker did it and I know it's old fashioned but we want to keep the top layer for, you know when. Not that we're planning to start a family just yet."

Then Hillary asks, "when will your photographs be ready?"

"About two more weeks, I think," Nicky replies. "I can't wait to see them."

I interrupt saying,"I've bought some in that I took." I turn to collect them from my bag in the cupboard. They are only snaps but I am pleased with them. We spend a few minutes looking at them and chattering together.

"You were so lucky with the weather," Hillary commented. And she was right. The day had been sunny and bright and the little Norman church, sitting at the end of a narrow country lane, made a wonderful setting. We had to drive past small cottages to get there and then the church came into view, surrounded by fields and countryside, it was idyllic. The church had been tastefully decorated by Nick's friends and family and it was a lovely, cheerful wedding service. Nicky looked absolutely beautiful and the few snaps I had taken outside the church were quite good, even if I do say so myself. I particularly liked one I'd taken just as she was about to get into the wedding car. All her guests standing happily around, and in the background the moss covered latch-gate and pathway to the old church. She commented on it too, saying how lovely it was, so I gave it to her.

As we are talking we are also keeping an eye on what is happening in the hall and I notice that we have some new toys, including some black and brown dolls. When I enquire about these new additions Hillary said, "I received a letter telling me that we must have a good selection of toys to appeal to any ethnic group, so that if and when we have children from other nationalities they will feel more comfortable and integrate better."

Well, I suppose that's politically correct, but I don't expect we had any financial help to buy them. The Powers That Be are always insisting on one thing or another but they are not very forthcoming with any money to help pay for them. Also, in all the years I've been here, we have never once had a foreign child. One child had an Italian father, if I remember correctly, but I suppose we must be prepared and be seen to be doing the right thing.

Hillary tells me we have to watch the children with these new dolls as some of them were frightened by the dolls yesterday. Jenny was in floods of tears for most of the day, and the dolls ended up being put back into the cupboard.

"Who's Jenny?" I ask her.

Looking round the room, Hillary points her out to me saying, "Oh, she's new. She's the girl with long red hair playing with Sally at the puzzle table."

"I hope she hasn't got the temper to go with her lovely red hair."

"If she has, we haven't seen it yet," replies Hillary. "I'm going to sit with Mandy and we'll be working with the children and I'd like you to sit with Julie and quickly check the record cards of all the children. Yes, don't look at me like that; we now have to have individual record cards for every child and adult here, another new rule. So my old address book has been made redundant at long last. I want you to make sure we have contact numbers of family and neighbours, and doctors' names and numbers. I've put a list of the new children's names on a bit of paper, it's on the desk. As you work through the list Julie can point the new children to you. Well, those who are here today. And this little lady here is Kadetta," she adds as she is tapped on the skirt by a quiet little girl. "I'll have her with me as she's rather shy and is finding nursery school a bit difficult."

I find the list and settle down with Julie.

"Kadetta? Kadetta? I've heard that name somewhere. Where have I heard it?" I say half to myself and half to Julie. "I know! I've seen that name on the telly. It's a car, for goodness sake. Hey Julie, were you ever tempted to call your son Vauxhall or Hillman?"

"No, but we did consider Cortina," she quickly answers.

"Mercedes might work but what about Skoda?" I counter.

"Or even Rover but not Beetle," she laughs.

"Rover that's what you call a dog, not a child," I laughingly add.

We have a few more suggestions and giggles but a 'look' from Hillary makes us get back to the business in hand.

Julie has another list in front of her, it's a list of the children who've gone to school and I have a quick look at it. I see we've lost Louise, Gemma and Catherine, also Steven and Michael.

"I'll miss Michael," I say to Julie. He was a cheeky little thing and we often had a laugh with him. "Do you remember when he came here with his pants on his head and would not remove them all day?"

"Yes I do," she grinned and said. "And when he came in with two different shoes on."

"Oh yes, I had forgotten that," I reply. I chuckle at the memory as Julie passes the boys' cards over to me saying, " You can do the boys cards and I will check the girls' cards." I notice we have gained three new boys Troy, Arthur (now there's a name we've never had,) and a David. David's parents certainly have a sense of humour!

"Hey Julie, will you look at this? David Oliver George. We don't often have children with three names. Oh, hang on. Just look at those initials. And with his surname too! Bowne. D.O.G. Bowne. I bet they never gave that a thought. Poor lad, I bet he keeps stumm about those middle names. I know I would. " That sets us off laughing again but it was quickly brought under control as we could hear crying. We both look round and see Topaz is sitting on the floor quite upset. I go over to her and sit on the floor beside her and ask her what the matter is. She sniffs and hiccups and says, "I don't like those dolls." Pointing to the new coloured dolls. I give her a little hug and suggest that she makes us both a nice cup of tea with the tea set, by way of a distraction. I hastily pick up the dolls and put them away in the cupboard. They could prove to be a complete waste of money.

The Powers That Be have been busy over the holidays making decisions about dolls and record cards, and in the relative quiet of milk time Hillary tells us, "I also had a letter just before half term asking if I had enough qualified staff? Well, as you know our idea of qualified staff is somewhat different from some pen-pusher in an office. I like to have people round me who know what they are doing. I'm not in the least bit worried if they have a certificate or not. I had to submit details of all of you and according to them I have to employ someone else. So I've been interviewing in the half term and have found us a new staff member. Her name is Tanya and she starts tomorrow. She's only young and this will be her first job from college."

This could be interesting I think to myself. I look forward to meeting Tanya on Thursday.

Thursday 22nd April

I arrive a little early today, it's a fluke, it only ever usually happens at the beginning of each term or if punctuality has been mentioned. Liz is already in the hall so I join her getting the last few items from the cupboard. I notice she has the painting easel out already, and the aprons, so I collect the paint powder and pots.

Tanya arrives and the introductions are made. She is shorter than I am and a bit on the tubby side with a very, very short hair cut. First impressions are not too encouraging as she seems a bit aloof, a bit reserved, but I shouldn't be hasty, she is new after all and probably a bit nervous and uncertain.

Hillary asks me to carry on with the painting and to explain to Tanya how we do it here. I used to hate being the 'new girl' whenever I changed jobs so I try to help her as much as possible. I show her where the paper is kept in the inner cupboard, and explain that the mixing of the paints seems to take forever. Then I get the bowl of clean water for hand washing and the towel, and put them on a couple of chairs beside her. I find us both tabards to wear and show her where the children's aprons are kept. Eventually, we're ready. Lulu is hovering around us and is our first willing candidate. I introduce her to Aunty Tanya and turn round to find Dilly has come over to us and wants to paint too. I introduce her to Aunty Tanya as well, and as Dilly and Lulu paint happily, I'm able to answer a few questions Tanya asks.

I collect the painting horse from the cupboard, ready for Lulu's painting to be hung on, and notice that Tanya and Lulu have both disappeared. As Brian is close by and is keen to start a painting, I soon have him in an apron. I put his name on a paper and peg the paper on the easel for him. Tanya re-appears and tells me she is quite capable of supervising the painting now as she knows what to do, and I get the distinct feeling I'm not now wanted.

I go and join the 'work' table and I'm happy to see the children are colouring a bride and groom and Liz whispers to me, "What do you make of her?" Indicating Tanya with a nod of her head.

"Well, I'm not quite sure yet," I answer.

"I must tell you something later. Remind me," she says quietly. This arouses my curiosity but she must feel she can't tell me just yet.

We all carry on with what we're doing but keep an eye on Tanya as well. She looks as if she is getting on very well with the children and seems full of confidence. Maybe my first impression was wrong. She chatters away to them and is happy to disappear down to the loo at regular intervals. Actually, she seems to be going down to the loo an awful lot. I decide to go back over to her and enquire if I can help in any way, and it comes to light that she's taking the children down to the toilets to wash their hands! I explain about the bowl of water and the towel sitting on the chairs next to the easel and I tell myself she is new, hold your tongue, and don't say anything rude or sarcastic.

I pop into the cupboard for some scissors and Liz comes rushing in and I tell her about Tanya and the trips to the loo. "Honestly, what did she think the bowl of water was for? A decoration?" We both raise our eyebrows skyward and shake our heads.

Liz can't wait to mention her bit of gossip too. She tells me that yesterday Tanya refused to go into the kitchen to wash up the children's cups Her reason being, and here Liz affects a false voice, 'I'm qualified to work with children and not to wash up!' Maybe my first impression was right after all.

"What qualifications do you need to wash up?" I ask sarcastically. "Do you have one? I've only been washing up for about thirty years I wonder if I'm doing it right. I think I'll ask Hillary if we can do a GNVQ course on it, so we'll know for certain we're doing it right."

"Shut up, you fool!" she laughs and hurries back to the colouring table.

At milk and biscuits time we all rush about, positioning the chairs, preparing the drinks and rounding up the children. We, being the royal 'We', and excluding Tanya. Perhaps she was watching and learning but I have my doubts. I end up sitting next to her and find she's not the easiest person to converse with, but I persevere and learn that she was the top student for her year. She has one brother and two sisters, and she just loves working with children. I ask her if she's okay to carry on painting or if she wants to swap, because sometimes doing the same job all morning can be tiresome. She says she's happy to carry on painting, so after we have tidied away the drinks and re-positioned the tables and chairs, I go and get on with making scrapbooks for the newcomers.

The day ticks along nicely, no major problems. As I sit 'gluing' with Brian, who is getting fairly confident now, I glance around the room and I notice Arthur putting a doll into the toy oven. I get up and go and ask him what he's doing and he says, "I'm cooking 'em to make 'em brown like the dolls we 'ad yesterday." I can hardly contain my laughter as I remove the dolls from the oven. I suggest he goes and sits at the table with Brian as I will need him to work with me in a minute, and I go over to Hillary and tell her what I've just heard.

"Hillary, I must tell you this. Arthur is only cooking some dolls to make them brown like the ones we had yesterday. Can you believe it? It's priceless."

Hillary chuckled and said, "I know, I can believe it. Some of the things that he says are so funny, and he has expressions way beyond his age. Do you know what he said to me yesterday? 'Okay, girl.' Yes, okay girl! I had asked him to do something and that was his reply. His family have moved down here from London and his father was a market trader and I think Arthur has picked up some of his fathers sayings. He is one to watch, that one, but in a nice way."

At half past twelve, we have all the lunch tables ready and again, I notice, Tanya was watching rather that helping. Ro is keeping an eye on the children sitting at the lunch tables and Liz is watching the going home children who are seated and almost ready to go. Then the fun begins! We start to hand out the paintings to the morning children, only to find, there are only three papers with names on, Dilly, Lulu and Brian, the children I started. Tanya did not think to name the papers. I must have forgotten to tell her, but it is so obvious that maybe I just thought she would know to do it. So we have to hold up each painting and ask, "whose painting is this?" and hope for the best. It takes a long, long time but in the end each child does have a painting. We just hope they have the right painting!

We're very late starting lunch, and know we will have to sort out and name the rest of the papers before we can start the afternoon children doing their paintings.

No one blames Tanya... much!

Tuesday 27th April

It's that time of the month again, and again I had to strip the bedding from the bed and re-make it with clean sheets. Then I put the messy sheets and my pyjamas into the washing machine. I have a stomach ache, I'm tired and I feel tetchy and grumpy. I throw my jacket at the hook and plod over to sign in and Hillary says, "Come over here and read this and tell me what you think? It's about our sandbox, the others have all seen it and I'm sure you would want to see it too." With that she hands me a letter, I'm not sure if I even look properly to see who had sent it, possibly the education department. I grab the nearest chair and sit down and begin to read.

Before I say any more, I'll tell you a little story about the sandbox. Five or six years ago we had a directive from someone in The Powers That Be and it stated all groups such as ours were to have sandboxes. No money was put forward, so we duly started fund raising, selling raffle tickets and having sponsored events, and it took us quite a few months to get the money together. Eventually we had enough money to order the model they suggested, which had a lid on it and was mounted on wheels for easy movement. We had to order it from a specific company, which we did, even though it was expensive and they wanted the money up front. At that time, we did not have enough money to order the sand from them but Hillary knew we could get the sand cheaper locally anyway.

The sandbox duly arrived. But, in the few months it had taken to achieve all of the fund raising and until the delivery , low and behold, we received another recommendation from The Powers That Be. The gist of this letter was, to tell us not to use sand! Sand is not to be used in play groups or nursery groups. Sand is messy, sand is dangerous, and sand gets in eyes etc. etc. etc. So it turned out to be lucky for us we weren't able to afford it at the time of ordering the box. But now we had a situation where we had a sandbox, which our 'parents' had paid for and wanted to see being used, but we were not allowed to put sand in it! What where we going to do? Hillary wrote a letter back to The Powers That Be and eventually a reply arrived suggesting we use rice.

Fine, our parents would be able to see the sandbox in use as soon as we could go and buy some rice. It would take a lot of rice to fill the tray, but again we were lucky as one of 'our' mums had a cash and carry card and offered to collect some from the wholesaler. Unloading it from her car was difficult as it was so heavy, and she admitted that she had had to ask one of the chaps at the wholesalers to load it into her car for her. At last we had rice. As we poured it into the sandbox we could see we only had about a quarter of the capacity but at least we could use it, it was enough to start with.

It proved to be such a popular game. There were always ten or more children pushing, shoving and yelling to have a go. So it was decided, for safety reasons that we should have no more than four children playing at a time and always with an adult supervising. As I mentioned it was a bit sparse on rice and the children had to reach down for it, but even with that degree of difficulty, rice was forever dropping onto the floor, no matter how careful we all tried to be. There was always rice everywhere; it couldn't be helped; it ended up in your lap, under your finger nails, in your hair and always, always on the floor.

We had plenty of sand toys which worked equally as well with rice, and the children definitely like to play with them. 'Yes isn't it fun when you wind that little handle and all the rice flies everywhere!' I smile and through gritted teeth agree with the children. This is a fun activity I ask myself? This maybe a fun activity for the children but definitely not for the adults. And if you had to walk anywhere near to the box, you had to be so very careful as the floor, within a ten pace radius, was lethal. Rice grains on a wooden floor were so slippery. We would try to position the box in a corner but still rice would fly all over the place and make the area quite dangerous to walk on.

I was so glad it was The Powers That Be decided that rice was the 'safe' option because, if we had to put in an insurance claim, the insurance companies would have been bound to ask questions, and we could have referred them to The Powers That Be, explaining we were only following instructions.

Sadly we didn't use the rice/sandbox very often, not just because of the safety aspect, but because of the weight of it. The tray and the lid were quite heavy on their own but add the rice/sand and the toys and it was a struggle to manoeuvre it in and out of the cupboard. And because the box had a nice flat lid on it, we seemed drawn to putting things on that lid, and sometimes it was all too much bother.

But now, back to this letter Hillary has given me to read, it says, in a nut shell that The Powers That Be, in their wisdom, have decided that the rice/sandboxes are dangerous! They have had complaints from other groups and nursery schools mentioning the slippery floors near to the boxes and also the weight of the boxes. Now there's a surprise! It goes on to say we must, have 'sand play'. Sand play is important and educational and we must use at least four different colours of sand and use a minimum of four different sized and shaped containers.' No more information. No other guide lines. One year sandboxes are to be used but the sand is dangerous and now the sandboxes are not to be used but the sand is okay! What are we supposed to make of that?

"I'm not in the mood for this today, Hillary." I say ill humouredly as I thrust the letter back at her. "I can't cope with all their gobbledegook. Just let me get though the day doing something easy."

She smiles that knowing smile and says, "go and sit at the play dough then."

"What! And have everything I make squashed in seconds. Not likely I'll sit by the sticky bricks, not that that is much better!" I grumble.

Thursday 29th April

I hope there are no more letters and silly new rules today, as I'm still very touchy and uncomfortable. Hillary calls out a greeting as I enter the hall and asks me to sit with Tanya and do colouring with the children today. Tanya has everything ready and I say good morning to her as I sit down. I notice a stack of papers with children's names on them, a lesson learnt there then Tanya, I think to myself. I also see from the papers that the subject for colouring today is a mummy elephant with her baby.

"Morning," she replies and continues, "I think we should stick to grey as the correct colour for the elephants and let the children use any colour they like for the eyes." That'll be exciting I think to myself, have you seen the size of an elephant's eye? A mere pin prick in comparison with the elephant. How nice!

After the first dull grey offering, I improvise a bit by suggesting to the children nearest to me that a hint of green grass appearing at the bottom of the page may look good, and some blue also appears at the top of some of the pictures. The more able children put in a big yellow sunshine, I wonder who allowed that? My children's pictures are looking a little more interesting, I think. I've had a few disapproving looks from Tanya who is just sticking to what is on the paper, a mother elephant and a baby elephant only. Why am I not surprised at that? She needs to loosen up a bit and be a bit more inventive.

My children's pictures look so good that I quickly commandeer the sticky tape and stick their work onto the walls. Unfortunately I have to tape up some of the dull ones too but they only serve to make mine look better.

As we work, I notice Tanya works well with the children next to her but seems to have no common sense. What I mean is, you can almost predict some situations i.e. a boisterous boy and a pencil can mean an accident to anyone within his arm's length, so we would explain to him to be careful. Also we don't allow one child to 'hog' all the crayons but to just take the one they need, and we stop rough scribbling which makes a tear in the paper. We aunties all know this, except Tanya it seems. I have seen her replace a few papers without saying a word to the child or explaining or helping them. Maybe it develops with time, I don't know, but she certainly hasn't got it yet. I feel I ought to say something to her about it but I think she would take it as a personal criticism, perhaps I'll just mention it, in passing, to Hillary.

Most of the older children are colouring beautifully now, but we do have to show the younger ones over and over. So many of them hold the crayon in their fist with a tip of crayon showing besides their little finger. They have no real control of the crayon like that, so we try to encourage a better way of holding the pencil or crayon. It can be a long slow process to get them to do it right, but it is so satisfying when they can produce a piece of work to be proud of.

Whilst the children are colouring, I glance around the room to make sure all is as it should be. I see one of the older girls, Annie, is reading to a younger girl, Jenny. Jenny only joined us at Easter but it looks as if she has made a friend already. Annie is patiently pointing out things on each page and talking about them. I wish I was closer and could hear what she was saying. Annie has two younger siblings so I suppose she's used to looking after smaller ones. In fact, one of her brothers will be joining us in September so I have been told. He has already been here with his mum for a few visits.

We encourage these visits, as we feel it helps the child to feel comfortable here and adjust to our ways a little more easily. Hopefully it helps the parents, too, to see that their child will be well cared for and in a happy environment. The children are usually okay and adapt very quickly, they see plenty of toys and lots of children happily playing and are soon joining in and having fun, but some of the mums! That can be a different story. Some are too scared their child will break something and follow their child about all the time. Some feel guilty about leaving their children and talk about it for ages as if trying to purge themselves of the guilt, and then there are some mums who can't wait to leave their children and rush out of the door and breathe a sigh of relief.

To be fair, the majority of the mums we have dealt with here have been very good indeed and they have helped us with fund raising and open days but, you do get the odd one. Hillary had to have a serious talk to one mum a few years ago about the language she was using. Her poor child was being called all the foul names under the sun, well actually, under our roof. Most of the other mums were embarrassed and we staff were horrified, but, this mother could see nothing wrong in swearing and using the 'F' word to her child.

As I look round the room, I notice some of the children looking at and discussing the elephant pictures which I have taped up. Some children tell us they are allowed to pin up their works of art at home; sometimes it's in the kitchen or in their bedrooms. I know from experience that they can look a bit of a mess after a few weeks, especially when the paper begins to go yellow, but they're so important to the children and we mums are so proud of their work that we put up with it.

I remember having my son's art work on the kitchen cupboard doors and on the fridge and hating having to remove them. Some would go all brittle and others had to be repaired over and over with sticky tape and the tatty ones eventually just had to go to make room for the new stuff. I think I still have some of his work in the loft. Is it in the loft, or under the spare bed? I think it's in the loft I might go up there and have a look, oops, I've 'gone off on one' as my mum used to say.

What's the time? Gosh! It's getting late. We'll have to get a move on to be ready in time today. I see Rosemary has started the loo run already. Liz is re-positioning the tables and chairs so I quickly start to tidy away some of the toys. Lego bricks into the big blue boxes. Dolls and blankets all together; plastic food and crockery together; the cars to the garage and puzzles in their correct boxes. Bending, carrying, sorting, transferring, separating, arranging and rearranging to make everything neat and tidy, and I spot Tanya just standing, standing doing nothing. I hear this voice in my head, dripping with sarcasm, say, 'No, that's fine Tanya; you just stand and watch us rush about like headless chickens, no problem. No problem at all…'

By the time I have finished lunch and repositioned some chairs and tables, my sarcasm has been put back in it's box. I ask Tanya if she needs me to help her with the few elephant pictures she has to do with the afternoon children.

"No," was the short reply I received.

I call over to Hillary, "as we've been doing elephants today, can I get the zoo animals out?"

"Good idea, we haven't had the zoo out for a while." She responds happily.

I commandeer two tables and push them together and fetch the box of zoo animals from the shelf. Jenny comes over to see what I'm doing and Arthur wanders over to join us. Between us we soon have small fences erected and the feeding troughs out and we're enjoying positioning the animals.

"I've bin to the zoo, Auneee Wendy," Arthur tells me.

"Did you like it?" I ask him.

"Yer, I liked the geerarffs best and the lions."

Joe appears at my side and says, "I saw a camel when I was on holiday, have we got any camels?"

"Yes I think so," I answer.

He found one and also grabbed a crocodile and then proceeded to stuff the camel into the crocodiles mouth. “There, that’s better,” he said. “I didn’t like that camel. He spitted.” What could I say? He obviously needed to get that off his little chest. He played for a while longer then went off to something else.

Other children came and went, and the zoo animals were moved here and there and back again. It was calming and pleasant and all too soon we had to pack away.

Tuesday 4th May

Cycling to work today is splendid as the sun is shining and has some warmth to it. When I opened up the tortoise run this morning, Henry was keen to get out into the garden. I had found some clover leaves and dandelion leaves when I was out with the Leo and washed them and put them down on the patio. So he was happy in the sunshine with his favourite food for later. I hope we have a good summer. Being slim I feel the cold and I hate it, give me the summer any day. As I glide into the car park on my bike, I see the mums look different today, I can’t put my finger on it but they seem brighter, happier somehow and they seem to be hanging about a bit, too.

“Hey, Julie, is something going on?” I enquire as soon as I see her.

“Come into the cupboard with me. I was just going in there to find the play-dough, and I'll tell you.” She then says with a sparkle in her eye, “It's Brandon.”

“Who’s Brandon?” I ask, intrigued.

“Brandon is a tall, handsome, athletic, young man who will be working here for a few weeks. He started yesterday and is doing some kind of community service.” We find the play-dough and we both go and play with the children. I can’t wait to see this mystery man who has aroused so much interest and I ask Julie to tell me as much as she can about him.

“Well, I don’t know much more than that really, except he is lovely.”

Hillary eventually gets rid of all the mums, all bar one, who has found that she has a free morning and wants to spend it helping out here. Fishy, normally wild horses couldn't keep a parent here.

Hillary comes over to talk to me and she explains, as Julie had, that Brandon will be with us till July. He will be working two days a week, usually Mondays and Tuesdays, and will do maintenance work, cleaning and gardening.

We have had people like this before and they've been utterly useless. Old Stan, for example, he was with us for two weeks and in all that time the only job he completed was to bang two nails into the wall for the hatch doors to tie back onto. He did make a mean cup of tea. Mind you, he had plenty of practice as that was all he did all day long, make tea and sit drinking it. We aunties could do many of the minor maintenance jobs better than he could, and we were so embarrassed by his ineptitude that we used to send him out into the garden all the time. And he used to sit out there with his cup of tea, watching the world go by and as happy as a lark. I remember, once he mowed the grass but he managed to leave tufts of long grass all over the place and it looked far worse than if he had just left it alone. I don't know if he was just not a practical man or just unbelievably lazy.

"There's the doorbell. I'll go." I call as I get up. I walk into the hallway, and there's this drop dead gorgeous bloke waiting outside with a bike. He's wearing a white tee shirt and you can see how toned and tanned he is.

"Who are you?" I say, before unlocking the door.

"I'm Brandon." This deep rich voice replies. I open the door and try to appear as unconcerned as possible. He must be nearly six feet tall with short dark hair and a voice that makes you go weak at the knees. No wonder all the mums were waiting about. He leans his bike on mine, (lucky bike) and follows me into the main hall and signs in, and he calls out a cheery, 'good morning' to everyone.

Hillary introduces us. "Wendy this is Brandon. Brandon meet Wendy," and she continues, "Brandon, would you mow the grass as the weather is fine and dry?" And she turns to me and adds, "can you show him where the mower is kept please?"

Can I? I have to take him outside to the shed and unlock it, how long can I make that last? I comment about the weather as we walk round to the back of the building and ask him about himself. He tells me he's twenty eight years old, comes from London originally where he used to help his dad in the family maintenance business, then he went on to work with disadvantaged kids. He tells me he is single, enjoys playing the guitar and has his own flat. I must remember not to leak that to any one, they will be following him home and queuing outside.

All too quickly we reach the shed and he easily manhandles the mower from beneath all the rubbish that's kept in there. I suggest he looks for the edging shears whilst he's in there. I know we have none, but he doesn't know that and oh boy, he has such a lovely bum. After a minute or two I have to admit there are no shears, I pretend to have just remembered that they had been thrown away. I have no reason to hang around any longer, so I make my way back inside and leave him to get on with the mowing.

"Jammy cow," Julie mutters good-humouredly as I go past her.

"Well, he is definite going to cheer up our days," I grin as I sit back down.

Nicky makes the drinks at break time and is told to take one out for HIM. She's all of a dither when she comes back in as he has removed his tee shirt because of the heat. I mention that he told me of his work with children, adding that I thought The Powers That Be had really slipped up this time. Fancy them agreeing to us having someone who could actually do maintenance work and has had experience with children. Now that is sensible and really doesn't sound like The Powers That Be that we know and normally have to deal with.

Hillary calls over, "remember, he's not allowed to ever be alone with the children."

"The reaction he has caused in just a day or two, I can't imagine he will ever be left alone, as there will always be someone who will want to be near him," Julie chips in.

"I know, and I also know he's been police checked, like us, but he's primarily here to help out with repairs," Hillary finishes.

This will make the next few Tuesdays a bit more interesting, that's for sure. Shame it is only for eight weeks.

Thursday 6th May

Everyone is talking about Brandon. We must all sound like love sick teenagers. Still, there's always something to bring you back to earth with a bang. We have an outbreak of head lice. As we do have to get quite close to the children, when helping them write or glue, this is the type of news we dread.

Apparently, Arthur's head is crawling with them. I've seen head lice before, unfortunately, but young Tanya says she has only seen pictures of them at college, not the real thing. I call across to Nicky and ask her if she has seen nits to which she replies, she hasn't. So we try to look closely at his head without him being aware of us. No chance! Arfur, as he has told us his name is, turns to us and says, "are yer looking at me nits?" He seems almost proud of them and the extra attention he is getting.

"Yes, I would like to show Tanya and Nicky," I say. "Is that all right with you?"

"Yer, carry on luv," he says simply.

He makes us smile with that comment. We look at his head and sure enough we quickly see the very small white eggs on his hair.

All of us are scratching our heads. It's psychosomatic. You hear the word 'nit' and you scratch.

"Liz, can you compose a letter for the parents?" asks Hillary. "Then we can hand out a copy to each child to take home, informing them of the outbreak. Wendy will you phone round the chemists and see if they have the correct shampoo in stock at the moment and then Liz can mention on the letter which local chemists have it."

We can do no more. The sooner we all get home, via the chemist, and wash our hair, the better.

Tuesday 11th May

As I open the curtains this morning I'm glad to discover it's sunny again and I'm sure it's feeling warmer too. I find myself wearing a rather nice blouse and a new pair of jeans. Wearing a new piece of clothing at work is like waving a red rag to a bull. It's asking for glue to go on it, or paint, or for one of the children to be sick all down you, but for some totally unknown reason I feel I have to make an effort this Tuesday and no, it has nothing to do with the fact that Brandon will be there. I notice all the aunties look rather nice today and some even have a bit of make up on.

Hillary calls me to her and asks if I would like to take a few children across the park to the play area, for them to play on the swings and slide. She agrees the weather is just too nice to stay indoors. She knows I love to be outside when it is warm, and adds, it will make a nice change for the children. I'm told I'm to take the older children and no more than six. Brian, Mark and Simon are the boys she has chosen and I have Dilly, Annie and Sophie. These six are given a lecture on doing as Aunty Wendy says, and they all nod and promise to be good.

I ask her, "what will we do about taking Jodie as she's not keen on dogs? And there are always some in the park."

"We'll cross that bridge later," she answers.

"Don't forget to go to the loo before you go," calls Mandy, "otherwise you know one of them will want to 'go' the minute you get there." So a quick visit to the loo for all of us, including me, and then I ask them to hold hands, boy girl, boy girl, and off we go. It's only a short walk across the grass and I try to steer a route around all the dogs' mess but Simon has to comment on it.

"There's lots of dogs' poo here!" he chirps. I ignore the comment and try to hurry them up. Once inside the play area I ask four children to sit down, well outside the arc of the swings, and tell them not to move. The other two I take over to the swings. Dilly jumps onto the swing, no problem, but Annie can't get onto her swing because it has bird poo on it. Simon has to come over to inspect it. Luckily the third swing is clean so we just move along a bit. Next Brian and Mark have their goes on the swings and I notice the four children on the grass are engrossed with something I cannot see. On investigation I discover that Simon has a hand full of rabbit droppings.

"These are rabbit poo," he announces confidently to all of us. After making him put the droppings down I decide to move the children along a little bit further, and Simon and Sophie eventually have their goes on the swings. Then we all transfer along to the slide. This was going well for a while, until Sophie noticed a small black, slug shaped lump near the steps.

"Is that poo?" She asks pointing at it. "What poo is it? Aunty Wendy."

"That's hedgehog poo," I tell her. Actually I wasn't absolutely sure if it was hedgehog poo but it was so like the little offering left in my garden most evenings after the hedgehog had done his rounds, that I felt fairly confident.

Simon examines it excitedly, "yes, I know this. It is hedgehog poo!" he announces confidently. "We have hedgehogs in our back garden."

These six seem fascinated by poo and Simon is so pleased that we have come across some more that he says excitedly, as he marks off on his fingers, "dog poo, bird poo, rabbit poo and now hedgehog poo. Four lots of poo, wait till I tell Aunty Hillary." She'll be delighted, I think to myself.

"Anyone would think you would prefer a poo hunt to staying here on the slide," I say half jokingly. The looks on their little faces, especially Simon's, confirm just that. So as they are all so much more interested in finding poo, I abandon the slide and swings and we go for a walk all around the park, in search of poo. If you can't beat them join them, I find myself thinking.

We find lots of dog poo. More rabbit poo. A smelly cat poo. Some large seagull splats and squirrel droppings! Well, I know that it's unlikely that they are squirrel poo but I told the children that's what they are. After all, I am an aunty and as such I'm supposed to know everything, and these droppings were unlike anything else we'd seen, and I was running out of animals by then. The children seem happy to believe me and there is an outside chance I might be right.

"Look Aunty Wendy, look!" Says Simon tugging at my arm and pointing with his other hand. "Look at that dog." And not far from us there's a dog, doing what a lot of other dogs had done on the grass. Simon is beside himself with joy and can't wait to tell everyone the minute we get back inside. I insist that we all go and wash our hands before we go into the hall but it's impossible to stop him telling everyone, everything he saw and found, as we sit down to our morning drink.

After milk time I have six more children to take over to the park. There are four girls, Sally, Lulu, Topaz and Jazzier, and two boys, Paul and Traydon. I overhear Hillary having a little talk with them so I hope that this group will be a bit more interested in the swings and slide. I'm pleased to say the girls are all very happy on the swings. Paul is a little anxious and I have to almost hold him all the time. There are no such problems with Traydon, who has mastered the art of swinging himself to and fro. I just have to watch he doesn't go too mad. They all enjoy their time on the slide too and soon it is time to go back to the hall.

As we reach the door, Brandon is there ready to go inside and he holds the door open for us. Julie is walking the dinner children down to the toilets and amongst them is Simon, who just has to shout out to Brandon and tell him about all the poo he had seen earlier in the park. I notice Brandon's eye brows raised a little higher on his brow but he didn't say anything except a non committal, "Oh, really."

My little group and I join Julie's group and go to the toilet and wash our hands. We make our way into the hall for lunch but I'm afraid to say, as hungry as I am, my cold sausage sandwich has lost its appeal!

Little Jodie calls me over to her and asks if she can go to the park. I tell her I think it will be all right and that I'll ask Aunty Hillary. I do mention all the dogs that use the park but she still wants to go. Hillary is happy to allow it and so it looks like my afternoon is going to be outside in the fresh air again.

Thursday 13th May

Riding my bike to school this morning, I have to admit to having a grin on my face as I keep thinking what the conversations were between my six 'poo spotters' and their parents. How I would have liked to have been a fly on the wall in those houses on Tuesday evening.

No Brandon today, so back to wearing old splattered jeans and a tatty sweat shirt and, I might add, most of the mums I see don't look as dazzling as they did earlier in the week. As I'm late again, I decide to wait and go in with the parents. If I ring the bell it will mean disturbing one of the aunties to stop what they're doing to come and unlock the door to let me in, only to repeat the process a few minutes later to allow the parents in. So I wait, and they're all so preoccupied with talking about Brandon, that they hardly notice me amongst them. One or two of them are even saying that they'll come in to help within the group, if they can come in on Mondays or Tuesdays. This is almost unheard of. We have tried and tried over the years to get parents to spare us an hour or two of their time, usually to no avail.

When the door opens I try to hide myself in the throng and I think I get away with it as nothing is said to me.

Hillary asks Ro to oversee and asks Liz and me to supervise the colouring.

"It's a little bit different today," she says to us, "as I want the children to colour in a Scottie type dog, which has been drawn on the paper. Then they can choose a plaid coat for it to wear and stick it on to the dog. The coats are small bits of colourful material which I have cut out and put in a dish for you. There are also a few bone shapes and balls which can be coloured and glued on by the more able children. Not hard work, admittedly, but it helps to have two of you as the coats and other bits are small and it could be fiddly."

"The shape of that dog is a bit like my Leo," I say to her.

"So it is," she replies.

We soon get set up and are able to have a good moan about things as we work, and the morning just rushes by. By milk and biscuits time we have a good display of work on the walls. We also have three black crayons in the glue pot and a handful of coats in there too. I gingerly pick the crayons out of the glue but leave the coats as they would be useless anyway now. Liz cuts some extra ones out of coloured paper saying, "I'm glad you fished those crayons out, I hate the feel of that glue."

"Oh, I enjoy gluing," I admit, "but don't you tell anyone."

After drinks we're back at the work table and the subject of Tanya comes up and neither of us feel that she is 'one of us' yet. Even though she's been here about three weeks now, she still doesn't quite fit in. We all try to be kind and helpful to her and she reacts as if she resents our help. I say to Liz, "I did wonder if it was just me she was funny with."

"Oh no, she's not really hit it off with any of us and we all find it hard to talk with her. If we ask her a question we just get an answer, no follow up, no chatter, no conversation. Whether she's shy or just has no people skills I'm not sure. But she is good with the children, look at her now, she's reading with Lulu but I've not seen her get up for a loo visit or even look around the room to see what's happening. She's good with one to one but she needs more than that, she needs to be more versatile and more aware of what's going on around her." I agree with her and mention the difference between her and Nicky.

Nicky, she hasn't been here that much longer than Tanya, (well, since Easter last year,) and yet you would think she'd been here years she fits in so well. If any of us see a job needs doing, we do it; we don't wait to be told. Tanya doesn't appear to notice. We have to ask her to do a job and she will only do it, if it suits her, and if it doesn't suit her she will explain why she won't do it. We really don't have time for a debate on everything and we're not used to that attitude. We all just muck in. There are things we don't like doing and there are areas where some aunties cope better than others. For example, I can cope with runny noses, but I'm hopeless with bums and not any good at all with sick (I have to join in if someone is sick near me.) Liz, on the other hand, is great with all leakages except noses. So I suppose we complement each other there and step in to help each other out. And with regard to the general running of the place, we all do whatever needs doing and don't make a fuss. If we go to the loo and the towels run out, you take some down. If washing up needs doing, you do it. If tables need moving, you move them. It really is all so simple to us. Liz and I aren't moaning exactly, just pointing out a few facts.

Hillary soon disturbs our chatter and reminds us it's nearly lunchtime. Hey ho off we go, putting toys into boxes and moving tables and chairs about, and organising the loo run. I notice Tanya is in the kitchen making our tea, very nice of her but what about all this physical work?

Hillary has to go out after lunch and Liz and I think it will be a good idea to get the dressing up clothes out for a change. We also think it will be good if Tanya can be in charge of it. Constantly having to dress and undress the children and doing up buttons and bows and zip fasteners. Having to help children into leggings and pulling sleeves the right way out and sometimes being made to wear ridiculous items yourself. Yes, we think it's a marvellous way for Tanya to spend her afternoon.

Tuesday 18th May

Hillary's not here today, so Eve has come in. She's an older lady and filled with common sense and she, too, is good fun to work with.

"We're not doing any specific work today," says Julie. "Hillary has asked me to try to get the children to do some cutting out. We have plenty of magazines and greeting cards so they will have a lot of choice. Tanya will you start off supervising the cutting out, please?"

Tanya doesn't say a word, just changes direction and heads towards the cupboard, presumably to get out some magazines.

"Julie, shall I get out the scrap books and the children can come to me with their pictures and stick them straight in?" I call over to her.

"If you like," she answers. "I have some paper work to finish but call me if you need me, I'll only be in the corner over there.

When Brandon comes to sign in, Julie has instructions for him to make a start on tiling the walls in the boys' toilet.

"No problem," he says cheerfully. "I'll go and see what needs to be done."

By the time I have our first trip to the toilets, I see Brandon has boxes of tiles; step ladders and tools laid out in the boys toilets, so everyone has to use the ladies loo. It's a squash and some of the boys are really piqued at having to go into the girls toilets, but needs must.

The morning rushes by and by the time I return from yet another trip to the toilets I see Julie has the chairs set out ready for drinks and has the children seated already. She calls over for us all to join her and tells the children. "We're going on a bear hunt." She makes it sound so exciting they quickly sit down and she begins to tell this wonderful story. It's about a walk through jungles, swamps, forests and deserts and the arm movements and sound effects which accompany you on this walk has everyone enthralled. The noisy animals you hide from, and the gloopy swamp noises are great and she encourages the children to join in all the noises. The children love it. She's a marvel with them. When the story finishes, Eve brings in the drinks and biscuits which are enjoyed by us all and I notice she whispers something into Julie's ear.

As soon as the drinks are cleared away Julie disappears into the cupboard and comes out with the doctor and nurses dressing up clothes. This is always very popular with the children as they love to dress up and nurse the dolls, teddies or even each other.

Eve and Julie ask us staff if we would be prepared to be the patients today and Eve mentions that she has bought some extra bits and pieces in with her in the hope we could play this game today.

Eve explains to the children that she has some pieces of bandage, some squares of sheeting for slings, and some boxes of plasters. She explains that the plasters must only be put onto us adults. She says she has brought in some very small coloured sweets to use as 'make it better pills' but these too, can only be given to the aunties. The children all agree with those instructions and can't wait to put on nurse aprons and hats, and doctor coats and start tending to us. They're having great fun. We aunties on the other hand, are injected, probed, prodded, plastered, bandaged, tucked into bed, (on the hard floor I might add,) given medicine, and have our knees hammered for good measure. I don't expect any of this is covered in official guidelines and would probably not be allowed but we supervise the children closely and everyone has a wonderful time.

Julie, Eve, Nicky and I are having as much fun as the children but I'm not so sure Tanya thinks too much of it though. I doubt if they covered anything like it at college but it's reassuring to see she did manage to crack a smile and even a small laugh at times. It would be a really wooden person who was not warmed by the fun and laughter generated this morning, and who knows Tanya may well stop going by the book and begin to relax a bit and look as if she is enjoying herself.

We're rather late getting ready for lunch and it didn't help when I had to go and answer the phone in the middle of it. It's Hillary, and she's phoned in to check if all is okay. She also asks me if I can swap my work day from Thursday to Friday this week as she can't seem to shake off a bug she's picked up. She has staff cover for Wednesday and Thursday and if I could help out on Friday it would help her a lot. No problem.

The afternoon children make straight for the doctors and nurses box when they have finished their lunches. So the game is played all over again with us aunties as the patients again. Tanya insists she should do some cutting out with the children but finds it increasingly difficult as none of the children want to sit down and miss out on all the fun going on around them. So Tanya grudgingly joins in and when she has to go down to the toilets with a bandage on her leg and an untidy bandage on her head; her arm in a sling and a big plaster on her nose, we all giggle rather unkindly. As we are letting her to go down to the toilets looking like that and knowing Brandon is working down there and he is bound to see her.

Friday 21st May

I can't, in all honesty, say that I'm looking forward to today. I know Friday is band practice day and therefore is a very noisy day. To help to muffle the noise, I've worn a floral scarf tied round my hair line and although it looks a bit odd on my short hair, it may help muffle the noise a little.

Dawn and Mandy are here before me. No surprises there but I do just make it in before Eve. She was parking her car and I whizzed past her on my bike. I enquire after Hillary and I'm told she's hoping to be well enough to come back next week.

I had been told that Mandy was in charge today. She's a short, fair haired lady and very qualified. I make my way over to her and she explains to me that we don't have much time for pieces of work on Fridays, so suggests I sit and supervise on the cutting-out table. She adds, "you will find we now have a large plastic basket with all the old club books, calendars, catalogues, magazines and cards in and they're on the middle shelf."

I collect it from the cupboard along with the scissors and as soon as I sit down Sally and Dilly sit down too and ask if they can start. Sally is a chatty little girl and both she and Dilly are very capable and soon have plenty of pictures ready for gluing into their scrapbooks. I have to tell them there's no time to glue now and that I'll write their names on the back of their pictures and pin them together. They're happy with that and go off to play together.

Topaz comes to the table and sits down, and I try to encourage a boy to come and join us and do some cutting out. The boys don't seem so keen on the activity but Paul's eyes light up when he sees I have some Lego leaflets and he studies the pages before he cuts into them. Whilst I'm watching these two with the scissors, Mandy comes over to me with a pile of newspapers in her arms, and asks, "would you mind cutting these into strips? They need to be about eight or ten inches long and an inch or two wide, don't worry about being too exact about it as they're only for papier-mâché work next week. Here's a carrier bag to put the strips in."

This is living up to my expectations of today. Dirty hands, newsprint on my tee shirt, and noise to follow. Great!

Eve comes over and sits with me and starts cutting the newspapers into strips. I'm not a very quick newspaper cutter but soon pick up a few tips from her and speed up a bit. Eve just comes into nursery twice a week, like I do, she has plenty of energy and she loves working here with the children and with us. She also spends some of her time as a volunteer in one of the local charity shops and she often has interesting and funny stories to tell us about her time there.

I ask her about her family and we catch up quickly with our personal news and then she tells me we need bags and bags of newspaper strips as all of the older children will be making one. And before I have chance to ask what, she's called away.

One what? I Puzzle. Next week is beginning to look doubtful.

I see Dawn is in the kitchen getting the drinks prepared and it is only a quarter to ten. Dawn has worked in the group for many years and has two young teenage children. She's a tall lady with pretty hair and has done various courses and training in childcare. She comes out of the kitchen to tell me that at ten we have to stop what we're doing and get the chairs positioned for drinks. Everything has to be ready for Lavinia to be able to begin at eleven.

At half past ten we take all the children down to the toilets. Actually I take all the children, boys in the first trip and then all the girls. Whilst I'm gone the chairs are drawn into a tighter circle than we usually make and the instruments are brought out of the cupboard. We have drums, cymbals, maracas, triangles, bells and tambourines.

Lavinia arrives a few minutes before eleven and after a quick hello to us all, immediately begins to match child and instrument according to ability. Then when every child has an instrument all hell is let loose. Mandy and Lavinia try their best to be in control but the odds are stacked against them. We hear Lavinia say, "we're going to play Baa-Baa Black Sheep." I'm glad she told us what it was supposed to be!

I notice that Dawn has moved into the relative quiet of the kitchen and is washing up and preparing for lunchtime. Eve and I go back to newspaper cutting and we discreetly move the table as far away from the 'band' as possible, but the noise level is well up. To be fair, some of the children do seem to have a grasp of timing, but they're well and truly drowned-out by the majority.

We have noisy renditions of Humpty-Dumpty; Rock-a-By Baby; Mary, Mary Quite Contrary. In fact, almost every nursery rhyme known to man - and only recognizable because Lavinia has the songs playing out loudly from a tape player.

Eventually we hear her say, "this is the last one for today as we've run out of time. I know it's one you all like; it's The Grand Old Duke of York. I'd like you to play it loudly."

Eve and I look at each other in astonishment. Could they possibly play (I use that word loosely) any louder? Yes they could!

At ten to twelve it's almost a pleasure doing the lunch time loo run. The relative peace and quiet of twenty four voices chattering together is nothing, nothing after what we've been through this morning.

I will never moan about the noise again. The scarf didn't help that much after all, deep down I knew it wouldn't. I can feel the start of a headache, but it does disappear quite quickly after I have a couple of pain killer tablets with my tea and sandwich.

There hardly seems to be any noise in the hall this afternoon. Dawn and I are cutting more newspaper into strips and not doing anything strenuous. I'm not sure if the children are quiet or if my hearing hasn't fully recovered.

Eve and Mandy are in the library corner quietly entertaining the children with stories and it's just the quiet countermeasure the day needs.

I must remember to be busy, very busy, on future Fridays.

Tuesday 25th May

I've not felt well all weekend and I've got a painful stomach. I hope I get a 'sit down and sit quietly' sort of day There aren't many of those kind of days at nursery school but I may be lucky. Hilary can see I'm off colour as soon as she sees me and she says, "We are going to be making a start on the papier-mâché pig money boxes and by the look of you, we'll need to find you something quiet to do."

"Ah! So it's a pig money box," I reply, and go on to explain that I had been wondering what all the paper strips were for.

I remember my son making a money box pig here many years ago and he still has it in his bedroom. It was his pride and joy for years and years and everyone who came to the house was shown this red pig. I'm not sure if he wanted them to admire the pig or to put some money in it, but it usually went back on the shelf a little heavier than when it came off.

The pig is made by blowing up a balloon and tying it. Then wet newspaper strips are wrapped over and around the balloon, and after the paper has all dried, it is painted. The knot in the balloon provides the pigs' tail and a cork nose and cork feet are added. Then a slit is put on its back and hey presto, a money box. Sometimes whilst cutting the slit, the balloon is punctured so a string tail is added. Hillary has a finished pig on the table we can use as a pattern and to show the children what the finished article should look like.

Hillary is talking again. "The jobs I want doing today are; blow up twenty or so balloons and tie string on to them; mix up loads of flour and water glue; help the children to wrap the paper onto the balloons, or, cut more newspaper." What choices! I opt for the latter as I've had practice and it may make my hands black but at least I can sit quietly whilst I do it.

I find the newspaper in the cupboard and the scissors and sit at a table quietly by myself, at the back of the room.

I see Nicky and Mandy have put aprons on and have covered a table with rough paper. There are two large pots of glue at the ready, and Tanya, I notice, is a dab hand at blowing up balloons. We still don't know much about Tanya, no one seems to have really befriended her. I don't think we can all be at fault. Maybe she doesn't like us, or perhaps she's just not happy working here.

It's a slow process covering the pigs with paper, as you can only work with one child at a time. Once the child has covered the balloon with a thick layer of soggy newspaper the pig is put to one side to dry and the aprons are removed. The plastic aprons are then wiped clean of glue, and the children have to be taken to have their hands washed under running water, which means a trip down to the toilets. It was found out early on that a bowl of water is not sufficient for gluey, papery hands because after one or two uses the water discolours and a scum begins to form.

Hillary joins me for a few minutes and explains, "we need to cover as many balloons as we can this week so they can dry in the cupboard over the half term holiday, and hopefully be dry for painting when we come back. We did a few yesterday and I'm hoping to get some more done tomorrow and Thursday. And we won't be here on Friday as it is an inset day at the schools, so I have decided it is easier to close one day early. I'm sorry to disappoint you as I just know how much you like Friday mornings." She added mischievously.

"Yes I do," I agree with a sarcastic tone and pulling a face at the same time.

"Don't be like that," she chides. "Anyway, as I was saying, I doubt we'll get much done on Wednesday either as Wednesdays are always hectic too. So we must do as much as we can today."

"I'll do as much paper as I can," I say as she gets up.

"Oh, I nearly forgot, I've some news you will like. We will only be working mornings during the next half of the term. No lunchtimes and no afternoons, until I can sort out a problem I have with the insurance company. So we'll all be finishing at twelve thirty."

It is turning into a rather more pleasant day than I anticipated. Me being able to sit down a lot and probably not being disturbed for the loo runs as the children will have the opportunity to go when they go to the toilets to have their sticky hands washed. Then thoughts of future afternoons to call my own, well that's an added bonus. Leo, my dog may get a slightly longer walk in the afternoons and I'll enjoy the free time. Things are looking up. I'm in a happy haze, dreaming of all I will be able to do in the coming afternoons and my morning flies by.

At lunch time we leave three tables with all the 'pig' paraphernalia on and position the rest ready for lunch. Once we finish eating and have cleared away the cups and lunchboxes we get some of the afternoon children started on their pigs. I look up and I see everyone looks happy working on the pigs and Tanya even looks like she's enjoying herself.

I have filled bags and bags with strips of newspaper and I'm ready to do something different so I go and sit at the library corner and I'm soon joined by a few children. I glance over to Hillary and she nods, which I understand to mean I can have the children with me that she no longer needs. The sun is shining and it's warm by the window and as I push up my sleeves I noticed the sun catches on my watch face, so I encourage the 'fairy' to come and sit with us. The children are delighted with her presence and if one of them gets too fidgety or begins to talk too much or spoil things for the others I make the fairy disappear.

"I will try to get her to come back but I think you'll have to be quiet," I say to them, and once they settle down again, I produced the fairy. It's such a simple ruse but it works time after time. The fairy stays with us while I read plenty of different stories and the children came and sat down for as long as they want to. It's calming and fun, and my afternoon passes very pleasantly.

Thursday 27th May

I can't help but see there are newspaper covered balloons everywhere in the hall. They are on the floor, on tables, sitting on toy boxes, some even in the kitchen, everywhere. They were probably put into the cupboard last thing and into any available space and poor Nora had to move them out of her way before she could get started. Nora comes in every morning to help us; she gets out most of the boxes of toys and stacks them against the wall. The cups and beakers she puts in the kitchen with the tea tray and biscuits, and most importantly, she now checks the heating has come on for us, not that we've needed it lately. She helps at any fund raising events or fêtes, any parties and the carnival, she's a real treasure and even though we don't actually see much of her in the mornings, we all appreciate all she does to get the day started for us, but I don't suppose she was too pleased at finding all those balloons.

"Well, what are we going to do with all these balloons?" asks Hillary to everyone in earshot.

"I suppose hanging them up would keep them all together," suggests Liz.

"Could you do that, Wendy?" asks Hillary "I have a few things I need to discuss with Liz."

"Okay," I reply and wonder where I'm going to hang them? I glance round the room and decide I can hang them one by one onto the curtain rails, where they will be out of reach and secure. I'll need the step ladder for this and I remember seeing Brandon had the steps in the kitchen on Tuesday when he changed the florescent tube. I wonder if they're still in there. Before I can go and look Hillary adds, "we've still got a lot more pigs to do and, as this is the last Thursday before the holidays and we won't see these children again until afterwards, we'll have to get a wiggle on if we're to get them all finished."

I go into the kitchen but the step ladder is not there. I walk to the store room and not only are the steps there but Brandon too. "Hello," I say to him. "What are you doing here today?

"I couldn't come in on Monday so I was told to come here today. So here I am, all yours," he finishes cheekily.

He carries the steps for me and between us we hang the balloons on the curtain rail. He's up the ladder and I pass the balloons to him and keep the children away. I still find myself glancing at his gorgeous bum every now and then. I expect there is a rule somewhere about using step ladders when children are about. And I expect we have just broken it. Hey ho.

I join Tanya and we work as quickly as we can with the children, pasting the newspaper onto the balloons with the children. Hillary and Nicky soon join us and Liz is left to finish a little paperwork and is asked to do the hand washing and loo runs. She looks delighted!

We have a good system and should, with luck, get finished today. One little lad, Brian, gets upset because he's having such fun gluing the newspaper strips onto the balloon that he forgets he needs a wee and ends up having a little accident. Liz goes for the mop and bucket and I take Brian to find some spare clothes. I find a pair of trousers he's happy to wear but he's not at all happy at having to wear girls' knickers! We have no boys' pants at all, I search everywhere. The knickers are blue and I had hoped he would not noticed. He noticed and he protested, but he has to wear them as we have nothing else He's not a happy bunny.

Whilst I was searching in the cupboard for spare clothes I came across some wire coat-hangers and decide to hang our wet balloons on them. I reckon I can get four or five on each hanger if I use different lengths of string. It'll be easier to move them about on hangers rather than individually. I'm rather proud of my time saving idea and soon have a full hanger to put onto the one of the remaining empty curtain rail. On another hanger, I also add some dry balloons from the other curtain rails to make them easier to gather up and put away at the end of the day.

At lunch time Hillary starts getting all the children ready, some to go home and some for the loo. Nicky and I tidy away the toys and position the tables. Tanya is still busy with little Jenny so we leave them to finish Jenny's pig. Brandon comes in to the hall and speaks to Hillary. She smiles and turns to Nicky and me and says, "Brandon is having lunch with us today, so put an extra chair out for him."

We get the chance to sit and eat and talk to him, which does not happen often. He tells us he's finished all the work he can do for now and he has a couple of hours before he needs to report to whomever it is he has to report to, and he would like to spend a little time with us and the children.

When we have all finished eating and start to clear away Brandon offers to help us with that too. He sees two of us pick up and carry one table between us and he says, "leave the tables to me." He just picks them up and re-positioned them, just like that. We've never been straight and tidy so quickly before. Liz,

Nicky and I resume working on the pigs with the children and Brandon comes over to see us.

"What are you doing here then?" he asks as he comes over to our messy table. We explain it all to him.

"I've never seen piggy-bank pigs made before," he says. "Just look at the way the children are enjoying themselves, I can't wait to see the finished ones."

Hillary calls to Brandon and asks, "Brandon would you like to help Tanya with the slide? We don't get it out very often as it's awkward to manoeuvre but it would be fun for the children to play on it for a short while."

"Just show me where it is and where you want it," he replies happily. He and Tanya soon have a queue of children waiting for a turn, and laughter and squeals come from their direction.

"Look," says Liz, "I do believe Tanya is laughing."

"Well, there's a first." I reply.

"Stop it you two," cautions Hillary with a smile. "Ten more minutes," she calls to Tanya, "then you must put the slide away."

Brandon has the slide put back in the cupboard with such ease and announces that he has enjoyed the afternoon.

"Did you get electric shocks from the slide?" I ask him.

"No." he answers and looks a bit bewildered as he heads towards the door. "Bye everyone," he calls out.

"I can't believe it, even the slide likes him," I say.

"Good taste, our slide," laughs Nicky. "Come on let's get started with the packing away."

It takes a while for all the children and parents to leave the hall especially as the balloons are hanging up and some of the children want to show mum or dad which is theirs and talk about them. But once they have all gone and all the toys have been put into the cupboard I proudly hang the coat-hangers full of balloons in there too, onto any 'hook' I can find. I quite enjoyed today. It was productive and pleasant. I must really be cracking up and in need of a week off. It's unheard of to say a nice thing at the end of a term, or a half-term. Normally we're all tearing our hair out.

It’ll be nice to have a week off and the weather is forecast to continue calm and sunny next week, so hopefully a few days can be spent in the garden for a change.

We say our goodbyes to each other and I head home for a nice weeks break.

HALF TERM WEEK

Chapter Four

Tuesday 9th June

Hillary must have been looking out for me because the minute I step inside the door she says, "hello Wendy, I'm glad you're in early, I want to have a word with you." As I remove my jacket I think, 'now what have I done wrong?' I'm always doing things wrong but often get away with it, now it sounds like I've been found out. But for the life of me, I can't think what she might be referring too.

"Two things, actually," Hillary continues with mock solemnity. "The first is, will you look in that cupboard and tell me what is the best way to un-stick all the balloons on those coat hangers?"

I can tell from her tone of voice that she's not really too cross about them. As I walk over to the cupboard I can see just what she means. They've certainly dried over the half term week and quite a few are joined together. Whoops!

"We separated a lot yesterday but left the really awkward ones for you!"She resumes as I turn back to face her. "And the second thing is, I've decided that we will do the carnival this year. What do you think of that? Oh, and another thing, while I think of it, and I know you will like this, we will just work mornings this term, all of the term not just half of it, and see how it goes. I've been in discussion with the insurance company and their premiums have gone up quite a bit and it would mean putting the fees up by quite a large amount. I've had a word with the other staff and they agree that if we can accommodate all the children in the mornings it may all work out to our advantage. What do you think of that?"

"Yes that is good news, I do like that." I answer as I struggle to carry the coat hangers and balloons out of the cupboard. There is no way of separating them until you can see clearly what you're doing and I'm finding it quite a challenge. Julie comes over to help and can't resist saying,

"Brilliant idea to put all these balloons on hangers. I wonder whose idea that was?" She knows full well it was my idea. I can only laugh with her as I would have said just the same if it had happened to someone else. Actually I would probably have said much, much more. Between us we get the balloons separated, some are shaped a little oddly, but not enough to matter, and at least we didn't damage any.

Whilst we are prising the balloons apart, Hillary and Nicky have covered some tables with rough paper in readiness for painting them. I see Mandy has the task of mixing the paints and Tanya is watching. Tanya still does a lot of watching, I expect it will come in useful one day. Mandy soon has four bright colours mixed and is still mixing the red as Hillary calls to Tanya to go and find the aprons so they can make a start.

Again I can foresee there will be the problem of finding somewhere safe for the balloons to dry and I don't like to suggest the coat-hanger idea.

"Hillary, where are we going to put the painted balloons to dry? Do you think we could use some of the scouts' tables to put them on? They may have an old one or two we could use." She and I go down to the scouts' cupboard to look and on the way she says, "you do know they don't like us using their stuff don't you. But if we only use old ones and cover them with paper, we may get away with it."

Brandon is down there fixing some chairs and he says, "good morning, I don't often see you down here, can I help you?"

Hillary explains our predicament and he says brightly, "give me a minute," and rushes off and quickly returns with a couple of old wooden saw-horses and says, "I knew these were in the shed and there are some planks about somewhere, you could make your own tables. You can put them against one wall where they will be out of the way. And if you like, Wendy, I could put some hooks on the planks so that you can hang some of the pigs up." He looks at me and grins. I suppose he knows all about the coat-hanger fiasco. He must have been shown the cupboard when he signed in this morning.

He continues, as we all laugh."I'll clean these up and make sure there are no sharp edges and bring them into the hall later if that's okay, Hillary?"

"Thank you. That will help us a great deal."

He's so capable and helpful and has proved to be a real treasure. He has tiled the walls in both the boys and the girls toilets and has painted the doors and skirting boards too. He regularly cleans our windows inside and out and keeps the kitchen and hallway tidy and clean. He works in the garden, trimming hedges and weeding the small boarders, and he mows the grass, all without complaint and with a cheery face. We've all got so used to him being around, and now he has even come up with a solution to this problem. We are really going to miss him when he leaves.

When we get back into the hall we see Julie and Mandy have aprons on and have two children in aprons who have started painting already. I grab an apron and join them and soon the talk turns to the carnival. It's always fun to do a float for the carnival, but, it's also expensive and very time consuming. We aunties are always keen to do it and are prepared to help all we can, but trying to get any help from the parents is usually hard. They all want their little darlings to be on the float but very few are willing to come forward with help.

"What is the theme this year?" Mandy asks.

Hillary admits she hasn't found out too much information yet as she wanted to sound us out first and, if we were keen, she would make further enquiries.

I say, "I think we should let slip that Brandon is willing to help us. That'll guarantee we'll get plenty of mums offering to help too."

"Hey that's a good idea," agrees Julie. "It's no good getting older if you don't get wiser and learn a thing or two about human nature, now is it?"

Julie offers to write a notice asking for helpers. We've done this in the past and received half-hearted responses or no response at all. Although, I must say at this point, there have been some years when we have been lucky and have had two or three parents willing to help throughout the term times. But when their children leave, so do they and we miss them terribly. We shall see what the notice brings.

We get the majority of our balloons painted before lunch and we remind Hillary to buy the corks needed to make the feet and noses. The children are excited over the pigs and can't wait to finish them and take them home. They have really enjoyed working on them, I suppose it's because it's unlike any other work they've ever done.

As I have a check-up appointment at the dentists at twelve thirty, I leave at twelve fifteen. There are two mums outside waiting to come in to collect their children. One of them is Dilly's mum and the other is Mavis. (I always remember her name now.) As I manoeuvre my bike Dilly's mother asks me if we are 'doing' the carnival this year.

"It's funny you should mention that," I say. "We've just been talking about it and it looks like we will be. We're all quite excited about it, even Brandon wants to help." With that I get onto my bike and cycle off with a big grin on my face. Job done.

Thursday 11th June

Liz grabs my arm as I walk in the door and takes me to see the notice that was put up on Tuesday lunchtime. The list of helpers is overwhelming! There must be at least thirty names on the list. She tells me that Hillary is so excited that she has arranged a 'helpers' meeting for this very afternoon and could us aunties stay an extra fifteen minutes to look after the children whilst she talks to them. This situation has never arisen before, so I suppose we must make the most of it. I must remember to tell Mavis and Dilly's mum more things in the future, as it must have been they who mentioned Brandon's name and the carnival in the same sentence and his possible involvement. The word has certainly spread! There can't be any other reason for this huge response.

"Hi Julie, what are you doing here?" I call to her.

"Hillary asked me to come in so we can discuss the carnival," she replies.

I see Tanya has set up the painting easel and call good morning to her, I notice she's busily naming long thin papers for the children to use and when I comment on the odd shaped paper she informs me that, when she was at college they were told to encourage the use of every size and shape of paper for painting and colouring. No hello or good morning from her, just that.

Before I can say anything, Hillary calls me over to join her and Julie, and Ro and Liz.

"Whilst we're setting up the tables and getting everything out ready for the children to put the final touches to their pigs, I want you all to think about the carnival and how it concerns us." She says. "And as you have all been involved in the carnivals in the past I want you to come up with ideas and pointers for me to use at the meeting this afternoon."

"Do we have a theme yet?" I ask.

"Yes," she answers. "The theme is, 'An Entertainment'."

"An Entertainment? What do they mean by that then? Have you got any ideas?"

"No, not yet, give me a chance," she replies."Anyway, that's what this meeting is about."

Well, the theme is a bit vague. If they were to say a children's film or something a bit more specific, I'm sure it would be easier. Well, at this stage it really is unimportant what the theme is because we're limited as to what we can do with the under fives. Safety has to be our number one priority. We have to have all our little ones seated and include as many aunties and or helpers as possible. And as the only competition category open to us is 'most colourful' , we know we will have to use creatively positioned bunting and crepe paper and as many colourful items as possible to catch the judges' eye.

We all talk excitedly and ideas fly thick and fast. Julie suggests we could be jugglers or magicians and other suggestions include something from the television or Punch and Judy with a seaside backdrop.

Julie says, "I'd better write down some of our ideas and I think I'll also start a list with the jobs that will need doing. People to dress the children on the day and do face painting if needed. Parents willing to ride on the float and others to walk alongside our lorry with collection boxes."

"We need some people to help design and make the float," Hillary reminds her. "And wouldn't it be nice if we could get someone to take a video of the day. Put that on the list, Julie, and we'll need wood and nails to secure the chairs to the lorry, paint, brushes, plywood and stiff card."

“We’ll need imaginative people to help with costume designing and costume making,” contributes Ro. “I wonder if Shirley could help us there?”

“We also need ideas, lots of ideas,” I add hoping someone else will come up with some.

“That’s a few items for the list and will give Hillary a guide for her meeting,” says Julie, “and if any of you have more ideas throughout the day then just let me know and I'll jot them down.”

When the children arrive we grab the ones we need to come over and finish their pigs. Only a few need to be painted and all have to have the cork ‘noses’ and ‘feet’ glued on. Then we aunties make a slit in the pig’s back and add a string tail if it’s needed, and hey presto, each child has a unique pig money box to take home.

Whilst we get on with our work we all think of possible ‘entertainments’ with plenty of cast, not too expensive, lots of colour, not too impossible to portray and one that is going to help us win ‘the most colourful cup,’ because if we are going to do it we’re going to do it properly. We have entered the carnival in past years and have always won something, so we have a reputation to live up to. Over the years we have also collected quite a few outfits and costumes which we may be able to utilize again this year. That may save us some money and time this year. We’re all very preoccupied with pigs and the carnival and the morning flies by. The children are excited about the carnival, I’m sure most of them are too young to really know what it is but they have picked up on our excitement and we’re bombarded with questions.

The finished pigs are put on the saw-horses and planks to dry off and placed safely in the corner of the hall. They are red, blue, yellow, orange and green and now they have faces and feet they look a comical group.

Julie and I keep all the children in the big hall, playing circle games and skipping and marching, whilst Hillary has her meeting in the small hall. There are a lot of parents in the meeting and it’s probably a bit of a squash in there. When they come out, they’re nearly as noisy as the children, all chattering and full of enthusiasm and we quickly hand over the youngsters and let them get home. I have to rush away immediately as I have a follow up dentist appointment, a filling this time, what fun.

Tuesday 16th June

I hurry into school today because I want to find out how the meeting went on Thursday. Hillary herself unlocks the door for me and before I even say good morning to her. I blurt out, “How did the meeting go? I couldn't stop and ask on Thursday.”

She beams from ear to ear and tells me that she was amazed at the amount of mums who have volunteered their time. I try to suppress an ‘I know something you don’t know’ smile.

“That's great, come on, tell me all,” I say as we enter the main room.

“The meeting was a great success,” she declares. “The most popular theme suggestion was for our float to be a circus. We have a couple of dads, one of whom is called Bob, who is willing to do videoing on the day, and another chap, I can’t think of his name just now, who has offered to take photographs. We have a group of men who have said they will make ‘the set’ and secure it safely onto the lorry; and the general opinion was for each parent to be responsible for their own child’s outfit.”

“I’m pleased everyone is so keen but isn’t it just typical they want to do their own outfits when we have quite a few we could utilize for a circus theme. I’m sure we have some furry animals and clown outfits and now they want to make their own.” I tut tutted.

“Yes I know, I thought that too,” agreed Hillary. “But remember the carnival is only three weeks away and there’s an awful lot to do, so our costumes may come in useful yet. Luckily we finished all the pigs last week and they’ve all been taken home so now we can devote all our time to the carnival.”

To get the children into the carnival mood, as if it were needed, Hillary has decided most of the work they do in the next weeks will have a circus theme. So today we have clowns to make. Nicky and I have been asked to keep the children busy colouring their clowns and do the loo runs to give Hillary and Julie chance to write up lists and rosters for the carnival.

By the time we sit down for morning drinks they have a pile of lists and notes to show us. Hillary has also been in the cupboard for the suitcase that holds all the costumes and she says, “I have found six red jackets which will do nicely for bandsmen but there are no trousers. There are also some colourful bits of material that can be used to make bunting.”

I offer to make the bunting as I have so many bits of material at home left over from a patchwork quilt I have just finished, and it won’t take too long to cut the scraps into triangles and machine them together. I can see Julie write my name next to ‘bunting’ on her list.

“You have to do it now,” she laughs. “It’s on my list, so it’s official.”

“Six pairs of black trousers for the bandsmen to be put on a list, please,” calls Hillary. “I have also found one lion, one tiger with only half a face, one rabbit, seven fairy costumes and nine assorted bits of clown costume.”

Mandy says, “we can surely use the lion costume and if the ears of the rabbit costume are shortened and re-positioned perhaps it could pass as a performing dog.”

“Good idea but I’m not too sure about the tiger outfit though,” adds Hillary. “The face is beyond repair but perhaps we can use the material to make a strongman outfit.”

“Yes, that’s a possibility and the fairy outfits can be altered to be trapeze artist’s costumes and the clown bits will all be useful,” adds Julie.

“I’ll take all the clothes home for washing and sorting,” says Hillary. “Then we will have a better idea of what we have and how it can be used.”

Drinks time is extended as we get the children to try on one or two of the outfits. Jodie wants to try on the rabbit costume. We explain to her it will not be a rabbit but a dog, knowing how she hates dogs we thought that would be the end of it. But no! She tries on the rabbit/soon to be dog outfit and it fits her perfectly. So it looks like we have found the first of our circus performers already.

Simon wants to be the tiger. I tell him that the face is ruined and it can’t be mended and we’re going to use the material to make a strongman outfit. He’s upset but curious as to what a strongman outfit will look like. So I take him over to the book corner and search through the books to find a picture. We find one in 'Noddy and The Circus', and he really likes the idea and wants to take the book home to show his mum. Hey presto, I think we have our strongman.

Hillary is helping Dilly into one of the fairy outfits and as she does so the wings fall to the floor and Dilly starts to cry.

"It's not your fault," Hillary tells her. "The wings would have had to come off, as we don't need fairies but trapeze artists." Dilly starts to cry even more.

"I would really, really like to be a fairy," she sobs, and we're all taken aback as Dilly never asks for anything or puts herself forward.

"We do need one special fairy," says Mandy, winking her eye and nodding. She has the attention of all of us now. "The lady that rides on the back of the elephant has to have that kind of outfit. Don't you remember? " We aunties suddenly realise what she's doing and quickly back her up and agree we really do need a fairy. Dilly is happy in the knowledge that she will be that special fairy. Dilly is smiling again and Hillary is relieved and order is restored once more. Well done, Aunty Mandy.

Julie is busy again, this time writing a note for the parents telling them that we have found some costumes, so those of them that can't make one need not worry. Also if any one has any black trousers for the bandsmen would they kindly bring them in, preferably name-tagged, especially if they want them returned.

Hillary asks us adults, "who of you wants to be on the float and who wants to walk?" I reply that I'll think about it.

"What's there to think about?" says Nicky. "Put me down to ride on the float." she says enthusiastically.

Julie can't make up her mind and Tanya says she'll let us know.

Hillary says, "I think it would be nice if all the adult helpers were to dress as colourful clowns. Would that be all right with all of you? Do you mind dressing up, Tanya?" She knows us long standing helpers and staff are up for most things but there's still so much we don't know about Tanya.

"I'll think about it," was the short reply she got.

We clear away the drinks and put the outfits to one side for now and finish the remaining few clowns pictures.

"Aunty Wendy," asks Joe. "Will you be a clown?"

"Yes, Joe, I expect I will."

"Can I be a clown then?"

"I should think so. We'll ask Aunty Hillary and your mum and see what they say. Okay?"

"Okay." He grins.

Ah, isn't that sweet?

The children are all excited about the carnival. They all have a clown to take home and a note for their parents. What another nice day today was.

Thursday 18th June

I hardly recognise the place as I walk into the hallway today. There are two large hardboard cut-outs of elephants, two large hardboard cut-outs of prancing horses and two more of seals with balls on their noses. There's a pile of tools and bits of wood, cans of paint and a couple of large, bulging, black sacks. I also see Shirley who is our movement and dance teacher.

"Hello Shirley, we don't normally see you on Thursdays."

"Hi Wendy," she answers and just then Hillary comes out of the kitchen and says in a mock surprised voice, "you're early again, Wendy, this is getting to be a habit."

"Ha ha ha," I respond good naturedly.

"As Shirley is very artistic," Hillary continues, "I have persuaded her to come in and help with the design of the float. She came in yesterday morning and drew the pictures of the horses, seals and elephants onto large hardboard sheets we had been given. A keen dad took the hardboard home at lunch time and came in with the big cut-outs first thing this morning. His persistent knocking on the door got poor Nora in a right old state. She's normally here on her own till one of us arrives. When she saw a man at the door she didn't know what to do." She eventually let him in after a long shouted conversation through the closed door. As we walk into the main hall she carries on. "There should be some parent helpers coming in today and I wonder if you would make a start with them painting the horses and elephants, you can do it out there in the hallway away from the children."

On the wall in the main hall I see a huge poster with the title 'What needs to be done' and another headed 'who's who', along with the items each child needs.

We have never been as organised in past years, I wonder if this is a good omen or not? I put my bag down and call "Hello" to Nicky, Tanya, Liz and Ro. I see Ro has the painting easel out already and Nicky has Tanya helping her name some pictures of performing seals with balls on their noses all ready for colouring.

At nine o'clock we open the doors and the children and parents come in, all in a rush, all talking excitedly about the float. The atmosphere is charged with enthusiasm and we must capitalize on this as it has never happened before and may well fizzle out.

A couple of mums say they are willing to help me with the painting and after a few words with Hillary they disappear into the hallway to see what tools and paints are there. Another couple of mums say they can stay and help this morning and I'm asked to look after them until Hillary is free. What Hillary really wants me to do is bar the door and make sure they don't do a runner when they realise Brandon is not here today. As soon as she can, Hillary introduces them to Shirley who has them sorting and repairing outfits in no time.

By nine twenty, my group and I have introduced ourselves and have a work-table erected in the entrance hall. We have found three cans of grey paint and June and Carol are putting some onto one of the elephants. June is Topaz's mother and Carol is Traydon's mum and they tell me they both work at the same place, but as work is slack they both have this week off. They're obviously good friends and they're talking as they work and are offering to organise a raffle to boost our meagre funds. They're turning into a star pair, these two.

I'm looking at the other paint cans when Hillary brings out a carrier bag and says, "there are some hammers, some more paint and D.I.Y stuff in here and I can see you have found the stuff Phil left in the hall. Can you put the items all together and make a list of what we have and if we need anything would you mind cycling into town to get it?" "Okay, I'm on it," I say.

I sort through it all and find we have plenty white paint, which will do for the horses, a little red paint and some blue and a couple of brushes. I think I'll suggest we get a small can of yellow paint because that's always a cheerful colour, and we will need some turpentine, plus a couple more brushes. That should keep us going for a few days. I go into the hall and see if she needs anything.

"Yes, crepe paper," she says. "I've had a thought. If we cut out the crepe-paper

and make them into flowers. That would be a colourful way to spell out the name of the nursery school. We can attach them, somehow, onto the sides of the flat base of the lorry. Not only will it add a great swathe of colour, it will also let everyone know who we are as we go past them."

"Have you got a lorry?" I enquire.

"Yes, the lorry's been booked. The local haulage firm, Bookers, are happy to help us again!"

"That's good, they were so helpful last year. I'll be off then. Outside it's dry and there's no wind so it won't take me long to get to the town and back on the bike. Those two in the hallway are quite happy and are working well together."I inform her.

At the stationers I choose red and yellow crepe paper and buy six packs of each and quickly call in at the ironmongers for the rest of the items. I didn't feel I'd been long but when I returned I could see my team of painters had finished the elephants and had put chairs round them to try to stop them from being touched. Also one side of each of the two horses has been painted. I help the ladies to lean them, wet side to the wall, to dry, and we all go into the hall for a well deserved drink. Time really does fly when you're having fun.

After coffee Carol and June say they will finish off the horses as it will only take a quarter of an hour or so and if they have time they will start on the seals.

"Do you need me?" I enquire.

"No, we'll finish and tidy up and then wait outside in the sunshine for the kids," answers Carol.

So I join Liz playing tea parties with some children and we're all talking about the carnival when she asks me if I'm going on the float or not.

"I still haven't decided," I reply. "I've done both in the past and just don't know what to do this year. Were you here when we did the court of King Arthur's float?" I ask her.

"Yes," she replies. "I helped in the hall getting everyone ready, and then I had to go somewhere, I can't remember where now, so I didn't go round the town. Were you on the float that year?"

"No, I was a walking helper and I don't know if I can face doing that again," I answer.

"What on earth do you mean? Was the walk too much for you or something?" she asks cheekily.

"No, nothing like that. Didn't I ever tell you what happened?

"No tell me now."

So I do. "I was dressed as a lady of the court and was wearing a long burgundy velvet dress with lace insets and a tall conical hat with a chiffon scarf attached to the point. I had comfortable shoes on under the dress as I knew I had a long, long walk ahead of me. I'd been given my collection box along with the other walkers and the weather was just fine, in fact the whole day had been sunny and at six o'clock it was still warm. It was fun talking to people gathered by the float and also to those as we passed by en route and everything was going splendidly. But, when I was called to the back of the trailer and handed a carrier bag with a potty in it and a boy with a weak bladder, well that was a different story." I say dramatically and continue. "He wouldn't just pee into the potty behind the crowds lining the route. Oh no. "Someone might see me." He had whispered to me. So I had to find somewhere a bit more private. I found a hedge to stand by and he said he was prepared to try to 'go' even though the pink potty was not to his liking! I'd put it on the ground and was attempting to shield him by holding out my full skirt in a kind of screen, anything to hurry up this shy lad, when a voice calls out asking us what we are doing. Not only is my boy shy and in full flow but he's nosy too, and turns to face the voice, peeing a perfect arc of urine across the front of my beautiful dress. The potty had a dribble of liquid in it and my dress felt like it had a cupful of liquid on it. Stop laughing, Liz I haven't finished. I hastily gathered together the potty, the collecting box, the child, and my dignity; and race after the float with a face nearly as red as my dress. As I stood in my wet dress, emptying the meagre contents of a bright pink potty down a drain in front of a host of strangers, I remember thinking to myself; it must be easier on the float."

Laughing with me, Liz asks, "well, was it?"

"Not really but that's another story, I'll tell you some other time. Come on let's make a start on that cupboard."

Tuesday 23rd June

I bring in yards of bunting with me today. It's a miracle I got it finished as Leo thought it a great game to sit on the material heaped on the floor as I was trying to sew it all together. I go across to the chart on the wall and cross 'bunting' of the list. I see there are lots of things with crosses through them, which is good, but there are also many extra items that have been added to the end of the original list. Why am I not surprised by that?

Nicky calls me over to her and asks, "have you decided if you're going to be on the float or walking?" There was a fake innocence to this question.

"Has Liz been talking to you?" I ask, knowing the answer even before I speak.

"Yes, we all had a good laugh yesterday, any more tales to tell?"

"Let's get organized and I promise to talk to you about it later," I say. "Wait till I see Liz," I add with mock anger.

I walk over to Hillary to find out where she wants me to put the bags of bunting. I also want to see what work we're doing today and to catch up on the latest developments on the float.

She has a broad smile on her face too. After saying good morning to me she tells me. "Eve has been bringing in odd things from the charity shop and all the mums are being great. Most of the children know what they're going to be wearing and some of our own costumes have been allocated. I told you they'd be useful. Other outfits are being brought in daily. Simon's mother has managed to get two strongmen outfits from the tiger material, so Simon and Arthur are going to be our strong men. If you speak to Arthur about it, he takes up a pose with his legs apart and his little arms raised and his hands clenched tightly and a scowl on his face. He is so funny.

Brian is going to be the human cannon ball, since his mother brought in a silver spaceman outfit in case it was of any use. We all looked at it for a while and someone suggested a human cannon ball and she's happy to redesign it for him. I can't believe it. It's all going so well."

It is encouraging to hear all the good news but I wonder if something will go wrong, I don't mean to be a pessimist but, I don't know, it's just that it all seems to be going remarkably smoothly.

Hillary is called away to marshal the days helpers, saying as she goes. "A backdrop of 'audience' has been made and hopefully it will get painted today and the horses are having their finishing touches painted on them. And we're making pop-up clowns today for the children, Mandy knows all about it so go over and see her will you, please."

"Morning Wendy," chorus Julie and Nicky, and as I look round I see they have pushed three tables together, so we can all talk together, or should that be work together? The clowns are already drawn on card and cut out, so all the children have to do is colour them and attach an ice lolly stick to their feet. Then the clowns are pushed up inside an empty loo roll, which also has to be coloured. Then the ice lolly stick can be pushed up and pulled down to make the pop-up toy. We have six children colouring and the others in the hall are playing happily and seem content. Some children are watching Shirley as she makes clown hats and others are discussing the completed outfits she has hung about the hall. Nicky tells me Shirley has been coming in whenever she has a spare hour or two and is getting such a lot done.

Julie calls across to Tanya and asks her to come and sit with us.

"Are you going to tell us about when you were on the float?" asks Nicky.

"Well Nicky," I begin. "I don't want my experience on the float to put you off, let's get that clear, and I'm sure it can never ever be as bad as it was that year." I took a deep breath ready to begin the story. "We'd got all the children into their outfits and..."

"What were they? What was the theme?" interrupts Tanya.

"We were space aliens or something spacey," I reply. "Anyway, they were here at the hall having a biscuit prior to getting onto the lorry…"

"How was the lorry decorated?" interrupts Tanya again, unusually.

"Moons and space ships as far as I remember," I answer. "As I was saying, we were just about to get onto the lorry when the heavens opened. Like stair rods, it was…"

"I hate rain like that, I don't usually mind rain but..." started Tanya.

"Tanya, can you take these two girls to the toilet?" says Julie and as Tanya left the room she adds, "I didn't think we would ever hear the tale the way she kept interrupting. What is it with her today, normally you can't get a word out of her."

"Thanks Julie, what's got into her do you think?" I ask not waiting for a reply. "Anyway, to continue my story. The day had been dull and overcast but we didn't expect heavy rain. I remember we all looked at each other, and then we all turned to Hillary wondering if we would continue or cancel. To cancel would have been awful after all the hard work that had been done and, would have been almost impossible as most of the parents had left with instructions to meet us at eight in the playing field at the other side of town. We tried to display an optimistic attitude as it may have just been a freak shower. Shirley was with us then. Hey Shirley, do you remember that awful wet carnival we did a few years back?" I call over to her.

"Do I?" she replies slowly. "It was just terrible. You're not telling them about it are you? You'll put them off."

"I am. They asked and I'm telling it as it was," I answer her. "As I was saying, it rained and rained and as Shirley lives close by, she had rushed home and came back with some golf umbrellas belonging to her husband plus a couple of her own smaller umbrellas. We found three umbrellas and some blankets and towels in the cupboard and Hillary fetched her umbrella from her car. A really kind gentleman from a nearby house came in with a huge roll of clear polythene sheeting offering it to us saying it might be useful. So we knew we would be able to protect the children and the float as well as we could. We had to climb a small ladder to get onto the back of the lorry and all of us got a bit wet doing that. The hard wooden chairs on the lorry were wet too and even though we wiped them dry, they were cold and you felt they were wet. The children were downcast and you could hardly see their costumes for the blankets and umbrellas. It was not a good start but off we set. It was no freak shower, the rain was lashing down. The driver of the lorry was very careful and only drove at about ten miles an hour. Fortunately we only had a short distance to go to get to the start area but when we got there hardly anything was left of our beautifully decorated float. What there was left was torn, tangled and wet. We sat on this tatty lorry, cold, wet, bedraggled and miserable, huddled under saturated blankets and towels, with umbrellas pulled low onto our heads. Some of our walking helpers came up to us as we waited. They too had umbrellas pulled low over themselves and it was hard to recognise them. Slowly we realised the rain was easing off a little. To try to cheer ourselves up and also to warm ourselves a little, we started a sing-song and one or two near-by floats joined in with us too.

The rain did eventually stop and the British 'never give up' spirit roused itself. We dried off as best we could and with the help of some dads we lifted all the children off the trailer and we all jumped up and down and marched about to try to get warm. We noticed other groups doing the same, drying off and trying to keep warm any way they could. We loaded the children back onto the lorry and had a more rousing sing-song to cheer us up. A mum appeared with a couple of flasks of coffee and some biscuits. Another mum produced some sweets for the children and soon everyone was almost happy again. The judges were kind to us and we won the trophy for the most colourful float. It was just a shame they hadn't seen the float in its glory, but seen it only as a soggy mess. They must have had good imaginations that year or perhaps the other floats were even worse than ours. The parade was due to set off at six in the evening and although it was not sunny, we were pleased it just stayed dry. We knew we had about two hours slow drive around the town ahead of us and we were all chilled but tried to keep cheery, hard as it was. We waved and sang more songs but after a while the cold set back in. The children were good, but when you have cramp in your legs and a cold, wet, numb bum, their asking for sweets, or drinks soon became tiresome. As did, 'I've got a runny nose.' 'Do we have to keep waving?' 'How much longer?' 'I want a wee.' 'I feel sick.' 'I want my dad.' 'My outfit itches.' 'I'm cold.' etc. etc. etc. After about thirty minutes my stuck on smile was forgotten and I, like the kids, couldn't wait for it to be over. I remember asking myself, is it really worth it? There now you know." I ended. "You've had two of my experiences. Now it is up to you."

I look at Nicky because she's laughing and she says, "It couldn't be that bad."

I don't argue. I don't say anything. We none of us know what the weather will be like on the tenth. We will just have to wait and see. And I still haven't made up my mind yet whether to try the float again this year or be a walker, decisions, decisions.

Thursday 25th June

It's raining and I have to use the bike as the car is at the garage for its MOT. I got very wet walking Leo and have had to change once already as my jeans were wet and muddy. Also the tortoise stayed put when I opened their little house up, they know to stay in the dry.

I've noticed that when I ride my bike it's either a real pleasure or it isn't, and today it isn't. The wind is against me, it never seems to help me along, Murphy's law, I suppose. The minute I stop I have to blow my nose, dry my face and catch my breath, I can't be that unfit, can I? I arrive at school, wet and puffed out, with a runny nose and I need the loo.

I see Liz in the hall and say solemnly I have a bone to pick with you."

"Oh, come on, I had to tell them, it was so funny," she says.

"Hello Hillary," I call.

"Hello to you both. Why did it have to rain today? "She says crossly. "I have three helpers coming in to finish some painting and I was hoping they could do it outside as it's some long sections of wood that need painting. I also wanted them to do the finishing touches to the audience back drop; which is too wide to fit into the hallway comfortably."

"Never mind," I say. "Perhaps we can make a start on the crepe paper flowers."

"Oh yes, that's an idea, thanks Wendy. Could you do that then?" She says hopefully.

Why, oh why, does my mouth do this to me? If my brain had been in gear I would never have suggested it. I can't remember how to make the flowers anyway and my memory of when we made them years ago is one of, don't ever get caught with that job again. Oh well! I've said it now.

Hillary goes on to explain to Rosemary what work she wants the children to do today and it really looks fun. There are men drawn onto paper and it looks like the children are to colour the men and then stick on furry leotards, hey presto, strongmen. I would have enjoyed doing that. Never mind. I find myself a quiet corner and try to make a crepe paper flower. At least I can try to look competent for when the helpers arrive. I have scissors and red and yellow crepe-paper on the table, and a rubbish bin part full of failed attempts. I'm deep in concentration trying yet again to make another flower, when a chirpy voice says.

"How are you getting on?"

When I look up I see Hillary, Liz and Nicky all laughing at the mess I'm in. What can I say? I haven't a clue how to make them. Hillary sits down next to me and quick as a flash, she makes a flower. She says, "I'll show you. I'll make the next one slowly so you can follow but I must say it was fun watching you struggle, because just like some of the children, you put your tongue out when you concentrate."

"I don't," I say indignantly.

"Oh yes you do," they all chorus.

We all have a laugh at my expense; then she gives me a quick refresher lesson on flower making and I'm all set. I have four or five reasonable looking flowers on the table when Mavis comes over and sits beside me. I explain to her what to do and I have just finished showing her when two more mums arrive. Introductions are made and Mavis and I show them the Rainbow Nursery School approved method of making crepe-paper flowers.

We all get on famously. David's mum, Ann, is very quick and able, as is Mavis but Simon's mum, Jill, well, let's just say, her flowers are very recognizable, not necessarily as flowers, but recognizable as hers. She must have realised her flowers were awful because she put herself in charge of cutting the crepe paper to the right sizes.

She then appeared with some black plastic sacks and put the yellow completed flowers in one and the red ones in another. She was keeping the three of us well supplied with crepe paper and keeping the tables cleared.

When we're called for coffee break, we have one full sack of yellow flowers and one and a bit sacks of red. We're all feeling very pleased with ourselves. At this rate, by lunch time, we'll have three or four full sacks.

We drink our hot drinks quickly and get back to flower making, not because we're really that keen, but because we're having such a good chatter. Home time comes all too quickly and I thank them for their help. They say they have enjoyed themselves and they offer to come again if they can. I can't help thinking again, that everything is just going far too well. I know the costumes are all almost finished; most of the set is ready for assembly onto the lorry and there's still a lot of parent participation. Going on our past experiences this is unheard of. I should be pleased but I just have this niggling feeling in my stomach.

Arthur and Simon are particularly pleased that they made strongmen pictures today. As they walk out with them clutched in their hands, they tell everyone that they are going to be strong men on the float. They both strike up the pose with legs akimbo and arms outstretched and raised at the elbows, scowling at each other and then laughing together, causing much amusement to those that see them.

Tuesday 30th June

"What's the matter with you? Are you feeling all right? You look awful," Hillary says to me the minute I walk in the door.

"I'm okay. It's just the usual, my period's due," I reply. I'd spent a few extra minutes putting on make-up to try to disguise how rough I felt. Obviously that was a waste of time.

"I'll just sit and make some more flowers if that's okay?" I say sorrowfully.

"Are you sure you should be here at all? If you want to go home again we can cope. All the aunties are here and Shirley too," she says kindly.

Go home and miss Brandon's last day? Never! The children have made a card for him and we aunties have clubbed together and bought a small memento for him to remind him of his time at Rainbow Nursery. It's an inexpensive watch with a small rainbow on the face. What it will do for his street cred I've no idea, but I'm sure he's man enough to cope with it.

"No, I'll be all right," I reply as I collect together the crepe paper and scissors and find a quiet corner to sit in and begin flower making. I had taken pain killers before I left home and was soon happy in a little world of my own quietly creating paper flowers. Ann comes in and joins me making flowers but she keeps reasonably quiet. I think someone must have warned her that I can be a bit crabby at certain times of the month. I'm pleasantly surprised when she tells me it's time to go and join the circle for morning break.

Brandon is sitting there too, looking particularly nice in a pale blue shirt and jeans. Hillary quietens everyone down and announces that the children are going to sing a few songs for him. The first song is more enthusiasm than choral expertise, but the following four songs are a joy to hear. The last song is 'If you're Happy and You Know It,' and all the aunties join in, and Brandon too, and it's a really noisy, happy rendition.

Biscuits and drinks are distributed and enjoyed especially as Brandon has brought in jam cream biscuits which both children and adults alike tuck into whether they should do or not.

Thomas has the wrapped watch under his seat and Dilly has the card. After the drinks are finished and cleared away onto a nearby table, Hillary calls to them both and they come forward and give the gift and card to Brandon. I'm sure he has a tear in his eye when he thanks everyone for the card, and much to our surprise and pleasure,

he put the watch on, declaring he liked it enormously. He then stood up and walked round the circle, shaking hands with all the children which they were highly amused by. When he got back to us ladies, he gave us all a kiss on the cheek and a hug. I'm so, so glad I didn't go home; I wouldn't have missed that hug for the world. Ann is included too and looks as pleased as punch. I'm sure she can't wait to tell all the mums about this.

I take the empty cups into the kitchen and wash up and put the cups ready for later. I am feeling a bit better but decide to take another painkiller just to help me through the next few hours. I make my way back to my quiet corner. After a few minutes Hillary and Brandon struggle up to my 'flower' table, with a huge roll of corrugated cardboard.

"This is for the flowers to be stuck onto," she says. "Brandon wants to see what it will look like before he goes and has asked if he can help us for the rest of the morning." Between them, then manhandle the roll the card onto the floor and Hillary tells us the flat bed of the truck is about twenty six feet long and we ought to allow a little extra for the attaching.

"I'll cut the card," Brandon offers. "How long do you want it then, twenty seven, twenty eight feet?"

"Do twenty eight," she replies. "Then I'll mark a foot at each end and know I have some spare. Then I'll write our name on it in pencil."

The full title of 'Rainbow Day-Nursery and Playschool' is far too long, so we agree on 'Rainbow Nursery School'. Brandon suggests it should be in capital letters to make more of an impact. Hillary has to write this out three or four times to get all the letters to fit and for them to look more or less the same size, and eventually she is satisfied with it. We decide to have the background yellow and the lettering red and she goes off to get the glue and Brandon and I grab a sack of flowers each.

There's quite a group of children watching what we're up to. So I suggest that if they want to watch then they are to sit along one edge of the card, which they do, happily. My sack of red flowers has somehow got shoved to the end of the line of seated children. When I ask for them, I'm amused at the way one flower is removed from the sack and passed, with reverence, down the line to me. I duly thank the children and ask for another which is transported in the same manner. I begin to stick the flowers onto the pencil outline and realise it will take all day to do a small section at the slow rate the flowers are appearing. So I have to move the sack closer to me and let one child help with getting them out of the sack and then keep swapping children so everyone who wants to help gets a turn.

Brandon and Hillary are doing the same and it seems everyone is happy with the arrangement. The children just love everything to do with the carnival and all want to help. Admittedly some of them get fed up with passing the flowers and go off and play but some stay for ages. Joe is sitting right beside me and chattering non-stop as I work. He loves to help; he's an adorable young fellow with a round, happy face and a funny, cheeky disposition. He'll make someone a lovely husband one day if he doesn't change too much.

After completing the 'R', I sit back to admire it. Brandon and Hillary are making good progress covering the non-letter areas with the yellow flowers and I think it's going to look great. The two bold colours are really eye catching. I carry on but run out of flowers on the 'B'. Two and a half sacks full of flowers and only five letters made. Gosh! We're going to need hundreds more.

"And this is only one side," says Hillary. "We need to do the same for the other side of the lorry too, don't forget. We will need some more help."

"I'm going to Worthing this afternoon," Liz mentions "I'll buy as much red and yellow crepe paper as I can find."

"And I'll collect some more from the town on the way home too," I add.

Hillary rushes off to write a quick note for all the parents and asks me if I can quickly copy out some diagrams on how to make the flowers. Brandon and Ann offer to cut the crepe paper, that we already have, to the correct size and put into bundles with an elastic band round them. They quickly get that task done and I'm able to add a diagram to each bundle of papers. Hillary says she's going to personally ask all the parents for their help as they come in to collect their children. Brandon helps to arrange some chairs around the name banner to protect it and then says his farewells and promises to see us on carnival day. When the parents arrive Hillary has the notes ready and the bundles of crepe paper and she is appealing to their better natures to help us out.

Thursday 1st July

"Hello Wendy," Shirley calls to me as I enter the main hall.

"'Morning," I say in a clipped and none too pleasant voice. "Have the flowers started coming in yet?"

"Yes, there are some in the cupboa..."

"I'll find them, I snap.

Who used the glue last and didn't wash the spatulas?

Where is the roll of cardboard?

Is this all the glue we have?

Is there a cushion I can kneel on?

I'm going to have to move the play dough table. Whoever thought to put it there?"

"Are you okay, Wendy?" Shirley asks with concern.

"Of course she's okay," says Liz. "Just ignore her, this is how she is at 'that time of the month'. Just leave her be and let her do what she wants. We've all been here long enough to know to steer clear of her when she comes in like that. She's not ill just uncomfortable and ratty. She'll be all right in a while."

"I don't want to be disturbed till break time." I announce to no one in particular. I grab a black sack of flowers and start sticking them onto the cardboard. I'm aware of activity around me but deliberately position myself so that my back is to the room. Bending like I am this morning is not doing my wretched stomach much good but, I kneel up straight and stretch and rub my tummy at intervals and soldier on. A new tub of glue appears at one stage throughout the morning and more bags of flowers arrive, but no one disturbs me.

Dilly pats me gently on the shoulder and tells me its coffee time. I go and collect a coffee and return to the sticking. I have completed 'RAINBOW NURSERY S' and have run out of red flowers, so I carry on doing the background with the yellow flowers.

Home time comes and I mention to Hillary that we still need many, many more flowers. We need to ask parents to ask nannies and neighbours to help too.

I position the protective chair barrier and as I leave I hear the others moaning about what a busy day it has been. Well, my morning was passable, painful at times, but passable; I don't know why they're grumbling.

Tuesday 6th July

This is the final week! The carnival is on Saturday. As I walk into the hallway there's an air of anxiety mingled with excitement about the place. People are sorting through black plastic sacks, more bags are arriving, and more people are arriving. Parents are chatting together. Hillary is there making sure the children get safely into the hall and she's also directing operations. There are sacks and sacks of flowers and Hillary asks me if I wouldn't mind dealing with them as it now seems to be my job. I grab a couple of bags and negotiate a path between the finished horses and elephants and the 'audience'. There's also more different size lengths of wood, tools and cans of paint which Brandon is carefully watching. Brandon? I do a quick double take but am too loaded up to stop and talk

I do notice my sack of bunting is there plus some other bunting which has been put on top of the bag. There's a carrier bag with brightly coloured clown wigs peeping out of the top and I see there's even a cardboard cannon someone has made and painted.

It's a little quieter in the main hall and I call out good morning to everyone there as I make my way over to the flower area. I see the list of 'Who's who' has every name crossed through, which must mean all the children's costumes have been delivered, allocated and named.

I can't help but see the adult clown outfits have been hung about the walls, all with name tags pinned on them. They're a colourful lot. Shirley has worked her magic on them and they look good. There's no outfit for Hillary as she has said she's going to be the Ring Master and is keeping her outfit under wraps till the day.

Mandy calls me over and says, "good morning, it's a bit of a mad house isn't it? Dawn and Liz have come in today to help out as there are just so many last minute things to do. Hillary has another list on the go, it's on her table over there, and it's entitled, 'Things we'll need on the day'. And she has asked that we all try to think of anything that we may need and to add it on to the list. Also, I've to tell you, Liz and Nicky are working with the children and will be colouring big top circus tents today. Dawn and I are to get every child to try on their costume and make a list of any items they may need and you..."

"Are to carry on with the flower banner," I finish for her and we both have a chuckle. "I expected to be doing that but tell me, what's Brandon doing here?"

"He made the canon in the hallway, did you see it? And he said he had nothing else to do today and has offered his services. She grins. "There are also two dads and Hillary's husband Philip, or Phil as he prefers to be called. sat over there, they're discussing where and how everything will be positioned on the lorry, what tools they will need and how much time to allow, all the nitty-gritty 'man' details."

Hillary flies into the hall, grabs a handful of papers from her table, goes into and comes out of the cupboard and then back out to the hallway. She looks harassed. Mandy and I look at each other but say nothing.

Two mums appear at my side and say they have come to make flowers. One is Ann who has made them before and the other lady introduces herself as Debbie. I just finish explaining what I need and settle them at a table close to the long cardboard frieze when Nora comes over. She pulls up a chair explaining she has a spare morning and wants to help too. Ann, David's mum, who is now a whiz at making flowers shows Nora how to do it. Ann is very methodical and she soon has a great system up and running with her table full of workers. And Debbie, she's Joe's mum, she's keeping all of us amused with jokes and stories and little anecdotes.

Hillary comes in again and looks calmer, whatever it was that had her looking flustered just now must have been sorted. She has a lot on her plate organizing this float, and as much as we all help, it is all ultimately on her shoulders. We're interrupted from our flower work when six 'band' people walk past.

"Look at us, Aunty Wendy," calls Sally as she goes by.

"My, don't you all look good," I smile.

"They do look colourful, don't they?" Ann comments as we all get back to work. A bit later on we hear, "look at me, mum."

It's Joe. He and Jazzier have come over in their clown outfits for us to admire.

"Oh, look at you," beamed Debbie. " Come here, let me give you a hug."

We enjoy the interruptions but quickly get back to work. Lots of flowers are made, lots more are glued into position and the morning just flies by.

Thursday 8th July

As I cycle to work today, I notice there's a lot of cloud about and I wouldn't be at all surprised if it didn't rain later. The tortoise didn't appear either when I opened up their house this morning. They are usually good predictors of the weather. What will the weather be on Saturday? It seems everyone is talking about the weather and the carnival.

There are quite a few parents outside the hall and they're all chattering excitedly. I have to leave my bike outside as the hallway is so overcrowded with carnival paraphernalia. I ring the bell to be allowed in and Hillary, smiling brightly, comes to the door.

"Hello, everyone, hello Wendy," she calls happily as she lets us in. "I think we're ready," she adds to me as we walk into the hall. "All the costumes are named and complete and all the scenery has been finished and painted. Will and his group are confident all will go well on Saturday morning, as there are plenty of helpers to get the jobs done. Mavis has organised some mums to bring in drinks and lunches for everybody on Saturday, and, if you carry on with sticking the flowers I'm sure you'll be finished today as you don't have that much left to do. I really think that's everything. Can you think of anything else?"

"I can't at this moment," I reply. To myself I think, this is all going far too well.

The painting easel has been erected and Liz is nearby naming the papers. She calls out to me, "morning Wendy, come over here a minute."

"Hello, what's up?" I enquire.

"I've picked up a little tip from Tanya," she says.

"Really," I answer, disbelievingly.

"Yes, I noticed that at the end of the day she always knew what the children had painted and would say, here is your lorry or elephant or whatever, and you know, as well as I do, that it's almost impossible to tell what they have painted let alone remember it till home time."

"Yes, you're right. What's her trick?"

"Well, she writes in pencil on the top edge of each painting whatever it is the child has told her the painting is of. Why have we never thought of that?"

"That's so simple," I agree with her. "We'll have to copy that."

"I am," she laughs. "I've got a pencil here and as the children are painting something related to the circus today, I'll be ready to write it down."

"Do you remember when she first started and did not even write the children's names on the papers?" I ask.

"Yes I heard about that. Now she writes everything on there. Well, she learnt a lesson and now so have we. It just goes to show, you're never too old to learn a new trick," Liz finishes.

I gather together everything I need to complete the flower banner. I only have the last four letters of 'SCHOOL' and about six feet of yellow background to do. That shouldn't take too long. Dilly and Brian come and offer to help me for a while and we talk about the float.

Dilly asks, "will you sit next to me on the lorry?" I gather she's a bit worried about the whole event but still wants to do it. Well, she's made up my mind for me, I'll be riding on the float this year after all.

"Yes I will, Dilly, and we'll have a lovely time," I say to her. We talk about elephants and clowns and the carnival in general, and Brian wants to know all about human cannon balls and did people really get shot out of cannons. They pass the paper flowers to me and we talk and work and we're all surprised when we're called for milk and biscuits.

I sit next to Nicky and tell her I've decided to go onto the float. She seems pleased and admits she would rather like to be on the lorry too. Hillary jumps up and rushes to get a pen and paper. When she comes back she says, "I've not worked out which aunties and helpers will go on the lorry and who'll be walking."

Julie says she will walk as she thinks she may only be able to accompany the float for a short while and it'll be easier for her to get away if she does have to leave.

While Hillary is jotting down names we aunties try on our clown wigs for a laugh and the children are highly amused. All of a sudden Hillary exclaims. "Hats! Hats! We haven't any hats for the band! It's probably too late to search the shops to buy any. What shall we do? We'll have to make some. There's not much time they'll have to be easy." She rushes into the cupboard and comes out with some blank paper in her hands. She rapidly sketches a couple of hat designs as we aunties quickly finish milk and biscuits and tidy away the cups and biscuit tin..

Hillary shows us the designs and one shape looks relatively simple. There are quite a few others she has crossed out.

Nicky and Tanya are asked to look after the children and I'm sent into the cupboard to try to find some suitable card. We only have white card but we do have plenty of it.

We make one hat to see if it's practical. It's just a tall cylinder of card with a small peak attached. We glue it together but also staple it. We don't like using staples as a rule but we feel we just have to this time, as the glue hasn't much time to set. It's a very simple design and at this late date it will just have to do. We have six band children so I cut out eight pieces of card just in case we mess one up and Hillary calls Lulu over and is measuring one up against her head.

"It looks so plain," says Nicky. "How about we paint thick red stripes down the length of the cylinder and maybe paint the peak red." She goes over to the easel and using the red paint draws a hat that shows us her idea. It looks good.

"I think it needs to be strengthened," says Dawn. "We don't want it to be floppy or collapse. Wendy can you cut out a circle of card and we can attach it to the inside of the hat, at the top, and it'll also finish it of properly."

We give it a try, and for a last minute thing, it looks very smart and passably strong enough. We all agree that they'll do perfectly and between us we cut out, paint, measure and glue all of them. Luckily they have almost two days to dry properly.

We all muck in to get the toys packed in the cupboard and Liz persuades Tanya to share the loo run with her to speed things up. I notice Liz has put a couple of glove puppets to one side and she entertains the children with them for a few minutes till the parents come in.

There are questions and enquiries relating to Saturday and we deal with them as best we can. The most asked questions are about times and places to drop off and collect their children. So I scribble in the diary in red felt pen to remind us to do a note for all the parents to be handed out tomorrow and a few extra for Saturday.

Now that the children have all gone home we finish clearing away the last few items and I very carefully hang the hats in the cupboard, keeping them very well spaced from each other. The phone rings. Hillary is nearest so answers it and from the one side of the conversation that we can hear, the news is not good. She replaces the handset and turns to us saying slowly, "We have a problem. We can't have the lorry that we were promised. It's broken down somewhere in Devon and will not be available for Saturday. Bookers have been very good and have found us another lorry but it's not quite the same. They have suggested I go and see it. So I'm off to see it as soon as we've locked up."

I knew it was all going too well, I think as I shake my head.

Friday 9th July

"I just had to call in to see if everything was all right," I say to everyone who is looking at me as I walk in unexpectedly.

"Hi Wendy, you can't spare a few hours, can you?" Hillary enquires eagerly.

"Yes, of course I can, but first you must tell me what happened last evening with the lorry you looked at."

"Well, the lorry they've said we can use is the same length, luckily, but it has two levels. One, the smallest area, is immediately behind the cab and then there's a step down to the rest of the flat area. Phil and I were discussing it all last evening and we think we can work round that but what is really worrying me are the sides of the lorry, or should I say, the lack of sides to the lorry. It's just flat and I'm worried about the children going on there."

"Can't we build it up?" I suggest.

"That's just what Phil said last night, he should be here any minute with Roger, one of the dads who has offered to help him on Saturday, and they're going to see what they can come up with, but in the meantime," I don't like the sound of this I think, "a couple of the mums have brought in some packets of balloons, suggesting that they may be nice for the children to hold onto on the float and add some more colour. I wonder if you have time would you start blowing some up?"

"If I can find the hand pump, you're on." I say.

"It's on that table over there." She smiles as she rushes off to answer the door bell. When she comes back in, Phil and Roger are with her. Phil calls me over to join them and I haven't blown up one balloon yet.

"Hello Wendy," he starts. "We've decided to build up the sides of the lorry with plywood and Hillary has just told me you had the same idea. Listen to this, we have two sheets of eight by four plywood left over. I was thinking that if we cut them in half, length wise, to eight by two, that will give us enough to do one side and part of the other side, of the flat edge of the lorry. If we buy one more sheet and maybe a four by two sheet, we will have enough to do both sides and the end. What do you think?"

He's asking me? All of that last sentence was just numbers, meaningless numbers. I only said 'can't we build it up' because it seemed the most obvious solution and not because I have any real ideas on the subject, but I'm rather flattered and try to look intelligent as I nod my head and agree with him.

"We don't have much time," he says. He's a master of understatement is Phil. "So if I start cutting the board we have, and Roger goes to buy the rest, perhaps you Wendy, would you look to see if we have any paint, as all the plywood will need to be painted?" He calls over to Hillary, "Is it all right if we keep Wendy to help us?"

Do I get a say in this? Obviously not! I go into the hallway and rummage about and find plenty of white emulsion paint and some red gloss. Most of the other tins feel empty but after further investigation I find a little bit of yellow and some black.

Phil has his work-bench set up in the garden area and is sawing the wood in half.

I go outside and tell him what I've found. “It'll have to be white emulsion as there's plenty of that.”

“That's fine,” he says. “Can you make a start?”

I grab an overall someone's left on the peg and go outside. I put the overall on. It's huge. I have to fold up the legs and roll up the sleeves but it'll do. I find myself a brush and after Phil has levered the lid off the tin I start painting. Phil joins me with the painting as soon as he's finished sawing and we've almost finished when Roger returns. The weather is fine with a slight breeze and the paint is drying almost as soon as we put it on to the boards.

Shirley has called in to deliver the face paints for tomorrow and comes out with a cup of tea for each of us and also to see how we're getting on.

“It looks a bit plain and uninteresting,” she comments. We all agree with her. They do need cheering up.

“Come on then, Shirley, you're the artistic one, you must be able to think of some way of making them look better,” I say hopefully. “But remember,” I add, “we don't have much time and there's only a little paint left.” With that I step back out of the way and let her think for a while.

“I know,” she says after a few minutes and goes back inside the hall only to return a few moments later with a pencil and paper.

“Look,” she says drawing on the paper. “I'll draw a few simple clown faces, you know crosses for eyes, a big dot for a nose and a big smiling mouth and you paint over them. In between the clowns I'll draw a few musical notes and maybe the odd ice cream cone. It won't take long and it won't use too much paint either. What do you think?” Another one asking for my opinion.

Phil, Roger and I all agree that will do perfectly and Shirley starts drawing on the boards straight away. She makes it look so easy, no mistakes and no rubbing's out. We three grab a can of paint each, one red, one yellow and one black and just paint whatever we feel would look right in that colour.

If I say so myself, we did a good job. The finished item looked really clever, it shouldn't clash with the flower name banner and it looks very jolly and colourful. Roger and Phil are pleased too and as soon as Shirley has finished she goes inside and brings Hillary out to see our work. She is also delighted.

As we pack away we all comment about the weather, hoping for a dry, sunny day, for tomorrow.

"It will be fine," says Roger confidently.

We all hope he's right.

Saturday 10th July

The weather IS fine! Roger was right. I don't have to be at the hall till one o'clock, but by eleven thirty I'm so fidgety and can't settle to anything. So I leave home. I walk to the hall and enjoy the warm sunshine. As the carnival finishes up in the park almost opposite to where I live, I won't have to walk all the way back to the hall after the parade, to collect my car or bike. I'm glad I'm walking as I pass one or two other places where carnival lorry's are being decorated. There is one outside the guide hall and it looks like the Oaks care home is entering a float.

As I get near to nursery school I can see our scout group have a float too. Our lorry is in the car park and it looks wonderful. The men have done a splendid job. The horses, elephants, the seals, the painted audience and the cannon have all been positioned. The hard, small uncomfortable chairs are back to back along the centre of the lorry, and securely fastened to the floor. The men are still attaching the newly painted sides and my flower name banner is there waiting to be fitted.

As I enter the hall the words 'organised chaos' jump to my mind. I am very quickly enveloped in the excitement, the busy enthusiasm and the happy chatter. It's infectious. I see Liz and Tanya are positioning chairs and Liz informs me she's going to name each chair with a child's name and put the corresponding outfit on it. Then when the children arrive they can undress and change into their costumes and they will have a chair to sit on, and a named carrier bag to put their cloths in. We will know whom we have done and who is left to do. Sounds like a good idea to me.

Shirley has two tables side by side and an array of face paints at the ready and I notice Julie and a group of mums are in the kitchen with the urn warming up and sandwiches and nibbles being put onto plates. Also I see two dads testing out their cameras and talking together.

I see Rosemary and Mandy, who are responsible for the items we will need on the float, have set up a table near the door, which already has umbrellas, rugs, sun cream, sweets, tissues, large bottles of squash and plastic cups on it. I see a large plastic bag on the table too; I expect that's the potty. I wonder who'll have that job this year.

Hillary has a group of people round her, all of whom are blowing up more balloons and tying wool to them. She calls me over to join them and says, "We're just going to finish these balloons then we're going to have a quick cup of something hot and a last minute talk."

"I know I'm a bit early but I couldn't keep away," I say excitedly to her.

"I think we all felt the same way as lots of us came early. I'm glad we did as there is still so much to do."

I join in with the balloon blowing but after one very slow, arduous effort I change to tying the strings on.

A bit later on Phil, Roger, and another man, I don't know come into the hall and announce that everything is done on the float. They accept a well deserved hot drink and we all troop outside to see the finished float. It looks wonderful, and I'm delighted to see my flower banner has been fitted and it looks bright and beautiful.

Hillary claps her hands with glee and we all are overwhelmed at how lovely it all looks.

We go back inside and just finish our drinks when the children start to arrive and the noise level goes up and up. I see Eve rush in and she comes over to help Liz, Tanya and me as we start to get the children changed. They're impatient to get into their costumes but once they're dressed a transformation seems to come over them, and although very, very excited, they're well-behaved. Thank goodness, because the time begins to fly and we have our hands full without extra trouble from naughty children. Dawn arrives and helps us and she takes a couple of children over to Shirley to have their clown face make-up done. I hear Nicky's voice so I know she has arrived, but don't have time to stop now. Costumes have to be put on, then the children sent over to Shirley for faces to be painted, a trip to the toilet and hands washed, something to eat and drink, another loo visit just to be sure. It's like a production line but with a difference.

Nicky takes my place so I can go to get changed. Some parents are already dressed as clowns, I notice, as I rush off to the toilets. I spend a penny before I change and still need another nervous wee before I go back into the hall to have my face painted.

Dawn calls out loudly, "It's a quarter to four, and we must get onto the lorry." As we make our way outside I see the scouts lorry has left. Hillary is by our lorry and looking splendid in her ring-leader outfit. It's bright red with gold braid and she has on a shiny black hat. She is organizing the seating and has decided that the band people will sit on the small raised area just behind the cab, and they are called to the front of the queue. We help Lulu, Sally and Jennifer-Marie to climb up onto the float and they're followed by Paul, Mark and Troy. They do look good in their red and black outfits. Phil comes rushing out with a clown costume on and offers to sit with them. I didn't realize he was going to be on the float but after all the work he has put in, I think it's only right. Once he's settled we pass the instruments up to him.

Hillary climbs onto the lorry next and has a quick check to make sure everything is just as it should be and then we all carefully climb up the short step ladder and get onto the lorry. Dilly gets on before me and has saved a seat for me and I have Simon, one of the strongmen, on the other side of me. Rosemary, Eve, Mandy and Dawn are also on the float so we have plenty of helpers.

Hillary claps her hand to quieten everybody down and once she has everyone's attention she says,"no child must stand up or attempt to wander about on this lorry. If there are any problems you children must talk to the aunty or helper nearest to you, is that understood?" There's a chorus of agreement and she goes on, "I want everyone to be safe and to have fun," she says it again in a happy sing-song voice. "I want you all to have fun. What did I say? What do I want?"

"You want us all to have fun." We aunties call back. And she says again, "What do I want?" We aunties have prompted the children now, and we all shout back. "You want us to have fun."

"I can't hear you,"says Hillary putting her hand to her ear.

"You want us to have fun!" We all yell back at her.

This has let off a bit of excited steam and we're all smiling and happy.

Some parents are tying balloons onto various places on the lorry and any child wanting to hold one is told they will be given one later. The supplies are loaded on and pushed under some of the chairs out of the way, and we're ready for the off.

The driver starts the engine and we pull slowly out of the car park to cheers and waves from our parents and helpers. A few near-by householders come out to see us off too. The sun is shining and there's hardly any breeze and it IS a lovely day.

We are driven very slowly to the line-up point, happily waving to anyone we see. There are about fourteen floats there already and as we park various parents, relatives and friends crowd round the lorry with encouraging comments and remarks.

More lorries arrive and everyone is cheerful and calling out to one another. People are taking photographs and more parents and friends arrive. Family and friends from other lorries stop to look at us and to talk to us too. We have eight beautifully dressed clown walkers and some carnival officials arrive to give them their collecting boxes and to give us some copies of the programme. We also have a dad, dressed as a clown riding about on a wobbly bike, who is entertaining our children and the public alike. Debbie and Ann arrive both dressed up as clowns and Joe and David are delighted their mums have dressed up. Apparently they did not tell their sons as they wanted to keep it as a surprise. Which it certainly was. We all chatter happily and give out the balloons to the children and we notice the judges walk past.

Strangers, acquaintances and people in fancy dress amble by. Some stop and talk others just wave and smile and there's excitement and anticipation all around. Brandon appears and talks to the children and takes photographs. There are a lot of photographs taken with him in them too, I notice.

The judges come back and announce that we have won the 'Most Colourful Float' and 'The Best Under Five' category and

Hillary is given two shields to keep. A big cheer goes up and soon the local press photographer is there to record the moment. Hillary asks our driver to display the shields in the front window of the cab so all can see them when we drive slowly around the town.

We're bursting with pride and the grins on our faces grow wider and wider. Time is getting on and we know we will soon be on our way as we can hear numerous bands starting to tune up. In the program it names the bands participating this year and there's the local scout band, the army cadet band, a local jazz band, the air cadets pipe and whistle band and the sea cadets band. There's also a comedy band from a nearby town that always plays and entertains the crowds with their antics. There are pom-pom groups, dance troupes, walking entrants, collectors, marshals, the police and the St. John's Ambulance Brigade.

Not far from us I can see that the local Stag car collectors group have a selection of cars. As it is sunny the roofs have been removed and there are beauty queens from surrounding towns sitting on the cars waving and looking pretty. There's also a contingent of old steam engines which have been beautifully decorated and are revving up ready for the off. One or two are miniature ones have amassed quite a curious crowd.

Our local beauty queen and her two princesses have an open float to sit in. It has been sponsored and decorated by a near-by garden centre and it looks so attractive. It is decorated with pretty flowers and plants and the girls have floaty pastel coloured dresses on and flower garlands on their heads. There's also the Fire Brigade and the R.N.L.I. who usually bring up the rear of the procession, carrying their hats or a giant flag to collect any spare change the towns folk may have left.

Our driver has started the engine and it looks like we're off. We're the fourth float to pull away and we're so grateful to be near the front. In years gone by we've been one of the last and by the time we have got to the end of the route and into the park, our little ones have been falling asleep especially if we've been behind the comedy band. They're so well known for holding up the carnival because they will keep stopping to play for groups of people, especially elderly or handicapped, or children or a particularly noisy group or anyone really. They heckle the crowds and try to encourage people to join in with them and no one minds because they're so much fun. We all like them but we're happy to be ahead them this year.

We wave and smile, and sing and shout our way around the town. As the weather is so warm and pleasant there are large crowds lining the route and everyone seems happy. We stop and start frequently on our slow journey as the driver has to negotiate narrow roads, tight bends and mini round-a-bouts.

The children are well-behaved. Admittedly we keep them distracted with crisps and drinks and have a sing-song every now and again, but the wonderful atmosphere and the good weather has affected them too and they cheerfully wave and smile at everyone. By the time we reach the finish some of them are very tired, after all it has been a very long day for them. Luckily there are a large group of parents at the rendezvous place waiting to take their offspring. But it's amazing how awake those tired children become when they see the funfair which is erected in the same field!

When all the children have been unloaded from the lorry and collected by their parents our job is done. Then we adults can make our own way, some to the fair, some to watch the arena events and some, like me, just can't wait to get home. Home, peaceful quiet home, with comfortable chairs to sit on and hopefully a nice hot cup of tea as well.

Tuesday 13th July

I can't wait to get to nursery school this morning. (I can't believe I just said that!) But it's true. I cycle like the devil is behind me, there's no wind at all and the sun is bright, and I'm going really quickly, it's exhilarating, childish, but exhilarating. I arrive ten minutes early, which is not normal for me and I ring the bell and have to accept the quips of, "Who are you?" and "Has our clock broken?" We're all in high spirits and allow ourselves a few well deserved praises and compliments. I see the trophies are standing in pride of place by the door and even a few photos are displayed as well. That was quick.

Hillary says, "good morning." And continues gleefully, "don't worry about getting much out of the cupboard today as we won't need many toys. My son in law, Tim, and Bob have edited the video and Bob wants to bring it in today to show us all. He wanted to bring it yesterday but he had to work."

"Oh what fun. That was quick," I say happily.

She adds, "we're only doing a small piece of colouring work with the children as time may be tight."

I only just get the crayons onto the table when the first children come in. The room fills with excited chatter and when Dilly comes in she walks straight over to me and sits down and starts talking happily about the carnival. She really enjoyed being a fairy and has already seen some photographs of herself, she tells me. She is so talkative, she hardly stops for breath. Soon Annie and Mark join us and Mark calls over to Sally when he spots her, and she and Jodie gather round. The talk gets louder and more animated by the minute.

"Calm down," I have to say to them gently. "We have some work to do, Aunty Hillary wants us to colour cardboard trophies and that means you will all have a special trophy each to take home." They seem pleased with that and they start chattering about Saturday all over again. Talk about lasting impressions. I think they will remember the day for the rest of their lives.

We have milk and biscuits early and rearrange the chairs round the television, in readiness for the video show. As if on cue the doorbell rings and we're introduced to Bob. He soon has the film ready and we're all sitting expectantly. The show begins.

He had started filming early in the day with us all arriving at the hall and talking and drinking tea. He filmed the hustle and bustle in the hall and respectful clips of us when we were helping the children to change into their circus outfits. He has also taken some footage of various children having their faces painted, which the children seem to enjoy seeing.

He has captured us aunties as we came back into the hall in our clown costumes and then having our face make up put on, and then struggling into our clown wigs. Next he has captured us all climbing onto the lorry; with some rather unflattering rear views, which I am sure he could have edited out. Then, there is a shot of the lorry moving out of the car park, and everyone waving and cheering as the float disappears slowly down the road and fades into the distance.

Somehow he managed to get to St. Winifred's Road before us and filmed our arrival. Then the waiting as all the entrants lined up and the officials checking we were in the correct place. He spotted one of our little acrobats showing her frilly knickers to everyone and then posing confidently when she sees the camera pointing at her. He also filmed Joe showing Sarah how to play the drums in our band group and Phil with his hands over his ears. Then there's Brian picking his nose, oblivious to the crowds. He could have edited that out too, but that's kids for you I suppose.

And of course, he filmed the presenting of the trophies and the accompanying applause and cheers. He had also captured the other floats which we had been unable to see properly. What was especially nice was the fact he had been able to film the whole of the procession which of course we hadn't been able to see either. It was a wonderful show and we were all so wrapped up in it you could have heard a pin drop. When it did finish we all burst into spontaneous clapping.

A glance at the clock shows we have just ten minutes to go until home time. Hillary and Bob talk with the children whilst the rest of us rush to put the few toys away. A quick loo run and the trophies are handed out to each child. I can honestly say I really enjoyed the morning.

Thursday 15th July

The last day of term and it's sunny and warm again and feels settled, perhaps we will have a good summer break with plenty of sunshine. We're all still on a high after the success of the carnival but I know I'm feeling tired and ready for a break. Liz greets me and says, "there are some toys that need cleaning and some odd bits of work to do with the children. Say you'll do the cleaning and I will too, then we can have a good 'ole chatter in the kitchen."

"That's fine by me," I tell her.

Hillary had come up behind us and says, " I heard you and I'm happy with that. I have some papers to work on and Nicky and Tanya can work with the children, and Ro is here too."

Liz and I go into the kitchen and I'm horrified to see we have the whole big box of the Duplo bricks to wash; all of the dolls, the garages and the plastic cars, and the sticky bricks; in fact most of the table top toys.

Hillary calls through the hatch saying, "don't bother with the dolls clothes, I'll take those home and do them in the holidays." I look at the tiny pile of dolls clothes. 'Oh, great, that will make a big difference' a little sarcastic thought pops into my head.

"I know what you're thinking," says Liz and we both have a laugh. Then she carries on. "I was horrified too, when I saw this lot but we'll soon get a system going." Which we do, and we talk and moan and laugh and grumble and the time just flies by. We are often interrupted to do a loo run and of course we have to make the morning drinks and wash up after them. We get on famously and we throw out everything that is broken or tatty and put them in the rubbish before Hillary can say anything. In fact we are enjoying ourselves so much we go back to the cupboard several times to find if any more things need washing. We do the tea-sets and the plastic fruit, the telephones and the tills. Then the many small prams and the sit on toys. And boy, do we catch up on our gossip.

"Liz, do you know where Tanya was on carnival day? I didn't see her at all once we left the hall."

"Yes I do, but I'm not supposed to say," she replied quietly.

"Oh come on," I plead.

She pops her head through the hatch to check no one is close by, then says, "Hillary is busy getting all the children's work together so I'll tell you quickly. Tanya went for an interview."

"What!"

"Shush! Yes, apparently she doesn't feel she fits in here. She came and helped us carnival day and had an interview that very afternoon. Now shush, and don't let on that I've told you."

Now that gives me something to think about and before I can comment we hear Hillary call, "have you two got time to wash the three large orange cars?"

She wheeled them into us and we had to rush to get them done as time was catching up with us. All in all Liz and I had a great day. I really can't believe I'm saying this again.

I must be in need of a holiday.

END OF TERM

Chapter Five

Tuesday 7th September

It's another bright and sunny morning and where do I have to go? To nursery school! I would much rather be here in my garden where I've spent most of the holiday enjoying the gorgeous summer we have had this year. I have had some wonderful walks over the Downs with Leo and really enjoyed the good weather. I feel rested but I'm greedy and I want more. If the sun is shining then I want to be out in it, not shut in a hall with loads of other people's kids. I really am in the wrong job! Still I can't put it off any longer, its eight forty and I'm supposed to be there before nine. I grab my lunch-box and get going.

"Morning all." I call out as I walk into the hall. Julie rushes over and quietly says. "You're going to love Antoinette." I don't like the tone of her voice but before I can question her further, Hillary comes over.

"Hello Wendy, did you have a nice holiday? It was lovely weather wasn't it? Have you remembered your lunch? I did phone you. I left a message on the answer machine to tell you we're having lunches again but not working in the afternoons, so we'll finish at one thirty." I nod my head and she continues, "I've had notification of one or two changes that we will have to make this term. I told some of the staff yesterday and I'll tell the rest when I see them." I hear my inner voice saying 'here we go again.'

Hillary continues, "The letter I had stated we must do more cooking with the children." I find myself nodding with her on that point. "Also the children are to be encouraged to bring in items for a nature table and to think about animals and possibly have a pet or two here, at school, for them to observe." I'm thinking, 'A pet? What pet?' She carries on. "Plus we must provide photographic evidence of all this and all other activities the children do. This we must enter weekly into folders for any interested party to see. And last but not least..."

My eyes have widened and my eyebrows have risen to the ceiling and I interrupt her. "And!" I exclaim. "And there's more? What now?"

"We must have a computer for the older children to use," she finishes with a flourish.

"What? A computer? A computer for four year olds? That really is the cherry on the cake. Some official HAS been busy. How much money have they allowed for all this?" I ask.

"None, none whatsoever," is the reply I receive. It was silly of me to even mention that really as I knew what the answer would be.

Hillary continues, "we will have to do some fund-raising this term so I need ideas." She knows better that to expect me to actually come up with an idea but it's kind of her to mention it to me.

Before we could talk any more Mandy calls out. "It's nine on the dot. I'm going to open the doors and let the children in." I look round the hall to find Julie, I must ask her about this Antoinette. I see she and Nicky have sorted out the day's work and she beckons me over so that I can talk, I mean work, with them. She explains we only have a simple piece of work today as we have to allow extra time for the new youngsters who have joined us this term.

She says, "I've already named all the papers and the work is to colour a patterned beach-bucket and a spade and colour in a sandy background. The older ones can have shells or crabs or sea-weed drawn onto papers for them to colour if they want. Did Hillary tell you about the computer and everything?"

"Yes she did, but what I want to know about, at the moment, is Antoinette." Before she can tell me Dilly rushes in and comes straight over to us. She really has bloomed and become much more confident over the few months we have known her. She can't wait to start a picture and she calls over to her brother, James, who is new this term. Dilly explains to him what he has to do and helps him to get started. Troy and Joe amble over. They're real friends now and what one does the other has to do too. They sit themselves down and are ready and willing to start colouring their pictures.

I think to myself, we had better have another new child or else we'll have all the new ones at the end and have to rush them to get the work finished. I glance round the room and see this very well dressed new girl standing quite still observing all about her. I stand up and go to fetch her explaining in my nicest new child voice, that she may come and join us and do a lovely picture for mummy.

"I don't want to do a picture and I won't, so go away." With that she turned her back and walked away. The encounter left me dumb-struck. I went back to the table and sat down.

"Do you know what she just said to me?" I asked in disbelief.

"I can imagine," said Julie. "You've just met Antoinette,"

I've only been in the door a few minutes and I'm not quiet ready for this. I know we have had difficult children in the past but I don't remember one quite like her. What a shock to the system she is. In between colouring and helping the new children, I find myself watching Antoinette a lot. She is rather haughty and seems to be looking down her nose at the rest of us.

At milk time, once the children are settled with their biscuits, Hillary says, "I think it would be nice to take the children on a trip to a farm, and it would tie in nicely with the animal and nature theme we've been asked to do this term. We have not had a trip out this year and if I can get a coach organized, and if the insurance isn't too high, and if we can get enough helpers, and if we can find somewhere not too far away, what do you all think?

"There are an awful lot of 'ifs' in that last sentence." I say.

"Yes I know, but if I can organize it, would you come along?"

"Yes," I say rather guardedly. "Put my name down."

"And me," says Mandy. "It sounds like fun."

"She is still so young and enthusiastic." I say to no one in particular.

Julie laughingly says, "we all know you really want to go, Wendy, so don't pretend otherwise. Put my name down too, Hillary."

"Well, it looks like we may be going to a farm if the others are willing to come along." Says Hillary looking rather pleased. "I will have a fair bit of phoning around to do, so Julie, can you please draft a poster, just leaving the date blank, and after I have checked with the other staff we can put it on the wall for the parents to see."

I find myself alternately thinking about a farm visit and Antoinette for the rest of the day.

Thursday 9th September

It's sunny again today so I'll take my bike and enjoy the sunshine. My bike must be twenty years old and in the holidays I gave it a good clean and some oil, so I hope I haven't shocked it too much. I also bought a new basket for the front and it looks rather nice.

I arrive at school, just as the mums walk in and I see we have Antoinette again. As I sign in, I look to see what days she comes. Mondays and my two days, great! I see the poster about the proposed farm trip has been pinned up and wander over to read it and and see quite a few names have been put on it already. Hillary calls me over and asks if I would like to do outdoor play today. Yes, yes, yes, anything to get outside into the sunshine.

"What do you want me to do out there?" I ask thrilled by the prospect.

"Take out the skipping ropes and balls, they're all in a box somewhere in the cupboard," she answers.

Nicky offers to help too. I leave her to rummage in the cupboard for the right box of toys while I go out to the shed for the fencing. The last time I came to the shed was with Brandon. Ah! Happy thoughts. There is just a small area we have to fence off as most of the garden is nice and safe after Brandon worked his magic on it. I'm happily putting all the pieces of fence together when Hillary comes out with some sun cream and sun hats.

I put my hand to my forehead and dramatically ask, "Are we allowed to administer sun cream? Am I qualified, can I be trusted with such a dangerous product as sun lotion? I know The Powers That Be say we have to use sun cream but have they really thought it through? What if one of the children comes out in a rash? Goes all blotchy? Faints from the smell? Gets it in their eyes? Swells up out of all recognition?"

"Stop being a fool," laughs Hillary.

"I need to sit and think this through," I joke. "I need to calm myself. I know it's only sun cream but it's enough to get one paranoid these days."

"Give over and get on with the fencing," she says laughing at my silliness."Or I'll have you back inside."

"Fencing!" I exclaim, feigning horror. "Am I allowed to put fencing up? I expect there is a ruling on that somewhere too."

"Stop mucking about and playing the drama queen, here comes Nicky," Talking to Nicky and pointing at me, Hillary continues, "Wendy is in a daft mood today, Nicky. Good luck with being out here with her."

"Seriously, if we were to abide by the letter of their silly rules we could turn ourselves from sensible adults to gibbering wrecks." I finish.

"No change there then," she chuckles as she rushes inside.

"What's that all about?" Nicky asks as she brings out the box of outdoor toys.

"Just me winding Hillary up," I answer.

Hillary is smiling as she brings out the first group of children. As there are two adults outside she has decided we can take eight children and she has selected a mix of old and new children and she tells us, they have all have been to the loo.

Well, we know what kids are like. They may have just 'been' but the minute you want to do something, they need to go again. I'm getting a bit like that too as I get older.

Nicky and I have great fun outside. Mark is a bit shy to start with but dear Dilly soon gets him playing with her brother James. We have footballs and soft balls, hoops, bean bags, a tunnel, rubber rings and a basket ball hoop. We allow the children a fairly free reign to begin with and then we introduce some team games. We try not to make too much distinction between winners and losers, (the under five's can tell the difference, even if The Powers That Be insists that they can't), and we keep swapping the team members about, so they all get the chance to be on a winning side. Hillary calls us in at ten o'clock and we are happy to go in for a very welcome cup of tea and a sit down. When everyone is settled, I ask her quietly, "how are you and the other staff getting on with Antoinette?"

Hillary considers her answer for a few moments. "She is a very head-strong and determined young girl, but then, so am I, and we are not changing our ways to suit her." That was all we were able to say on the subject before she is interrupted for something else.

After drinks Nicky and I take another group of eight to the loo, before going outside for some fun. We have Antoinette this time and don't we soon know it. She informs us primly, "I do not need the toilet so I won't try. I wanted to go outside with the first group. I've waited a long time. I want to go outside, now!"

I find myself counting in my head to calm myself down, one, two, three, four, five, six, seven, eight, nine, and ten.

I stick on a smile and say in my sickliest voice,"Antoinette, won't you at least try to go to the toilet," Then I add. "If I have to bring you in to use the toilet once we have gone outside, then you will have to stay inside."

"I won't," she scowls.

I find I'm counting again, one, two, three, four, five…

"You will," I say quite firmly and think insincerely, what a little treasure you are.

She stomps into the toilet and does a wee. She glares at me as she pulls up her knickers and washes her hands in silence.

Eventually we go outside. I don't think I'm going to enjoy this session quite as much as the first one.

Antoinette wants a straw sun hat like the one she has at home and we don't have straw ones only cloth ones.

"Well I won't wear one then." She says. I explain that she must wear one or go inside. She is quiet for a while, and then she snatches a hat from the pile, plonks it on her head and off she goes.

We follow the same format as we did with the first group and allow the children to run off some steam. Antoinette wants a bean bag. Antoinette wants a ball, no, the red one. Antoinette wants the hoop. (I know what Antoinette wants and if she carries on like this she may just be in luck if my itchy palm has anything to do with things!) I find I'm doing a lot of counting to ten in my head.

We play catch the ball and then try to encourage the children to walk with the bean bags on their heads. Some children try their hand at shooting the ball through the basket-ball hoop and all is going well until Antoinette decides to practice her skipping right in their way.

"Leg it, girl," calls Arthur. This makes me smile, as she is obviously getting on his nerves too.

We try to play down her bad behaviour as much as we can and try not to draw too much attention to it, as it seems the more we try to talk to her the more unpleasant she becomes. We decide to get the children into teams for a bit of competitive fun, and Antoinette is having none of it. She's playing with the hoops now and will not come to us. We need the hoops for the obstacle course we have devised so something will have to be done. If Antoinette is allowed to carry on like this she will well and truly disrupt the whole group. Nicky tries talking to her, first asking her nicely, then trying to persuade her to be in the team, trying to find her nice side, which appears to be well and truly hidden. All to no avail, Antoinette is stubbornly refusing to cooperate.

The other seven children are well-behaved and enjoying themselves and this one is being a right pain in the bum. She had earlier snatched a rubber ring from Jenny, she had gathered all the softballs and sat on them, she had skipped right in front of the basketball hoop so no one could use it and now this, well, I have had enough. I march over to her and ask her to go and sit by the empty box as we don't want her in any of our teams at the moment. I accompany her over to the box and wait till she sits down, and then I turn my back on her and join the others.

"That's better," remarks Arthur.

"Now, now Arthur," I say quietly, even though I do so agree with him.

She stays there, much to our surprise and she is quiet too. We keep a surreptitious eye on her all the time and after two or three minutes I go over to her and ask, "are you ready to join us now?"

"No I'm not," is the frosty reply I get. So I let her sit there a bit longer. The other children are enjoying the races and take no notice of her at all.

Hillary knocks on the window pane and taps her watch face, indicating our time is up.

We pack everything away and go in. Antoinette does not speak to me, nor I to her and the look she gives me was none too pleasant either. I really don't think anyone has ever stood up to her before, always allowing her to have her own way. I think I shocked her into silence by sitting her on her own and ignoring her, just as she had shocked me with her rudeness on Tuesday.

We take the children into the toilets to wash their hands and as we enter the hall we see all the tables are ready for lunch, so our group are seated straight away.

Oh well! I think to myself, I have five days to recharge my batteries before the next confrontation with Antoinette next Tuesday. But then, she has five days too.

"Antnet was a real pain, Aunee Illary," says Arthur in between mouthfuls of sandwich. "I'm fed up wif it, I can tell yer."

We aunties try to stifle our laughter at this little outburst. Secretly most of us agreed with him.

"Thank you Arthur," says Hillary. "Eat up your lunch now."

I know I am being stared at by Antoinette. I can feel it. I wonder what she's thinking. After we have eaten our lunch, we pack away and a few songs are sung before the parents come in.

"Before you go, Wendy," calls Hillary, amusement still bubbling out from her. "We ARE going on a farm trip. I have just got the coach and insurance sorted. Are you free on Saturday 18th?"

"That's next weekend!" I exclaim.

"Yes I know. The coach was available that weekend so I said I'd have it. I have phoned Mandy and Eve and Dawn and they can all make it. And I have left a message for Ro and Julie to get back to me as soon as possible. It should be fun."

"Whereabouts is this farm?" I ask.

"It's near Petworth. It will only take thirty or forty minutes to get there. David's mum went there in the spring to see the lambs and she said her children really enjoyed it. She gave me their name and number so I phoned them up and they are happy for us to visit."

"Well that was quick. And yes, I think you are right, it will be fun," I agree with her.

Tuesday 14th September

Hillary is waiting at the door for me as I arrive and takes me into the small hall for a quiet talk. It's about Antoinette. Why am I not surprised? Apparently her mother has been on the phone and was asking a few questions about the activities on Thursday. I had already told Hillary what had happened and as she had already spoken to Nicky, she had a rough idea of events. Between us we know the child needs some discipline but it is never easy telling the parents this. We discuss different ways to deal with Antoinette and we both agree that she is the one that has to change her ways, not us.

Whilst I have Hillary's ear I ask, "where's Tanya? I haven't seen her."

"She's not with us any more," answers Hillary. "She told me she wasn't particularly happy here and she wasn't sure if this area of childcare was quite what she wanted. And let's face it; she didn't really make that much of an effort to fit in. I've promised I'll write her a reference, which could be a bit difficult. We'll be okay staff-wise for the time being because I've had the local senior school asking if we would be interested in having a student come in for work experience, so I think we'll be able to manage. Will you work with the new children for a while this morning, letting them colour their rainbows whilst you get their scrap books started?"

It's a pleasant enough start to the morning although I must admit, I'm not really looking forward to working with Antoinette but I expect it will be interesting. I notice a van pulling into the car park and a man getting out and wandering about. He then climbs back into the van and drives off, only to return about ten minutes later.

"Are you expecting a delivery, Hillary?" I call to her.

"No, why?"

"There's a van in the car park. This is the second time he's been here in the last few minutes."

We're all curious and on our guard. You never know what unsavoury people there are about these days. He gets out of his van and looks around. He obviously knows we're watching him and soon we hear the door bell. Hillary and Julie go to the door and Mandy stations herself close to the phone, just in case of trouble. We soon hear talking and even laughing coming from the hallway, so we know we're not in any danger.

Hillary comes rushing in and explains that the man had an arrangement to give a talk in the nearby church hall but no-one is there and a passer-by suggested he try here. Hillary has decided he can come in for a short while. She asks Julie and me to position the chairs in a semicircle, like we do at break time but with a table in the middle, and he will be in, in about five minutes time.

Hillary says his name is Mr. Bates and he has a nice surprise for us. We're all sitting expectantly when he walks in with a dog on one lead and a fox on another. Hillary has positioned herself next to Jodie. Jodie who dislikes dogs. Hopefully she will feel safe and reassured with Aunty Hillary next to her. The rest of us adults sit in amongst the children.

The dog is a shiny black Labrador who sits down on the floor as requested by Mr. Bates. The fox is beautiful and has everyone's attention. He seems very tame and obedient and sits on the table while Mr. Bates tells us all about him and foxes in general. We learn that this fox is called Rouge and Mr. Bates found it whilst he was out walking with his dog, Rex. The fox had a nasty gash on its side and an injured leg. He was very young at the time and was thin and sad looking. Mr. Bates nursed it back to health, and his dog Rex helped enormously by licking the wound and sleeping close to the fox to help keep it warm. This was about three years ago and the dog and fox have become good friends and are rarely ever apart from each other.

At the end of his very informative talk he indicated to Hillary that the children could touch the fox, a few at a time, if they wanted to. Obviously Hillary has to consider the safety aspect of such an offer and also the value of such an experience. She stands up to speak and was almost knocked off balance by the speed of

Jodie's rush to be the first one to touch Rouge. Well, that sealed it. Hillary is going to allow the children the chance to be close to a real live fox. Actually we haven't got a ruling on touching foxes from The Powers That Be but I expect we will, should they ever get to hear about this visit.

Thursday 16th September

Today is another warm and sunny day. We've had the most settled and sunny summer I can ever remember. My tortoise have eaten and eaten and I'll be happy in the knowledge that they will have a good weight to go into hibernation with in about a months time.

Riding my bike in this weather is so much better than fighting with the wind and rain. I'm a bit late again but in a happy frame of mind as the postman delivered me a really nice little windfall from the premium bonds. I call a cheery, "good morning." to everyone in the hall as I enter.

"I hear you had a fox in on Tuesday," Ro says to me as I put away my bag.

"Yes he was gorgeous. I've never stroked a fox before and the fur, under his chin, was so soft. You know what they say about people growing to look like their pets, well, Mr Bates had red-brown hair and a pointed nose."

"Only you would think of that," she says shaking her head. "Do you look like your dog, Leo?"

At that moment Hillary came over to us and asked me, "will you be in charge of painting today, Wendy?"

I really stick my neck out and ask, "can we do it outside in the garden?" Before Hillary can reply Nicky chips in with, "what a good idea and maybe I can take a few of the children on a small nature walk!"

That swings it and we're out in that lovely sunshine again today. You're a treasure Nicky. "Thank you, Nicky." I mouth to her over the top of the children's heads and behind Hillary's back. It's amazing how quickly you can set up something when you really want to. We have the papers named and the paints fully mixed, all the clean water and towels together and are out of the door before anyone can change their minds. We put the easels in the shaded area so we don't have to bother with sun hats and sun cream.

Hillary has Amy, Arthur, Sally and Jodie waiting and ready for me and I soon have Arthur and Jodie into aprons and started painting. Sally is sitting on the grass next to Amy and chattering happily. As Nicky walks past us I notice her little group consists of Annie and her brother Jake, and Dilly and her brother James.

Arthur finishes his painting first and Amy takes his place. He gets a bit fidgety sitting watching with nothing else to do. I ask him to stand next to Amy and help her, explaining that, as she is new to us, she may need a 'big boy' to help her. I'm sure I could see his little chest puff up at this and he happily stands next to her. As I help Jodie out of her apron and get Sally ready, I suggest Jodie looks at the other two doing their paintings and then talks with them about them. This is different because usually they just go off and play and never take much notice of each other's work.

Nicky comes back from her walk around the grounds and is ready to start painting with her four children. As my group are all finished we set off on our nature search. We find leaves and daisies and dandelions and even a few early hazelnuts. There are some grasses with their seed pods and we pick one of each as our offering for the nature table, which at the moment is an old tray, but it serves its purpose. I hear Nicky calling to us, "we're finished and ready to go in." So we join her and all eight children are happy and chatty as we enter the main hall, via a trip to the toilets and hand wash. We can see the chairs are set out ready for drinks time.

Hillary asks me, "how did you get on? The children look happy enough." Nicky and the children take the nature offerings and put them onto the nature tray on a table which has been pushed up against the far wall. We can see them re-arranging everything so that all items can be seen clearly. I answer saying, "we all enjoyed it and it's lovely and warm out there."

"Stay and have drinks and you can take another group out afterwards."

I see Nicky has Antoinette in her group this time. Hillary has tried to persuade me into thinking that she's not a naughty child but just stubborn and strong willed and she is the way she is because she has been allowed to do whatever she wants to do.

Well, we're all entitled to our own opinions, but I know she has an attitude about her which seems to dare you to try to cross her and she has a look that could stop buses. I'm not convinced.

"Do you want me to paint first again?" I ask Nicky.

"Yes, let's follow the same pattern as before," she answers happily.

I have Alison, who is one of our new intake, Mark, Topaz and Joe. Joe stands right next to the easel struggling to put on an apron, keen as can be to do anything is our Joe. He's such a happy-go-lucky boy, cheeky at times but always polite and funny. He has managed to put his own paper on the easel and has started painting. I help Alison into an apron and it's soon obvious she hasn't painted much before. In no time at all there's paint running down the easel and along her arms and there's a real danger of the paper being ripped by the force she is using.

I clean her up a bit and explain she must wipe the excess paint from the brush and be gentle when applying paint to the paper. She's very enthusiastic and excitable, and she talks and talks, and she forgets what I've just said. As she talks her arms and hands and paintbrush are flying about all over the place. Off we go again.

I give her yet another sheet of paper. Again I explain to her that she need only use one brush at a time and that she only needs a little paint on the brush and to wipe it on the side of the container. I have to stay with her and keep on and on repeating myself over and over, but it's worth it in the end, as eventually she has a painting that is so much better. She tells me it's a tree and a garden, I can't see it myself but it's certainly an improvement on the soggy and torn mess the first efforts produced. The important thing is, she really enjoyed doing it.

Topaz is altogether different, she's a neat and tidy little girl and she really does not like paint on her hands so she takes her time and carefully produces a bright picture. Mark is quiet and shy and is not happy being watched by the others. He uses each brush just once, dabs a bit of colour on the paper and moves onto the next colour. It only takes him a very short time but the picture looks good for all that. Joe is confidently washing and drying his hands himself but it takes me quite a while to get Alison cleaned up. I only just finish drying her hands when Mark and Topaz have finished painting and want to rinse their hands and dry them. Soon we're ready for our wander round the garden looking for more items for the nature table. I look up and see Nicky indicates she is ready for the swap over to painting

Nicky soon has her group at the painting area and I can hear Antoinette is not impressed with the choice of aprons the children have to wear. I hear her say she wants purple paint, which we have not got. I glance over to them and can see Nicky is coping and I'm not needed.

When we take the children in, I quietly ask Nicky, "what was the problem with her this time?" Indicating Antoinette with a nod of my head.

"I'll tell you later."

"Have you got time to squeeze in another group?" calls Hillary. "There are just six children left."

Nicky and I take three each and quickly have a painting and nature walk accomplished and get them back to the hall just as the tidy up is starting. Ro takes the children from us as I call out, "we won't be long, we'll just get some water and clean the easels before we bring them in." Back outside I say to Nicky, "come on, spill the beans."

Nicky took a deep breath and started, "apparently Antoinette likes to wear the red apron with the cat on and it was not out here. I tried to be understanding and commiserate with her, and I was gently persuasive in trying to get her to wear another, but on being told to 'Go in, now, and get the red one!' I just told the child to wear the one available or not to paint at all. She stood her ground for a while, seemingly to weigh up in her mind if she would get away with a tantrum or not. She then she put on the apron and did a wonderful painting. If only she could have done that without all the fuss."

"I know what you mean," I agree with her. "She has an amazing knack of winding us all up but we know we can't let her get away with it. She's going to be a real challenge, that one. Did I hear her comment about purple paint?"

"Oh, yes. Purple is her favourite colour. I just said 'we don't have any', but you could try to make some by mixing red and blue paint together. She pulled a face, totally ignored me, then produced a beautiful painting.

We soon finish and carry everything back inside. As we enter the hall we see most of the toys have been put away and all the tables are ready, so we're able to join the others at the lunch table. Hillary calls us over to sit on two empty chairs next to her and says.

"I've been talking to the others about fund-raising this morning and Rosemary has offered to organise a sponsored slide on Wednesdays, with her little ones, to help us out. And we've been talking about a fête-cum-singing event for the parents. We didn't have any singing at Easter so I think it is a good idea. What do you two think about that?" We mull it over but before we can say anything she continues, "the general idea so far, seems to be, to have a raffle, and a few stalls around the edge of the hall, with, say, tombola and possibly a second-hand clothes stall, and toys and maybe even have cake and teas for sale. Then we invite the parents and any relatives to come and hear a singing concert and whilst we have them in the hall, we go round with raffle tickets and encourage them to visit the stalls"

Nicky and I both nod our heads and agree it's worth a go. "Do you have a date yet?"

"No, not yet, but I think it should be near half term sometime, if we have it any later it will be too close to Christmas. I'm glad you both like the idea as I've just asked Liz to write a poster asking for parent helpers and ideas for the event."

Just then Liz walks over to us and shows us what she has written. "This'll have to do for now. I've mentioned we need to raise some money and that we're thinking of hosting a singing event and that any other ideas are most welcome. I'll stick it onto the wall by the door and the parents will see it as they come in."

Hillary says,"remember to ask for any consent forms and payments for the farm trip while you're at it. And do tell them, their children will not be able to go to the farm without consent or payment up-front. Be firm about that."

"What time do you want us here on Saturday?" I ask.

"The coach will be here at ten, so half past nine ish."

We've run out of time, the parents are arriving and queuing up outside. Time to get a move on.

Saturday 18th September

The weather forecast last night said the weather would be warm and a bit overcast today and that is just as it is as I ride to school. The ground is dry and it should be just perfect for our day out.

I leave my bike in the hallway, and head into the main hall. There are a lot of people already in the hall and I join them.

"I'm glad you're here now Wendy," says Hillary. "I was just about to go over the plan for today. I am expecting about forty two children, five or six mums and a dad. Unfortunately Ro can't make it and Eve is unwell so won't be coming. But there should be enough of us adults to be responsible for three children each. And," she adds, "it goes without saying I want all the children to use the toilet before we get onto the coach."

"And me too," I call out.

"Well yes, I think we had all better go as the facilities at the farm may not be brilliant, but at least they do have some."

"Here's the coach," calls Mandy. "And a few cars are arriving."

"I must have a word with the driver," says Hillary and off she goes.

The hall begins to fill up with excited children and we check they have sensible shoes or Wellington boots, a jacket or coat, lunchboxes, and that they have paid and returned the consent forms, only then do we let the parents leave them with us.

I see Bob and his daughter Sally have arrived and they have a buggy with a little one in it. I am puzzled by this and just about to go over to say something when Ann walks in with her son David, and she has a buggy too. Then I hear Bob call over to her. "Hillary told me there was another parent with a buggy, I'm glad I'm not the only one." That must be okay then, I think to myself.

Mavis comes over to me and says, "I'm a little worried about my Jodie. She wants to go to the farm but is a bit anxious about the animals. Normally I would come too but I'm five and a half months pregnant and don't I know it," she adds with a deep sigh. "Even this far along, anything and everything seems to make me sick and I don't want to spoil everyone's day."

"Don't worry I will keep an extra special eye on her and I'll make sure she is in my group. When is the baby due?"

"Mid January, and it can't come soon enough," she answers.

I see Jill walk in with Simon and looking at the two lunchboxes in her hands it looks like she is one of our helpers.

We are asked to start the loo run and I have the chance to ask Julie about the buggies.

"Bob and Ann both wanted to come to the farm but had no one who could look after the toddlers, so Hillary agreed they could bring their little ones as long as they didn't advertise the fact to too many others and that they agree to be responsible for them all day. Bob is the dad who filmed the carnival, do you remember?"

"Yes, he seems a really nice man," I reply and continue, "I've seen Jill arrive, who else is helping?"

"I think Debbie put her name down and a couple of others, I can't remember now," she answers.

Soon we are all ready and queueing to get on to the coach. I notice Antoinette and her mother are the first on. Hillary asks if the adults can sit in an aisle seat and have one child sitting with them and two children across the aisle. This should enable them to keep an eye on the two across the aisle and be able to act if necessary. I notice Antoinette and her mother have sat in the front seat, behind the driver and the other front seat is where Hillary has put her bags. When we are all settled the driver stands up and claps his hands and we all quieten down.

"Hello," he says. "My name is Reg, Reg Smith and you can all call me Mister Smith. I have been a coach driver for many years and I have developed some very special powers over that time. I can tell when a child is going to be naughty." With this he narrows his eyes and sweeps the whole coach looking at each child in turn. "I will not have naughty children on my coach." He says slowly enunciating every word. "If I have a naughty child I will stop and they will have to get off."

He certainly has everyone's attention, and he continues. "Have you all got that? I won't have naughty children and I won't have children sitting on the front seats either, so you missus had better move back." He says this to Antoinette's mother and Antoinette. Neither of them look too happy about it but before they can say anything he carries on. "It's for safety as much as anything, so hurry up and we can get going."

They end up sitting at the back of the coach and they do not look very happy at all.

Off we go then," calls Reg as he settles back behind the wheel and starts the engine. We only go a few yards when he stops and looks back saying. "There is a little boy thinking of standing up. He had better think again if he wants to go to the farm."

This Reg is very clever, I think to myself. I look at my watch and see it is nearly ten thirty and calculate we should be at the farm just after eleven. We leave the car park behind us and head out of town towards Arundel. When the castle comes into view Hillary calls out for everyone to look at it. It is a complete castle not just ruins and it always looks so wonderful nestled at the bottom of the hills. The town itself is very pretty with a large cathedral and plenty of antique shops and tea rooms. We leave it behind us as we continue on our way and soon we are travelling down the very steep Bury Hill. Again Hillary calls out for the children to look at the splendid views over the countryside and she indicates where the river Arun meanders through the fields.

It is not long before we are driving under the dark canopy of trees in Fittleworth woods, then we burst out into the brightness again. After a little while, Hillary stands up and holds onto the back of her seat and announces, "we're nearly there, and when the coach stops, I want you all to sit still until the farmer says we can get off." Just then Reg slows right down and turns into the narrow roadway leading to Lowergate Farm.

As the coach comes to a standstill a rather squat little man emerges from a barn and Hillary gets off the coach and has a word with him. They both return to the coach and she introduces him as Farmer Hewitt.

"Hello children," he says. As he speaks his weather-beaten old face breaks into a smile. "I have a treat for you." This has our attention. "I have got my two trailers ready and hitched up behind my tractors and we can go on a ride before you have lunch. How does that sound?" Off he goes without waiting for a reply.

Amid a lot of excited gabble Hillary manages to regain control saying, "shush, shush. Sit still for a moment longer, I just want to tell you what farmer Hewitt has arranged. Firstly we will have a ride on the trailer, and then when we will come back here to the barn and have our lunch. Then we will divide into three groups and look at the smaller animals. As we are the only visitors here today, Mr Smith will leave the coach unlocked so the adults, and I mean adults, not children, can have access to the coach. I have brought spare clothes should the need arise. I also have a first aid kit, some wet wipes, some spare Wellington boots. There are also some aspirin should any of you adults need them," she adds with a chuckle looking at us adults.

Farmer Hewitt has driven a large tractor and trailer up close to the coach and there is another slightly smaller one behind. Hillary tells us to leave our bags in the coach and we all file out. Farmer Hewitt helps us to climb onto the trailer.

"My son George is driving the other one," he tells us. "There's plenty of room for you all. You may have to squash up a bit but you'll be fine."

I find myself in the second trailer with my three children, Jenny, Jodie and Arthur. Once everyone has a seat, we jerk to a start and bounce our way towards some cows in a distant field.

"I ain't seen real cows up close," Arthur informs us all.

"I don't know how close we'll get," I answer.

"Can I ride one?" he asks.

"I don't think so," I reply with a smile. He really is a townie boy.

Bob is in the same trailer with Sally and his little son is in his arms, and he says, "people usually ride horses not cows. Cows give us milk."

"Do they?" Asks an interested Arthur. "Where is the milk then?"

Before we can say any more there's a click, then a crackle sound and a voice comes over the tanoy on the roof of the trailer. "Hello everyone, I'm George. We are going to go into the field with the cows and we'll stop there for a few moments. Cows are curious animals and this herd are all very friendly and are used to people, so they may come over to see you. If they do, don't shout or squeal or you will frighten them. They may look big and scary but they are really just great big softies. Dad has opened the gate and driven into the field and I must close the gate behind us after we have gone though. So don't worry if I hop out of the tractor cab for a second."

Once in the field we stop next to a feeder with hay in it and after a few moments we can see a big brown and white cow getting closer to the trailer in front of us. Another cow brushes its body along the side of the feeder as if scratching an itch. I could feel Jodie squash even closer to me.

"Don't you like them?" I whispered to her.

"I don't know," she whispered back.

"Aint it big!" Arthur exclaimed. He is fascinated and watching closely.

Three cows come towards us and stop a few feet away and just look at us. One licked its lips and the end of its tongue went up inside its nose.

"Did ya see that? I wish I could do that," says Arthur trying really hard to push his tongue out and up as far as it would go.

Just then the engine starts up again and we continue on our way. Once out of the cow field we bump along a track beside a field where there were many, many sheep.

George came on the trailer tanoy again and explains that we are going to see some horses and donkeys in the next field. The horses are beautiful and look at us over the hedge as we trundle past. Some of them walk along in the same direction as us, still looking over the hedge at us. George then drives us into another field and we stop beside his father's tractor and trailer. He jumps out of the cab and walks back to us and suggests we walk the last few yards to the barn saying, "I'll help you all out and the short walk will give the children chance to release some energy before eating."

As we enter the barn we can see that our coach driver, Mr Smith, has put all the bags and lunchboxes in there. The barn has hay bales all over the place and the children soon find places to sit. Most of the boys just want to climb and play and Hillary tells them that they can do just that once they have had their lunch. It takes a few minutes to match the correct lunch box to the correct child. And Hillary desperately tries to get the children to wipe their hands on wet wipes before they start eating, but in the mêlée the odd sandwich gets a bite taken from it before she can get there.

Farmer Hewitt comes into the barn and claps his hands to get our attention then he says, "listen up everyone. I must tell you, the cats here on the farm are working cats. They look all soft and fluffy like your cats at home but they are wild and will scratch and hiss, so it's probably best if you leave them alone. The small animals you'll see after lunch are fine for petting but leave the cats alone."

It is warm and roomy in the barn and everyone is chatting and eating. There are some children I hardly know as I don't go in on the days they come into school, but everyone is mixing together and enjoying themselves. Everyone except Antoinette and her mother. They are sitting together and a bit away from anyone else and they seem a little uncomfortable on the hay bales.

Julie is sitting next to me and I quietly ask her, "what is Antoinette's mother's name?"

"Cynthia," she replies.

"I hadn't noticed until now but look at her outfit and her hair. You'd think she was on a fashion shoot not visiting a farm,"I whisper to Julie." Is she wearing a Barbour Mac? They cost a fortune. And look at those wellington boots. You have to be a certain type of woman to get away with pink wellington boots with multi coloured assorted sweet pictures on them. Mine are just plain."

"Stop it, Wendy, don't get me started. Shush here comes Hillary."

"I'm about to split you all into three smaller groups," says Hillary in a loud voice. "There are four areas of the farm to see this afternoon, they are, the chickens, the pet sheep and goats, the rabbits and the old tractor. If we spend about half an hour in each area that should take us up to three o'clock or thereabouts."

"The time has flown this morning," I comment.

"Yes it has," Hillary agrees. "Julie, in your group, I want you to have Bob and his two children, Antoinette and Cynthia and Ann and her two little ones. Wendy you are responsible for Jenny, Jodie and Arthur, and Julie you have Annie and Jake, and Dilly. What about her brother? Where is he?"

Mandy calls out, "he is sitting next to his friend Mark. They have both been good and are no trouble. I'm happy to have them both in my group if you agree."

"That's fine," Hillary answers.

"Julie, yours is a slightly smaller group than the rest," Hillary continues, "but you will have both the buggies with you. Will you be okay with that?"

"Yes, we'll be fine," answers Julie looking at me and smiling.

I'm happy to be with Julie, and our group of children are usually well-behaved in school. Bob and Ann are a nice people and appear to be happy to join in. It is just Antoinette I'm a bit worried about.

As if reading my mind Julie says, "we'll be all right."

Hillary has one last instruction for us. She says,"when you have all finished eating, pile your lunchboxes by the door and then you can start off in the small animal barn." Handing Julie a scrap of paper, she adds, "follow this route round and we will all meet back here around three o'clock."

She then goes to talk to the others and we start to gather our little group together. Antoinette and her mother stick to each other like glue and Sally stays close to her dad and holds onto the buggy. We all move off through an adjoining door into a small barn where we see a large pen with rabbits in. There is a sign on the gate saying you can go in and touch them. We don't want to risk opening the gate and the rabbits getting out so Bob offers to lift the children over for us. It is only a very low fence and Julie and I climb in and help with the children. We suggest we all sit on the straw and let the rabbits come over to sniff at us.

The rabbits are so friendly, hopping on and off laps and chasing each other around and the children are having a wonderful time stroking them. There are so many rabbits, all pretty colours and different sizes. I was a bit worried about Jodie but she has a big grey rabbit on her lap and is happily caressing its ears.

Ann has elected to stay outside with the buggies and she says she can see, there are guinea pigs in the next door pen and a few young calf's in the one next to that.

We stay a little longer with the rabbits and then climb in with the guinea pigs. These are just as much fun as the rabbits and we all enjoy their antics. There is some food left in the feeders and we hold some on the palms of our hands to see if they will feed from us. They do and the children are delighted to have a go.

"Has anyone here got a rabbit or guinea pig at home?" asks Julie.

"No," says Arthur. "But if me pockets was bigger I could take a small one."

"We're not allowed to take anything from this farm, or anywhere else," says Julie, trying her hardest not to let her smile show. "Come on lets look at the calf's and then we must move on."

Everyone clambers out of the guinea pig pen and Arthur can't wait to get up close to a calf. We don't have much time as we are scheduled to go and play on the hay bails and the two old tractors next, but there is just time for everyone to stroke the calf and to let a couple of children into the pen for a few moments.

The boys are really excited about climbing all over the tractors and run ahead. I happen to be walking behind Antoinette and I see that she must have sat in something as there is a dark, damp, rather unpleasant patch on her coat. Do I mention this to her or her mum? No. I decide not to.

Ann is close to me and she points to the mark on the coat and raises her eyebrows as if in question and I just shake my head and ask, "has the farm changed since you came earlier in the year?"

"It is a bit different actually. It was spring time therefore we saw lots of lambs and only a few of the smaller animals. I think there were some chicks under a heat lamp and a few duckling too. But we didn't have a trailer ride or go out onto the farm itself. David is really enjoying himself. I'm so glad we came."

As I glance round I see the girls are having as much fun as the boys and are enjoying a bit of freedom to run and play. I don't suppose many of them have clambered over hay bales before.

Ann and Bob, Julie and I have all tried, at different times, to engage Cynthia in conversation, but she just answers whatever question we put to her but offers no other conversation, so we have tended to rather leave her to it. So when we hear her exclaim, "Oh no!" Julie and I look at each other to see who is going to see what's wrong. I end up going over to Cynthia, as I am the nearest, and she says, "look at this." She holds out one side of Antoinette's coat and one pocket is hanging off. "She has just torn this on that old tractor." She complains.

"Is she hurt?" I ask, thinking perhaps there was a jagged edge or something.

"No, but look at the state of her coat," Cynthia demands.

I do look at the coat and can see it will be easily repairable with just a couple of stitches to hold it back in place. Luckily the pocket itself is not torn or ripped.

"A couple of stitches and it will be as right as rain," I say as I rummage in my bag. "I have a safety pin in here somewhere, here you are." She doesn't look very pleased at all. Wait till she sees the mark at the back!

"Come here children," calls Julie. "We are going to see the goats and some pet sheep."

Outside in a small field behind the farmhouse is where we find the goats and sheep. There are three sheep and about seven or eight goats. Jodie holds back a bit, she tells me she is not sure she wants to go in with them. So I wait outside with her. Bob offers to stay outside with the buggies and mentions to Ann to go in and he will keep an eye on her little boy.

One goat comes over to the fence and I lift Jodie so she is able to reach over and touch it. It keeps turning its head looking for food and Bob pulls up a clump of grass and the goat greedily eats it up. He pulls up some more grass and gives it to Jodie to feed to the goat.

She very bravely puts the grass on her palm and offers it to the goat.

"His nose is all tickly," she giggles.

"Look at Jenny and Dilly, they have a little goat that they are stroking," I say.

"Come and see this one," calls Dilly. "He is really lovely."

"Do you want to?" I ask her.

"Maybe in a minute," she answers tentatively.

"Look Aunee Wendy," calls Arthur. "Me 'and disappears, look."

He is with a sheep and the wool is so thick on its back that his hand does disappear into it.

I can hear Cynthia's shrill voice. "Get off. Give it back. Get off."

Now what, I think to myself. Julie goes over to her and I can hear Cynthia saying, "that wretched animal has eaten one of Antoinette's hair ribbons. What are you going to do about it?"

Julie looks on a bit bewildered then says, "I think it is time we moved on now."

"But my ribbon!" Shrieks Cynthia.

I don't know what Cynthia thought Julie was going to do about it as there really is nothing she can do.

"There's nothing I can do about it, is there?" Julie says echoing my

thoughts."So come on, lets get a move on, if we are going to have any time to see the chickens and chicks we had better go now."

"Chickens! We can't see any chickens. Antoinette has an allergy to feathers," exclaims Cynthia.

"Well chickens are the next stop," Julie replies patiently. "Would you rather go back to the barn and wait for us there?"

Without a word she turns on her heel and off they go. The rest of us wandered over to where we could see the chickens in an enclosure near the farmhouse. There are a few ducks too and again there is a notice giving permission for us to go in and walk amongst them. The ground is a bit slippery so we remind the children not to run. The chickens won't keep still for the children to touch them but nevertheless it is interesting to be close to them. The girls are picking up feathers and tickling each other and giggling.

A woman comes out of the house and I assume she is the farmers wife. She introduces herself as Mrs Hewitt and asks if we are ready to see the chicks. "Come this way," she calls. She takes us into a room with what looks like filing cabinets against the wall, and she opens a drawer and inside the drawer are rows of eggs.

"These eggs are incubating. Do you know what that means?" Everyone was quiet, so she continued, "they are going to turn into chicks."

"'ow?" enquired Arthur.

"We keep them warm in these cabinets and after a few weeks the shell cracks and out comes a chick," she answers kindly.

This has them all puzzled but before any more questions are asked she says, "come with me."

We follow her into a small but very warm barn with a large lamp hanging down low in the middle of a fenced run. There before us are about thirty or so tiny chicks enclosed in that space. They all look so soft and fluffy and yellow.

"Would you like to hold one?" she asks the group and got a resounding yes from us all. Even us adults. She carefully picks one up and gently holds it in her hand whilst explaining that these chicks are only two days old.

"I don't think we should actually hold one," said Julie. "Perhaps we could touch the one in your hand."

She accepts that and very patiently and slowly walks amongst us so that we all can touch the tiny yellow bundle. The children seem to know to be gentle and they were quiet and seemed to be thoroughly enjoying the experience.

She put the little chick back with the others and we make our way outside. I prompt the children with, "what do we say to the nice lady?"

The children chorus,"thank you Mrs Hewitt." Then we head back to the barn. Nearly everyone is there and Farmer Hewitt is near to Cynthia and we could hear him saying, "I told 'e those cats were wild. Young 'uns never listen these days. Anyway its only a scratch."

"Only a scratch!" Cynthia exclaims loudly. "Only a scratch."

"I have antiseptic cream and a plaster in the first aid box," says Hillary quickly. "Do you want Antoinette to have one?"

Cynthia answers "Yes," then begrudgingly, "thank you."

After sorting Antoinette out, Hillary calls out to get our attention. "As most of us have very mucky boots can you all go over to Mandy and Dawn by the tap and they will clean you up a bit. Then come back here to me. I'll be standing by the bags and boxes and after I have wiped your hands with a wet wipe you can collect your lunchboxes and get onto the coach.

The Mrs Hewitt appears with a pile of papers and hands them to Hillary. Once we were all seated on the coach and ready to go Hillary says, "I have just been given some sheets of paper with pictures of farm animal on them. There is enough for you all to have one each. You can take it home to colour in and it will remind you of your visit. I'll fold them in half and you can put them safely into your lunchboxes. She walks down the coach and hands all the adults a few pages each so that we can help the children and get the job done a bit more quickly.

We can hear Mandy say, "come on Simon, open your lunch box. Come on you're holding everyone up. No you can't hold the picture in your hand, we want it in the box." Very reluctantly he opens his lunch box and we can hear Mandy exclaim, "Urgh! Give that to me." She walks down the aisle holding the box at arms length saying, "he's only got a selection of animal poo in here!"

A lot of us adults are trying desperately to smother our laughter. Trust Simon!

Thank goodness we found it and not his poor mum.

Monday 20th September

I had a phone call from Hillary yesterday evening, just after I had been watching an Antiques program on the television. She wanted to know if I could swap my day from Tuesday and do a Monday instead. I know Monday is the day Shirley comes in for a few hours and does music and movement with the children. I have not seen that before and I'm not sure what to expect but I'll soon be finding out as I'd said, yes I'll do it.

I decide to drive to work as it's raining heavily. Where has the sun gone I ask myself? Please don't let this be the end of the summer yet. It's still pouring with rain as I park and in the short dash to the door I get drenched. I shake off some rain from my coat but my feet are wet. I notice some of the mums who have had to walk are absolutely soaking wet. What misery they have to put up with just to get their children to school. I'm so glad I have the option of using the car when I need to.

I see Mandy, Eve and Dawn are all here and I know Hillary has an appointment as she had explained to me last night. Mandy approaches me and says, "Hello Wendy, what a wet morning! Thank goodness it wasn't like this on Saturday or our farm visit wouldn't have been half the fun it was." I nod my head in agreement as she continues. " Would you do a little work on the scrapbooks until Shirley comes in at nine thirty?"

I hardly have time to get everything out and the first child gluing when the doorbell rings and Shirley arrives. She calls a cheerful, 'hello all' to us and to me she adds, “nice to see you, Wendy, we don’t often see you on a Monday. I can’t stop as I’ve a lot to do.” And with that she heads towards a cleared area of the hall and sets up her music system.

Half the children are instructed to go over to her and the rest of us, I presume, carry on with what we’re doing. She talks to her group of children for a few moments then BOOM. BOOM. BOOM. The music starts and it IS loud. The children are marching and swinging their arms. I look over at Mandy and Eve and they’re laughing at my pained expression. They knew what to expect. I didn’t.

“How long does this go on for?” I mouth across the room to them.

“All the morning, on and off,” Is their reply.

“Oh! Wonderful,” I mouth back gently shaking my head.

No wonder Dawn has found something of utmost importance to do in the kitchen. It must be important; it needs the hall door shut and the hatch doors shut too. Mandy comes over to me and we both work on the scrap books but we don’t get to talk to each other very much. The noise level of the music drops a little as Shirley encourages her troupe to be trees, gently swaying in the breeze, we hear her say.

“Is it always like this?” I just get the question out and the noise increases as the children are encouraged to join in with sound effects. There is a lot of whooshing and blowing and it sounds more like a gale now, not a gentle breeze. There’s no point at all in trying to talk but we do get a fair amount of work done.

The usual hubbub and chatter of milk time seems positively tranquil but, of course, does not last long enough, even with the introduction of fifteen minutes singing practice. Mandy explains to me that Hillary wants us to try to find time each day to do at least fifteen minutes singing in readiness for the concert, which is to be on Thursday the twenty first, just before the half term break. Only three weeks away.

“I’ll have to put that date in my diary. Has anyone said they’re willing to help us?” I ask.

“One or two parents, yes,” she answers.

"Talking of parents," I say. "I found Ann and Bob very easy to get on with on Saturday,"

"Yes they are nice," she agrees. "It was good at the farm wasn't it? Did you enjoy it? I have had a lot of mums talk to me about it and I know Hillary was pleased with the way it went."

"I expect Cynthia had something to say," I couldn't resist saying.

"Don't," she cautions and laughs at the same time.

"Well, they were a disaster the pair of them. Antoinette was scratched by the cat, she tore her coat, she somehow managed to get mess on the back of her coat and the goat ate her hair ribbon. No one else seemed to have so much trouble. Did they?"

"No they didn't, you're right."

"At least the chickens didn't 'do' anything to them," I laughed.

"No, but that's only because they didn't go near them due to some allergy to feathers or something," added Mandy.

"Thank goodness for that," I say. "I dread to think what else could have happened to her. At least nothing went wrong while they were petting the rabbits, unless that was were she got that mess on the back of her coat."

"Could have been," agreed Mandy. "And don't forget she had to sit at the back of the coach, I don't expect she'll forget the trip to the farm for a long, long time." We both laughed, we couldn't help ourselves. It was unfortunate but very, very funny.

We didn't have the chance to say more as Shirley has called for the second group of children to join her for music and movement. I gather together a few cups and quickly head towards the kitchen to wash up, but find Eve has beaten me to it.

Back to the scrapbooks and the noise. I don't know what Shirley's up to now but the music is thumping away at a fair old rate. As the morning progresses, I find myself willingly offering to take the little ones to the toilets and savouring those moments of relative peace. I don't think I even notice how cold, and smelly it is down there. Nor that the water is freezing cold How your assessments can change in different circumstances.

As I've mentioned in the past there is nothing of any use in our first aid box, so I ask around to see if anyone has an aspirin as I've a headache. That is a bit of an understatement as I have the mother and father of all headaches. Luckily Eve has some aspirin, brings them every Monday apparently.

It's gone quiet! I look about me in disbelief and see Shirley is packing away all her speakers and music. What a welcome sight that is.

That must mean it's nearly lunch time and so we start to get the hall ready. The children seem quite excitable and noisy over the lunch time, probably from the active, noisy morning they have had.

I sit next to Mandy and she tells me that Ro brought in her pet rabbit on Friday.

"What, on band day?" I exclaim.

"No, she came early, before Lavinia arrived. Can you imagine how frightened that poor rabbit would be with that noisy racket going on? Anyway the children loved it, they sat round and watched it hop about for a bit and Ro had brought in some food for it to eat. Then Ro picked it up and the children were all allowed to stroke it if they wanted too."

"I would have liked to have seen that," I say. "I dare say we will be colouring rabbits in the next few days."

After all the children have left Mandy asks me, "Have you enjoyed the day?"

I think the look I gave her was answer enough but just to be sure there could be no misunderstanding, as I put on my coat, I said to her and the whole room. "I am never, never, never going to do a Monday, ever again. Mondays and Fridays are definitely out."

"What about Wednesdays?" Called out Eve with a grin.

"I'm not even going to answer that," I say as I fish in my coat pocket for the car keys.

Thursday 23rd September

I feel awful. My head hurts. My stomach is aching and I've got to go to school. It's a quarter past eight and I haven't even had breakfast and I'm still not dressed. Leo won't be getting a walk and it looks like I'm going to be late, very late.

I arrive just as the last of the parents are queuing to sign in and I merge in with them and hope no one notices me. Dilly has, and quite clearly says, “hello Aunty Wendy. I was looking for you, will you come and draw with me?” Thanks for that, Dilly. I can’t be cross at her though as she is such a delightful girl. I throw my jacket on a chair and go and join her. I’m happy just to be sitting down. I do ache. Amy joins us and Kadetta comes over too. I look round for Dilly’s brother, as he has stayed fairly close to Dilly since his arrival. He is not with her for a change and it appears he is finding his own friends and getting more confident.

“Can you draw me a cat?” Kadetta asks pleasantly.

“I can,” I answer, and to myself I think, but it may not be very good. My drawing skills are next to none and the only cats I can attempt are the figure of eight shape with a tail at one end and triangle ears at the other. She seems quite happy with it. Amy asks for a dog but there is no way I can do dogs, so I persuade her fish are prettier and draw a passable fish for her.

Before they all start asking for any more animals that I can’t draw, I start on a tortoise. Dilly likes that and wants to colour it. One or two other children are curious about what we’re doing and so I begin to draw a few more tortoise and fish and cats, and I throw in a butterfly or two for good measure. A limited choice, I know, but a choice nonetheless.

Hillary comes over to see us and asks,“what are you up to?”

“Just drawing a few animals,” I reply.

“Oh that’s fine, especially as pets and nature were mentioned as part of this year’s curriculum. Can you draw some farm animals too?”

“Do rabbits count as farm animals? I can draw them like my cats but with longer ears. I can’t do cows or anything like that. If we have some pictures of farm animals, I could trace some animals,” I add trying to be helpful.

“Are you feeling okay? You look a bit pale.”

“I think it’s near that time of the month,” I reply.

“Aha,” she says in a ‘I know what to expect type of way'. She pulls up a chair for herself and says, “well, you just carry on doing drawing then and I'll find some farm animal pictures in a moment. Did you hear that the reaction to a mini fête has been good. Tombola and raffle prizes have started to come in already. One of the dads has offered to organise a couple of table-top games for the children. There have also been suggestions for a book, puzzle and toy stall, a cake stall, and jumble and white elephant stalls. How about that? Have you any preference which stall you would like to run?"

Was I asked if I wanted to run a stall? I think, but say, "Of course I'll run one and I don't mind which." She has one of her lists in her hand and tells me the dad running the games table will need a hand and no one has, as yet, offered to take charge of the jumble table. What a choice: dusty, smelly clothes or noisy kids, I opt for the kids. C'est la vie.

She leaves us to our animals and suggests that I tell the children we'll be keeping them to decorate the hall, so that it will be bright and colourful for the singing day. I don't mind what we do with them just so long as I can get through this day with no mishaps.

I am feeling more and more uncomfortable as the morning goes on and I am grateful when our hot drinks are ready. The extra minutes sitting listening to the children's singing is nice, and brings a smile to my lips.

I head back to the drawing table and soon have a couple of children colouring.

Antoinette arrives to see what we're doing.

"Would you like to do an animal for the wall?" I ask her, pleasantly.

"Yes, I'll have a tortoise and a fish," she demands.

"Yes, I'll have a tortoise and a fish, please." I repeat looking at her and willing her to say please. I was subjected to one of her looks and a few moments pass but she did say please eventually.

"She's rude aint she, Aunee Wendy?" Blurted out Arthur in his usual blunt way.

I do so agree with him but have to say, "now, now Arthur, carry on with your colouring.

Little Brian has been sitting next to me on and off for most of the morning, He has four completed animals for the wall. Jodie and Dilly have three each, they both enjoy colouring and keep coming back to do more and it seems a shame when I have to ask them to move away to let someone else have a go.

All of the children come to me at some time or other and all of them have at least one animal for the wall. I notice my rabbits look very similar to the cats, only the ears are larger and the tails are shorter, but none of the children seems to notice.

The morning drags slowly on. My stomach still hurts and my head feels heavy and I'm feeling sorry for myself. Eventually it's time to pack away. I'm pleased to see we have a large collection of colourful animals. The tortoise look especially colourful as some of the children have coloured each section of shell a different colour. The butterflies are striking too. Some are stripy and others have bright spots on them. I suppose I should have checked what colouring rule we are supposed to be following this term, but it's too late now. I'm going home to curl up with a hot water bottle.

Tuesday 28th September

It's lovely to see the sun is making a brave effort today, after the wet and miserable weekend. I, for one, appreciate it and decide to take my bike. I felt under par all weekend and hope a little bit of fresh air might make me feel a bit better.

As I enter the hall I notice there are a lot of toys out today, the easel is already out and the paints are mixed. I also see Hillary and Julie both look particularly smart today. What's going on I wonder?

"You want me to do the painting today?" I call out to Hillary.

"Yes please," she replies. "I'll be over in a minute." As I get closer to the cupboard to get some paper, I see Mandy. "Hello Mandy, that's a very nice blouse." I say to her as I pass. When all the parents have left, Hillary approaches me and says, "You remember Rob the photographer? He's due in today."

Rob comes here once a year and photographs the children. He has no formal sittings, nothing fussy or false, just natural pictures of them at play. I must admit his work is superb, he certainly knows his job. I notice Antoinette looks convincingly casual in a bright pink party frock and satin bow in her hair. Obviously her mum wants a really natural photograph!

Rob arrives about nine thirty and we try not to make a fuss about his presence but it is difficult to act naturally when you know a camera may capture a pose of you at any time. Luckily the children don't take much notice of him after a while and we leave him to do his own thing. He's a young man, slim and quite studious; he obviously takes his work very seriously and doesn't like to be disturbed too much. He sits in at the work table and the jigsaw puzzle table and wanders around the various toy areas capturing the children in all sorts of natural poses. He waits by the painting easel and he also takes some photographs at milk time. The parents just never know what actions he will capture and it makes his pictures special and unique.

At ten to one the doorbell goes and the rest of the staff members enter.

"What are they doing here?" I query.

"Rob is to take a photograph of each one of us," explains Hillary.

"Us!" I exclaim, looking at Hillary in disbelief. "Now I know why you all look so clean and tidy. Look at me all mucky and dishevelled. Why did no one tell me?" I go rushing down to the loo muttering as I go, "look at this old tee shirt I'm wearing. I don't have a comb with me, I'll have to try to comb my hair with my fingers and I've no lippy either. I'll just have to do the best I can."

"Why have we got to have our photos taken?" I ask a bit irritably when I return. "If I'd known in advance at least I could have worn something half-decent."

"I'm sorry,"replies Hillary."I thought I had told everyone. Anyway you don't look too bad. I had a letter saying that we have to have a picture of every member of staff and it has to be mounted and displayed for all to see. Are you sure I didn't tell you? There was also a note in the diary," she finishes.

"Is this another one of the ideas The Powers That Be thought up over the summer holidays?" I grumble.

"Yes it is, and actually, for a change, I think it is quite a good one as all the parents will be able to see at a glance who is who," she answers.

"They'll know me. I'll be the scruffy one," I say gruffly. "But it does make sense, I suppose," I add grudgingly.

Thursday 30th September

The children have been busy over this last week, drawing, painting, colouring and making animals. I notice most of the pictures have been mounted onto long friezes, which can be put on the walls later.

Hillary calls me to her and says, "would you mind painting another background paper. I would like you to do a blue one for all our fish and crabs, and the weeds and sea horses that we have made. Have you seen the green one with lots of your animals on?"

"Yes I have, they look good don't they?" I reply

I soon have two pots of blue paint mixed up and Hillary has found a part roll of wallpaper, which will do nicely. Dilly walks over to me with her new friend Sophie and she asks,"what will we be doing today?" When I explain I've been asked to paint this wallpaper blue, she quickly has herself and Sophie into two aprons. Talk about willing. It is pretty monotonous painting large areas in one colour but they are chatting away and seem quite happy.

"I'll go and mix up some more paint, will you two be all right for a moment?"

"We'll be fine," Dilly answers confidently for both of them.

I leave them to it for a few minutes and whilst I'm mixing the paint, I hear raised voices, one of which is Dilly's, which is most unusual. I hurry back to find Antoinette standing with hands on hips glowering at Dilly who is still kneeling on the floor next to the paper.

"What's going on?" I ask.

"I want to paint," Antoinette announces.

"You can have a turn in a minute. I'm just mixing some more paint and I won't be long," I tell her. But that's not good enough for her.

A stamp of the foot accompanies, "I want to paint, now."

"If you go away and play nicely, I'll call you when you can come over here to paint, but," I continue slowly and deliberately because I can see she is not a happy bunny, "if you make a fuss, you will not paint at all today. Is that understood?" She stares at me for a while, I can almost see her debating if I mean it or not, so I decide to help her out a bit by saying, "you know I mean every word, don't you?"

She turns on her heel and flounces off. She and I will never be bosom buddies but we are getting to understand each other.

Milk and biscuit time comes round and is followed by more singing practice. The children are encouraged to sing solo or with a friend if they wish too and it's lovely to watch them. Antoinette stands up and says, "I want to sing on my own."

"What would you like to sing, Antoinette?" Hillary calmly asks.

"Mary, Mary Quite Contrary," she answers primly.

What an appropriate choice, I think to myself.

"Dilly and Sophie are singing that song," Hillary tells her. "Would you like to sing it with them?"

"No. I want to sing on my own."

"How about Twinkle, Twinkle Little Star?" Hillary tries patiently.

"No."

"Or Jack and Jill?"

"No."

"Humpty Dumpty?"

"No."

Hillary tries another, "how about I'm A Little Teapot, everyone always loves that song. Actually, lets all sing it now."

We all sing the song and do the actions too and the doorbell interrupts us. Liz goes to see who it is and comes in with a lady in uniform. Hillary greets her and introduces her as the Green Cross Code lady. Her name is Ann, and she has come to talk to the children about safety on the roads and pavements.

Ro and I quickly clear away the cups into the kitchen and Hillary, Liz and Nicky stay with the seated children. Ann starts her talk and illustrates it with pictures and posters and easy questions for the children. It only takes about half an hour and the children are very good, listening and answering her intelligently.

When she has finished we allow the children to go and play at whatever they want especially as they've been seated for such a long time. The noise level goes up a bit but it's not for long as we'll have to get the tables ready for lunch soon. The time has gone quickly today. Am I complaining?

When the parents come in, Antoinette marches over to her mother who says, "How was my little darling today?" She says this partly to Antoinette and also to me, as I happened to be near the door at the time. I think to myself, 'she was a right little horror and if she was mine I would be ashamed,' but my mouth actually says, "she is a little headstrong at times but she is settling-in okay."

Before we can say anything else Antoinette interrupts us, "I'm singing in the concert and I'm singing I'm A Little Teapot."

"That's nice, dear," says Cynthia as she turns to go.

I must remember to tell Hillary Antoinette has decided to sing that song in the concert.

Tuesday 5th October

There's definitely a nip in the air today: it is dry and I'm on the bike but it's colder than I realized, much colder.

"Hello Phil, I haven't seen you here since the carnival. What are you up to?" I say to Hillary's husband as I dismount.

"I've been roped in to put up the bird table." Bird table? I think to myself as he carries on talking. "Perishing cold, isn't it?"

"Come inside and have a cuppa first," I suggest to him. "You won't be able to do much till the children are safe inside and the parents have all gone away."

"Good idea, that," he agrees and we go into the hall together.

"Brrrr, it's not that much warmer in here," I say as I disappear off to the toilets. It's really very cold in there and on investigation I discover someone has left a window open in the boy's toilets. It must have been the scouts because one of our last jobs before leaving is to check all windows are shut, check the taps are not dripping and turn off all lights. Thank you, scouts.

I glance in the kitchen as I pass by on the way to the hall. Phil has the kettle on and an array of cups ready.

"Do you want one?" He calls.

"Yes, please," I reply and think to myself, I need warming up and if the bladder starts to play up, as it has started to lately, then I'll just have to offer to do the loo runs. I remember my mum telling me once, 'you don't appreciate your bladder till it starts to play up!' I didn't fully understand what she meant then but I'm beginning to now.

Whilst we're drinking our tea, Hillary can't resist saying, "you're early today Wendy, are you all right?"

"Yes I'm fine," I reply cheerfully.

She carries on, "Shirley has drawn lots of different African animals and a truck or two, so we can have another frieze to go on the wall. I have some yellow paper which hopefully will be large enough. It will be smaller than the others but that won't matter. Some of the animals have been cut out already and the others will need to be cut out after they have been coloured in. Would you and Nicky mind doing that today?"

Nicky and I move our work table near to the hatch as we still have some hot tea left to drink. We position our cups just out of reach of the children and get up every now and again for a sip.

Some of the mums want to spend time chatting about the mini fête, some have bags of books and toys, and others are laden with clothes for sale. Hillary and Julie are kept busy with them all. As the parents leave, Mandy hands out books of raffle tickets for them to try to sell.

Nicky and I have had a productive and uneventful day. The animals have been crayoned, cut out and stuck into place and the completed safari frieze is ready to go on the wall. The bird table has been erected by Phil and he stayed and listened to the singing practice at coffee time and commented how good it was. The plans for mini fête are well under-way and it's time for lunch before we know it. My kind of day, that.

Thursday 7th October

Have I mentioned Fiona? I don't think that I have. Fiiiiooonnnaaa. It's one of those names that can be slowly drawn out and slowly pronounced. It fits perfectly with one of the young students from the local secondary school. She came here for work experience and to help us. Did I say help us? Silly me. We have had a few students come and spend time with us and help out where they can but Fiona is one of the more memorable.

She arrived in the second week of term and was painfully shy. She wore a long skirt and a long shapeless sweatshirt and trainers without socks. I know most of the youngsters wear trainers these days and I've nothing against them, but they do seem to have passed all of us by. I'm sure Nicky has a pair, only she's too afraid to wear them here with us oldies with our sensible sandals and sensible shoes. Fiona is quite over weight and it took a while before we could really see her face as she tended to keep her head down and her long hair would hide most of it. Over the weeks we have slowly encouraged her to talk and we have found out she has a good sense of humour, which helps enormously in this job.

Everything about Fiona is slow. She doesn't walk, she ambles. She doesn't sit down, she plonks herself down. She doesn't jump up from her seat, she hauls herself slowly to her feet. When you have to be alert and nimble to match the antics of three and four year olds, she really isn't the ideal choice.

On the whole we are a friendly bunch of women, well...the others are, I have my moments. We do try to help Fiona along and encourage her as much as we can, not just with our ways here at school but in general too. After all it's always difficult when you're the new face and a teenager as well, so we all try to be gentle with her. It was a big improvement when she started to wear a headband and we could see what a pretty girl she really is. We all try to make allowances as she is still learning our ways but sometimes it is an uphill struggle.

She's been here about a month now and I must say, in her favour, she has unending patience and will sit for long periods of time colouring, reading and playing with the children. She's also very cheerful and chatty now, it's when we want some real help that she isn't very good. Let me try to illustrate what I mean.

At the end of each session one of the last jobs we do is to sweep the floor. The broom is a wide-headed industrial sized one and we whiz up and down the length of the hall in about twelve sweeps and have all the debris bagged up within minutes. She has seen us all doing this and one particular day Hillary asked her if she wouldn't mind doing the sweeping up.

When we sat down to lunch just after twelve o'clock she wandered over to the broom cupboard saying, "I'll start now if it's okay."

Well, it really wasn't a good idea to start whilst we were eating, and before we had even made any food mess, but we didn't want to dampen her enthusiasm. So it was suggested she start at the far end of the hall well away from the lunch tables.

It was frustrating to watch. Fiona brushed against the grain of the floorboards, so left half the bits of paper and play dough in the grooves. When it was suggested to her that she should go up and down the floor with the grain of the floorboards, she replied that she couldn't as we were in the way. Well, she did have a point there, I suppose. She carried on in her way and swept a small area of floor, leant the broom against the wall and headed towards the broom cupboard. After an age she reappeared with the dustpan and brush. She sauntered back to the broom and dropped the brush and dustpan onto the floor and bent down and picked out the odd pieces of trapped paper from between the floorboards. She swept a little bit more then rested the broom against the wall and strolled back to the pan and brush. She laboriously swept a minuscule pile of rubbish into the pan and ambled over to the rubbish bin to empty it. This went on and on.

We could hardly believe our eyes. We had our lunch and our cups of tea and we tidied away all the lunchboxes and tables and Fiona was still messing about with the broom. She then moved into the messy dinner area and slowly began to sweep the crumbs and the odd crisp and biscuit. We had all the children seated ready to go and Fiona was still sweeping up.

So you can maybe understand my dismay to be told, as I arrive at work today, that Nicky will be in late, as she has a doctor's appointment. Liz is off sick and Ro has had to go into her daughters' school for a meeting.

Leaving just Hillary, me and Fiona to do all the work! Need I say more?

Tuesday 12th October

I received a phone call from Hillary last night to tell me that we will be cooking today and to remind me to bring a clean apron, which I immediately fetched and put somewhere safe. Now this morning I'm talking to myself because I know I put that clean apron somewhere, but where? I can't search for it for much longer or I'll be really late. I'll have to go without it and use one of the spare ones at nursery.

I put on my coat and grab my lunch-box and there sitting underneath the lunch-box is the apron. I remember now, I put them together so I would know where it was. My memory!

I arrive at school with just a minute to spare and put my lunch-box in the kitchen with the others. I notice we have icing sugar, basins, spoons and rounded butter knives out on trays and there are two packets of plain round biscuits and a pile of paper plates. We must be making iced biscuits for drinks time.

I see through the hatch that Julie is in the main hall and has covered some of the tables with pretty plastic table cloths. I quickly put on my apron and call out a general, "hello all," as I walk into the hall.

Hillary answers me saying, "good morning Wendy. Mandy will let you know what to do. I have some phone calls to make but will join you as soon as I can."

Mandy soon has us organised. She suggests Julie, Nicky and I have a table each and whilst we wash our hands and collect our ingredients, she takes six children down to the toilets and to wash their hands.

Julie chuckles to herself and says,"hey you two, do you remember the Sunday evening programme a few years back where they had contestants who had to do a challenge within a certain time?"

"No," says Nicky.

"Yes, I do," I piped up. "Wasn't it with Bruce someone? I can't remember his surname."

"Yes, that's right," continues Julie. "I feel like one of those experts."

"What are you two talking about?" quizzed Nicky.

"Shall I tell her or will you?" says Julie but carries on without really expecting an answer. "There was a show on the television on Sunday evenings with singing and dancing and sketches. There was a slot in the show where members of the public were invited to participate, usually father and daughter or mother and son. And almost every week there was a guest person trained in a particular and often, unusual skill. Maybe sculpting with butter, or origami, or theatrical make-up, or hat making and the contestants were shown this skill, then were expected to do it themselves in a short time period. Usually with funny and disastrous effect."

"Was it any good?" asks Nicky.

"Well, most of the nation used to watch it but it would be considered a bit dated now, I expect," replies Julie. There is no time to say more as our six 'contestants' have returned. Fiona has arrived too and comes over to see what we're doing. I explain to her that the aim is to get the children to cover a large round, plain biscuit with icing and then to make a face on it with small round jelly sweets.

"You can help if you like," I say to her. "Go and find an apron, and wash your hands." When she comes back, I add, "the children are allowed to make two biscuits each, one to eat at milk time and one to take home. Once they have finished their biscuits we lay them on a paper plate with the child's name on. Do you want to name two plates for me? I've got Annie and Jake here."

Fiona sits herself at a nearby table and watches me as I work with the children and has the plates named and ready for the biscuits to go on. As the children finish she takes the plates from me and the other two tables and puts them in the kitchen for us.

I notice Hillary is in the main hall again and is helping out where she can as we need to have all the biscuits ready and set so the children can eat one at milk time. It's pretty intense but it's also good fun too and the children all seem to enjoy themselves.

"How are you getting on?" Hillary calls across to me.

"Nearly done I think," I answer.

"We'll have to have drinks a bit later this morning because the children need a little time to go and play," Hillary says.

Fiona has been helping the children to remove their aprons and wash their hands. We aunties all look a mess and our aprons and hands are sticky and white. The floor is a mess and will need a quick mop over and the kitchen is a bit untidy too but we've all had fun.

As we sit down, rather belatedly, to milk and biscuits, we're happy to see the children discussing their biscuits before eating them. Mandy is still in the kitchen putting fine plastic film over the remaining ones ready for home time.

It seems the children only have a short time of play before we need to get the tables ready for lunch. Some of the tables are still a bit sticky despite having had table cloths on them and having been wiped, but it was an enjoyable activity.

At lunchtimes, we all try not too sit too closely to Fiona. She usually produces a smelly, sweaty sandwich of either egg or tuna fish from the depths of her clothing. It's often squashed out of all recognition and has to be peeled from a perspiring polythene bag and mixed with the pong from her trainers it's not something we rush to share. Hillary has been trying to help her gain more confidence and often spends time talking with her. I think she needs to mention sniffy foods and how to keep them nice in a plastic box.

It seems unkind to pick on her smelly sandwiches and smelly feet but they don't have the monopoly. She has a whole range of odours to choose from and as we sit drinking our tea and coffee, we have long conversations on the merits of certain shower gels, bubble baths and deodorants. I even saw an Avon book on the hatch recently, I wonder if it was for all of us to look at or for Fiona's benefit. As yet all our efforts have had little or no effect whatsoever.

She also suffers from uncontrollable flatulence! We suffer too, I might add. And the children, being children, make a big thing of it and pinch their noses with their thumb and index finger and pull faces. I sometimes wish I could do the same. I will try to remember to bring in some more air freshener on Thursday. Am I being catty and unkind? No, I'm afraid I am not. I'm just being truthful.

Another subject for Hillary to broach.

Thursday 14th October

There's definitely an odd odour as you enter the hallway. I can't put my finger on it but it's a bit like some of the charity shops have, not nasty, but just not right. A few squirts of 'Meadow Fresh' should help a bit.

"Morning all," I call as I remove my jacket and put my bag away.

"Come in here a minute, I've got something to tell you and you'll love it," whispers Liz from the toy cupboard. I join her in there and we bend to pick up puzzle pieces that have accidentally on purpose been dropped on the floor at our feet. It gives us a legitimate excuse to be there for a little time.

"What is it?" I ask, intrigued.

"Well, yesterday, Fiona was asked to see if there were loo-rolls and hand towels in the toilets. Well, she ambled down to the toilets to have a look, came back, collected one loo roll from the box and took it down to the loo. Then when she came back she took another one loo roll from the box and took that down. Then she came back to the cupboard and opened a packet of hand towels and took about six. Six! I ask you how long will that last? Then she took one more loo roll from the box and disappeared again. When she came back that time, Hillary asked her what she was doing. She had had five journeys down there and still hadn't completed the task. Hillary gave her the rest of the pack of hand towels and a couple of loo rolls in an effort to get the job done. Well, she didn't come back for ages, so Hillary went to look for her and do you know what she was doing? She was putting the hand towels in the dispenser one by one! She didn't think to remove the top cover and drop them in. Oh no! She pushed them up from the bottom through the little slit."

"Never, I can't believe it!" We laughed and laughed as we picked up the puzzle pieces and were surprised when Hillary interrupted us and said, "Fiona has arrived now and you're not to say anything."

"How did she know I was telling you?" Liz said. "She's cleverer than we give her credit for."

"No, I think she just knows you and me very well," I reply.

We are asked to work on the frieze. The children get a lot of colouring and glueing done and Liz and I catch up on the gossip.

At milk time Hillary talks about the day Ro brought her rabbit in and I don't know what possesses me, but I find myself offering to bring in my two tortoises for the children to see.

Hillary jumps at the idea. I mention that it should be on a day that I was not working as I didn't want to leave them in a box all morning.

I also add,"it will have to be soon as they are nearly ready to hibernate."

"What are you doing tomorrow?" she asks as quickly as anything.

"Not a lot, I could come in tomorrow, what time?" I reply.
"Could you come early?" she asks hopefully.
"I'll be early," I say and get a few raised eyebrows from the aunties nearby. "I can do early," I say indignantly. "Anyway I will want to be gone before band practice. I'll come just after nine."

What has my mouth done to me now? It has spoken out loud before my brain has time to register what is being said. How did it happen is all I can think about for the rest of the day.

Friday 15th October

Henry and Ethal are not used to being disturbed this early in the day and at this time of the year when it is cooler. They are still sleepy as I put them into a cardboard box. I drive carefully to nursery and arrive about nine fifteen. I ring the doorbell and Hillary greets me in with a smile.

"I've got the chairs out ready and I have told the children you are coming," she says. "Can I have a peek?"

"I would appreciate it if you can take the box from me for a moment while I take my jacket off, if you don't mind," I reply.

I notice she has a handful of tortoise pictures in her hand. I expect the children will be colouring them later.

I remove my jacket and open the top of the box for her to look in.

"They are bigger than I expected," she says. "Come on let's go in and show the children."

As we go through the door some of the children come up to us and Hillary quickly ushers them to the chairs. The aunties and other children soon follow.

I have remembered to bring newspaper with me and I put some on the floor, prior to removing the two tortoises from the box. I lift Henry out and he decides it is time to wee. Luckily I have him over the newspaper and it is soon sodden. The children start giggling. I think they enjoy that naughtiness. Thank you Henry, I think to myself, why couldn't you have done it in the box or just waited till we got home. I quickly remove the soggy, soiled paper and replaced it with clean. I soldier on telling everyone that this tortoise is called Henry and he is very old.

"How old?" some voices ask.

"He is about sixty, probably as old as some of your grannies," I tell them. "And this one," I say as I lift out Ethal, "is called Ethal and she is even older. She's about seventy."

Henry has perked up and is looking around and takes a few steps. The children are all watching and Alison pulls her legs up under her as if she is afraid. I notice Dawn goes over to her, and after a quiet talk, they both leave the group.

Henry walks about and appears to be looking at some of the children. I retrieve him back onto the paper and start to tell the children a little bit about tortoises. Then I ask if any of them have a tortoise at home. It turns out none of them have. I ask the children if they know what tortoise like to eat.

A few odd suggestions are called out, including. Sausages. Cake. Sweets.

I say, "I don't think so." Then go on to tell them that my tortoises like to eat some flowers they find in my garden. They like pansy's and ice plant. And when I take Leo for a walk I look for weeds like white nettles, thistle leaves and clover leaves. Very occasionally they have some banana as a treat. I tell them another food the tortoise like is dandelion leaves and I have bought some in with me and put them on the newspaper. Ethal starts to eat some, but Henry is walking off again, much to the children's amusement, and I have to fetch him back to the newspaper area.

The children and aunties ask a few of questions and it is obvious that most children have not seen a tortoise before. One child asks if tortoises can run. Another asks if they like chocolate. Arthur makes us all laugh when he says, "they look like the burnt pies me nan cooks."

I tell them that these two tortoise will be going to sleep soon, for a very long time, and how they don't have Christmas because they sleep through the whole winter. This makes the children stop and think for a while. And Arthur pipes up again, "whot, they don't get presents?"

"No, Arthur, they don't have any presents but in the Spring when it is warm they have a nice long bath and some tasty food."

"I'd rarver ave presents," he says. I change the subject and ask the children ask if they want to touch the tortoise. I'm happy for them to do this but ask them to be gentle. When I hold Ethal near to them, some are very reluctant to touch the constantly moving leathery legs, but don't seem to mind patting her shell.

As I am walking round the circle of chairs with Ethal held firmly in my hands I see Henry has wandered off yet again and is soon under a nearby table. The children laugh and point at him. He now has the attention of everyone in the room and he proceeds to do a poo. I know it is coincidental but it just seems as if he waited for an audience.

"Look. Look at that," shouts Simon with glee.

I hastily put Ethal back into the cardboard box before she can embarrass me as well, and ask if one of the aunties would pass me some tissues. The children are laughing and chattering and getting quiet excitable and Hillary has to talk to them to quieten them down. I scrabble under the table to clear away Henry's mess and I grab hold of him and put him back into the box. Hillary insisted the children say 'thank you' to me and I get a little round of applause too. Then off they go to play and possibly start colouring in the tortoise pictures.

I hastily clear away all the newspaper and use the mop and bucket and clean the floor area under the table and the area where we were inside the circle of chairs. Then I pick up the cardboard box with the errant tortoises in and take my leave.

The visit didn't go exactly as I had planned but I'm sure it will be remembered, especially by Simon.

Tuesday 19th October

We're bound to be singing again today. We've had singing practice every day for the last fortnight and the children are really singing beautifully now. The solo singers are so cute. Some of them are so bold and confident and others are very shy and look at the floor the whole time. Some stand swinging their arms and others fidget from foot to foot but they are all so engaging. I hope the parents enjoy it as much as we do.

Mandy suggests we should make glitter headbands for the children to wear for the concert and Hillary has asked Julie, Fiona and I to make it our job for today. So that will keep us busy this morning, cutting out cardboard, colouring, gluing and sprinkling glitter. That sounds like my kind of morning.

Just as we have settled the doorbell rings and Hillary goes to answer the door. She is smiling as she returns and says, "look! The photos have arrived. Give me a minute to undo them and then we can have a look at them."

After a few minutes she holds one up and says with amusement, "look at this."

It's a photograph of Arthur with a book on his lap, his hand is scratching his head and he has a slightly worried expression on his face. "It's just him," she chuckles.

We aunties all go to look at the photographs. The varied shots Rob has captured of the children are wonderful. I'm not keen on black and white photos myself, but I have to admit these are really good and clear and crisp.

"Don't forget," Hillary reminds us. "These photographs must be paid for before we allow the parents to take them home. I'm not having another year like last year, when I had so much trouble getting the money from some of them. Where are the staff photos? I want to mount them on card as soon as I can and put them up on the wall in the hall."

She would, I think to myself. She and all the others look clean and tidy. I, on the other hand, look a real scruff-bag, messy hair, no lipstick and a really fetching dark paint blob on one side of my chin. Why did no one mention that on the day?

We leave Hillary to sort out the photographs and go back to headband making.

When we're called at milk time, Julie quietly says to me,"shall we get one or two of the children to wear their headbands? I know some are still a bit wet, but there must be one or two dry enough for the children to wear."

I tell her that Dilly's should be okay as she was one of the first to complete hers. Also the ones James and Joe made should be dry. I go over to the table where the completed ones are drying to check. I find the one Topaz made feels dry enough and Simon's and Sally's too. I carry these back and we call the children to us and put the headbands on them.

Those six children are happy to put the headbands on and they walk proudly to their seats and sit happily accepting the admiring glances from their friends.

I have to rush down to the loo before I can have my coffee and when I return I see the only chair vacant is the one next to Fiona. Thank you friends, I think to myself. I can't help noticing the air is not as fresh as it should be just here.

"Fiona's going back to school after drinks," Liz mentions to me as I accept my coffee from her. "That's why she is having her dinner now." That's what the pong is, she is eating a garlic sausage sandwich! Someone should tell her that stinky sandwich fillings are best eaten at home and not in company. Phew! Another subject for Hillary to discuss with her.

I don't want it to seem that I dislike Fiona because I don't. She's very good with the children and she has changed and opened up a little since she arrived here. When she first came she seemed to have a 'I don't want to be here, I don't really want to be anywhere,' aura around her, but she is now a lot more talkative and friendly. She still wears the same shapeless clothes day in day out as if trying to make herself invisible, almost as if she doesn't want to be noticed. She has lovely skin, thick dark hair and big brown eyes and a happy disposition. In a few years she could be so different, if and when she manages to gain a bit more confidence in herself.

Julie and I sit together after drinks and finish the last few head-bands. We check and double check that every child has one and whilst we're at it we cut out enough for tomorrow's children.

I call Hillary over and show her and Julie a toy that had been given to me as a child. I always called it a click-clack and ask if I can show it to the children.

"Keep it till lunch time and you can show it whilst we clear the tables, talking of which, we had better make a start fairly soon," she finishes as she glances at her wristwatch.

After lunch I position a table away from the others and put chairs in a semi circle round it, close enough for the children to see but far enough away that they can't keep touching. They don't need much telling to come over and sit down, they're just like us adults really, something different going on and they like to know what it is.

"Now children, has anyone here seen one of these before?" I ask as I hold the click-clack on the palm of my hand. It consists of six pieces of wood each measuring two inches by three inches and a quarter of an inch deep and the pieces are hinged together by webbing.

"No," they chorus.

"Watch." I grasp, with my thumb and forefinger, the top-most wooden slate and they lift concertina style into the air. As I hold the outer, narrow edges and swivel my wrist forward so that the top wooden oblong bends right over and touches the one below it, it starts a chain reaction and all the oblongs begin to tumble one after the other, and because one side is painted red and one side painted blue you see a colourful tumble of colour and hear a slight click clack sound as each slate touches the next. I twist my wrist up, and the back of the wooden block touches down onto the one below it and as I keep twisting my wrist so the tumbling continues. The children seem to like it and one or two call out and ask if they can have a go.

"Wait a minute, I have some more to show you," I tell them, and I do a few tricks with coins making them disappear on it, which they all seem to enjoy.

Hillary comes over to me and says, "you will have to stop now the mums are waiting." Then to the children she says, "did you like that, would you like Aunty Wendy to bring it in again?"

After the noisy chorus of yes had died down she said, "would you mind letting us all have a look at it another time. I'd like to see it and I'm sure the children would enjoy seeing it again."

"Yes," I agree. "As it's only small I can leave it in my bag for another day."

Thursday 21st October

Today is the day of the concert. We aunties have been asked to arrive extra early as there is a lot of furniture moving to be done before the children arrive.

"Hi Wendy, you made it then," calls Liz cheekily from the kitchen. "Hillary's in the hall, she'll be glad to see you."

"Hello Wendy, I hope you've had a good breakfast as we've a busy day ahead," was Hillary's greeting to me as I remove my coat.

I answer cheekily, "I'm rearing to go, boss." And raise my hand as if in salute to her.

She smiles and continues, "we will need all the tables and chairs we can find, even the spare ones from the store room. That's the first job as we must have all of them in position before the children arrive. I've selected the toys I want taking into the small room. And when that is all done there are quite a few black sacks in the store room containing donated items and they must be brought though to the hall."

I go to help Nicky and Liz collect some chairs. Carrying them two at a time along the corridor and positioning them is a laborious task. When Mandy arrives she helps us carry them from the store room and Eve stays in the hall positioning them. That really helps speed things along. In the store room I see the black sacks and also the second-hand clothes hanging on a rail, so, when all the chairs have been taken, I wheel the rail into the main hall.

"Where do you want this?" I call over to Hillary.

"Pushed against the back wall please along with the tables. Each table must have one of these labels on them telling us what they are to have put onto them." She hands me the papers and I turn to fetch the sticky tape.

"The relevant boxes and bags can be put underneath the corresponding tables in readiness for the contents laid out a bit later on," she adds.

Nine o'clock comes round quickly and the children are let in. There's excitement in the air and we adults all try to stay calm as we don't want the children to become over excited. There are toys and games set out for them in the small room and we usher them in there. The small room leads off from the main hall and is used only occasionally by us. Sometimes Dawn will go in there when she is doing her needlework or Hillary will go in there for the odd meeting or to do paperwork if she wants to be undisturbed. And today we are utilizing it for a short time to keep the children occupied and calm before the concert. We have laid out games like puzzles, colouring books, fuzzy felt pictures, puppets and the farm animals all of which the children can play with sitting down. No play dough or anything too messy as it is beautifully carpeted in there and we don't want to be the ones to spoil it.

Dawn, Mandy, Eve and Ro have been asked to be in there and that leaves Hillary, Nicky, Liz and I to add the finishing touches to main hall.

The kitchen fills up with cakes and biscuits for the cake stall, all of which have been kindly donated by the mums. Julie goes in to get the urn on and to sort out the kitchen in readiness for the teas. She also displays and prices the cakes whilst she's there.

"Those chocolate ones look good, Julie, keep a couple by for me please," I ask nicely. "Actually I could eat one now."

"No chance, off you go," she grins.

A few parents offer to stay on to help us and, as the singing is due to start at ten thirty, we are very grateful to them. At nine forty five we have a very welcome hot drink and admire the hall, which has been transformed. All the children's pictures, paintings and friezes are on the walls. The tables are laid out with a tombola stall; a books, puzzles and toys stall; a colourful handicrafts table; a white elephant table; the cakes table has been positioned near the hatch and more overflowing cake plates are lined up to replenish those sold. The raffle prizes are nicely displayed and two games tables are ready too. The chairs have been put in to a large semicircle for the parents to sit on and the little chairs are arranged by the back wall for the children to sit on. There are two non slip rugs laid out in front of them for the solo singers to sit on.

The children not normally due in on Thursdays, but who are wanted for the singing, begin to arrive at ten and, as we take them into the small room, we have to bring out some of the toys as space is getting tight in there. All the children have a drink and a biscuit, and then the mammoth loo run begins.

The eager parents are queuing outside so Hillary decides to let them in a few minutes early and asks Liz to try selling them some extra raffle tickets at the same time.

We search to find extra chairs as there are a lot more people than we had expected and allowed for. There are older brothers and sisters, grandparents, friends and neighbours and even the head-mistress of the local junior school. We have all the chairs we can find, even the ones belonging to the scouts, and still some people will just have to stand at the back.

Once the audience are all in the main hall and the outer door locked, the door to the small room opens and a hush falls over the room. Hillary pokes her head out and nods to me. This is my cue to have a few words with the parents. I stand up in front of them and start by saying, "Hello and good morning to you all. Thank you all for coming. We want everyone to enjoy themselves. We know some of you will want to take photos and videos, which is fine, but all we ask is that you are as discreet as possible and try not to distract the children too much. That's the speech over, now let the show begin."

Hillary opens the door wide and the children come out into the hall in pairs and holding hands. They're all wearing their headbands and walk nicely to their appointed chairs. The 'ah' factor is running high as they do look like little angels. Liz and Nicky have come out with the first of the children and are helping to direct them into the correct places. Some children wave shyly at a parent, others wave frantically, as if they haven't seen each other for weeks. Arthur is determined not to be missed, by anyone. He stands still and shouts," 'allo mum. 'Allo dad. Look at me 'at, aint it nice?" And waves both arms till Liz goes and has a little word with him.

Once all the children are seated Liz and Mandy sit on the floor facing the children slightly to the right of the group and Nicky and Ro sit on the left. Hillary and Mandy sit down on the floor in the centre facing the children and the concert begins.

There is a little bit of a shaky start but once the children get going the singing is lovely. They sing three songs as a group then Sophie and Dilly stand up and hold hands and start to sing Mary, Mary, Quite Contrary. It is very quiet but clear and beautiful and I'm sure they bring a tear to nearly every eye in the room, and they get a big round of applause.

Then Simon, Arthur, Joe and Troy stand up and sing a song about Postman Pat. In all the excitement the verses were completely missed out and we have about five repeats of the chorus. This is only brought to a close when Hillary starts to clap, which we aunties, and then the audience all follow suit and eventually drown the boys out. They sit down smiling and well pleased with themselves.

It is now Antoinette's turn. She stands up and she really looks a picture. She is wearing a check dress and has a matching ribbon in her hair. She gives a little twirl to show off her dress, the little madam, and then there is silence. Everyone is waiting and still nothing happens. Hillary goes to her and has a word, after a few moments we see Hillary remove the card headband. Hillary then sits on the floor a few feet to the side of Antoinette and Antoinette starts to sing. She sings I'm a Little Teapot. She has a loud voice and she performs all the actions and is, in fact, quiet funny with her expressions and movements. She is doing very well and the audience laugh and clap.

"Don't laugh at me," she yells.

Hillary rushes to her side and I expect is telling her that it is good that we are all laughing and enjoying her performance.

"I don't want people to laugh at me." She stamps her foot and marches off to the side where I can see Mandy is ready for her.

Hillary gets the singing under way again and we have three or four more songs which are all sung as a group and are all well received.

The last song is 'If you're Happy and You Know It'. The children sing it boisterously and then the audience are invited to sing a verse on their own. Hillary stands up and says to the children, "they didn't sing it as well as us did they?"

Of course all the children shout back a loud, "no!"

"Let's sing it again and show them how it should be sung," encourages Hillary.

"Yes!" They all shout back.

After another, even louder verse, one of the dads stands up and says to the other parents. "We can do better than that can't we?" So they all the sing the song again. Everyone is having fun and the atmosphere is wonderful. The children are highly amused by it all. Hillary finally suggests we all sing one verse together which is just what we do and very nearly bring the roof down. Everyone is clapping and happy and shouting for more.

Hillary holds up her hands for quiet and slowly the noise level recedes.

"I want to thank you all for coming and hope you have all enjoyed our concert today. Please can I ask you to keep a close eye on your own children whilst going round our mini fête. There are teas available and drinks for the children. I can see Julie has some ready on the hatch and so it only remains for me to say, that there is only an hour for you to spend as much as possible before we draw the raffle."

This raises a chuckle and, I thought, was very cleverly put. Whilst she has been talking, the helpers and aunties have quickly and quietly gone to their assigned places and the selling can begin.

The cake table quickly empties and the toys and books are popular too. Tim, Hillary's son-in-law, has a large crowd around him at one of the games tables. The children and adults alike are waiting to have a go at his 'feely boxes.' None of us know what he has put into them but the laughter and squeals have us all wanting to have a go.

Another game he suggested is also a huge success. This is the game I'm supervising. He has spent ages explaining it to me. I have an upturned clay flowerpot on a tray and the idea is to get as many marbles as possible through the small hole on the bottom of the flowerpot in one minute. That doesn't sound too complicated until you realized you can only pick up the marbles with a wooden spoon and no matter how hard you try it's very difficult to pick up marbles with a wooden spoon. It's addictive. People want more and more goes and the banter and laughter is drawing more people to try. We had decided to award a prize for the highest score but we can't get people to stop trying to beat their previous scores. So in the end we decide to award a booby prize instead, for the lowest score, and one happy Brian goes home with a bag of sweets and the wooden spoon as a memento.

The tables are emptying of goods. The raffle has been drawn. Cups and plates are cleared away and people begin to leave, and for once I can honestly say I'm sorry to be going home as we have all had such a good time. The children have been well-behaved and the parents all say how enjoyable it has been. All the hard work has been well and truly worth it.

I pay for and collect my chocolate cakes and put them in my bag. I call goodbye and take the few squashed cakes that have been on the floor and crumb them onto the bird table. It is still dry and I smile as I cycle home knowing I have a whole week off. Ahhh!

HALF TERM

Chapter Six

Tuesday 2nd November

The weather is awful. It's raining and windy and cold. Those tortoise of mine have the right idea, to hibernate till the warm weather comes again. I decide to take the car, It will take me ages to go on my bike and I will be drenched by the time I get there. No, the car it is today.

At least it had stayed dry on Saturday night for the fireworks display and bonfire. Every year, on the last Saturday in October, Littlehampton stages a big torchlight procession, weather permitting of course. Although having said that, I can only remember it being cancelled once or twice in all the years I have lived here.

Other Bonfire Societies come and join in the fun. Some societies come from as far away as Uckfield, Henfield and Crowhurst and of course Lewes, which is by far the most famous Bonfire Society in the south. They gather in the town and there are events and activities all day long, including fancy dress competitions and mini processions. In the evening all the societies march together in their colourful outfits and carrying burning torches. There are also decorated floats and steam traction engines and marching bands too. They all parade through the town and then on to the seafront where there is a huge bonfire waiting to be lit.

It was a good evening on Saturday and my family and I thoroughly enjoyed watching the parade and, because the weather was dry, the streets were lined with thousands of people. It's lucky the greensward beside the beach is so large because everyone gathers there to await the lighting of the enormous bonfire. There are usually hot food vans and candy floss sellers and sometimes fair ground rides on the promenade. There is usually just time to buy a bag of chips and a hot drink before the huge firework display rounds off the evening. Littlehampton

Bonfire Society goes all out to provide a wonderful and safe evening, and they succeeded once again this year.

I had left home in good time this morning but actually got into school a tad later than planned as there is a refuse lorry manoeuvring into our small car park. I have to wait, but eventually I park the car and rush inside.

I call out, "hello," to everyone and Hillary gathers us aunties all together and has a quick word. "I hope you all enjoyed the half term break. Did any of you go to see the procession?" We all either nod or reply quickly as she continues,"if you are painting or colouring or drawing with the children, then encourage them to produce a firework related picture. Also I want you to talk to them about the dangers of fire and fireworks. Many of the children may well have bonfire parties to attend and we want them to be as safe as possible." She turns to me saying, "Wendy, would you mind starting off at the painting?"

Fiona offers to help me and as we set everything up we talk about Saturday night. She tells me she had gone to see the procession and fireworks and had stayed till late at the funfair on the promenade. I admit to her that I find the rides a bit scary these days especially the 'twisting turn you upside down' ones.

`"Yes," she said. "I was sick when I got off of one of those on Saturday night."

There's a delightful thought to keep me going.

The children come into school chattering as usual. The weather really doesn't seem to bother them at all. But all the adults are griping about it.

Simon comes straight over to Fiona and I and calls out to David to come over too. They tell us they both saw the procession on Saturday and how they enjoyed it and when I suggest they paint a picture of it they can't wait to start. Fiona, who has pulled up a chair and is sitting close by, offers to keep an eye on them as I go over to Hillary and ask her about the fête.

"What a wonderful success that was," she says. "We made four hundred and twenty six pounds profit. The sponsored slide by the toddlers made one hundred and three pounds and a donation of twenty pounds by one of the dads made us a healthy five hundred and forty nine pounds."

"That's brilliant," I agree.

"We'll soon have that computer," adds Julie

"Oh yes, I think we will but the main thing is everyone enjoyed it so much. I have had no end of comments about it and people praising all the hard work. Also, in the half term holiday, I heard from Cynthia, Antoinette's mother. She..."

I interrupt her saying, "sorry to interrupt you but what was all that at the singing? I never did get round to asking you."

"The headband you mean?"

"Yes."

Hillary puts on a posh voice and says, "Antoinette could not possibly sing with that on her head. It spoilt her hair."

"Why does that not surprise me?" I tut and shake my head.

"Anyway," Hillary continues, "Cynthia informs me Antoinette will not be returning here, she has enrolled her at Normanton Manor Private Pre-School, which is probably very exclusive and probably very expensive too."

I find my mouth insincerely saying, "oh what a shame! How we're all going to miss her!"

"It will certainly be easier without her," Hillary agrees and with a smile on her face she sends me back to the painting area.

Thursday 4th November

The weather is still bad with heavy rain forecast for the whole weekend. Unfortunately that may spoil the Guy Fawkes celebrations planned all over the south of England.

It's easier to park in the car park as I'm a little late arriving today, and most of the parents cars have left. As I've confessed before, I'm often late. I really try not to be but something always puts me behind. Today I try to slip into the hall unnoticed.

"There you are, Aunty Wendy!" A shrill little voice calls after me as I quickly unzip my jacket. "I've been looking for you." Dear sweet Dilly has blown it for me, now everyone knows I'm late again, still, that'll come as no surprise to anyone here. She's bursting to tell me about a birthday party that she went to yesterday, so we go and sit down together for a few moments.

A short while later Hillary informs me she wants us to colour with the children today, again with a firework theme, and to remind them again how dangerous fireworks can be. Liz joins me and we are soon ready to go with clean, named papers and crayons at the ready. We draw whatever the child wants relating to bonfire night, a bonfire, a rocket, a fireworks party, a Guy Fawkes. My drawings are not as easily recognizable as Liz's but I console myself, that once they are crayoned over they hardly resemble what they started as anyway. Liz has Sophie and Arthur sitting next to her and I have two new children with me, Alison and Annie's brother, Jake. Neither Alison nor Jake let me down, their colourful scribble perfectly covers my bad drawing of a firework party.

"Look at me rocket," Arthur exclaims gleefully. "I'm 'avin' a firework party and we got indoor ones an' all. Me dad says they're fun but I aint never seen any."

We had some indoor fireworks one year and they were a real disappointment. I don't say anything to Arthur as he is clearly looking forward to his.

Whilst working with the with the children we have a lot of talk about fireworks and how lovely they can be but also how dangerous too. The pictures are an unusual mix of blacks and red with splashes of different colours and as each picture is finished, up on the wall it goes.

At milk time I ask Hillary, "why didn't we have sweets for the children after the singing this time? We usually have sweets for the children after a singing concert."

"You of all people ask me that!" she exclaims. What can she mean? "Don't tell me you don't remember?" Remember what? I'm puzzled. I haven't a clue what she means.

"Lily," she prompts.

"Oh yes. Lily. I remember now," I say rather sheepishly.

"Come on one of you, spill the beans, I want to know what this is," says Nicky her curiosity having been aroused.

Hillary takes up the tale and explains. "One Easter we decided to sing for the parents and as an inducement to make the children sing beautifully we had a basket of small chocolate Easter eggs. At each practice session we told the children if they sang well at the concert they would receive a chocolate egg. On the day of the singing, the children had Easter rabbit headbands and were led into the hall to 'ohs' and 'ahs' from their parents. Wendy here, and another helper sat on the floor on one side of the children and Liz and I sat to the other side. I could see Wendy had to talk to Lily on more than one occasion even before the singing started. The singing went well, or so I thought although I was told later that Lily was really misbehaving. She would not sit still and she did not sing one word. Wendy had to speak to her a couple of times throughout the performance. Sometimes we do that if we see they are fretful or anxious, so I wasn't overly concerned. At the end of the singing Wendy handed out the chocolate eggs to all the children but not to Lily. Her mother created merry hell when Wendy would not give Lily an egg. I know it was wrong of me but I really wanted Wendy to give her an egg just to shut them up. But you wouldn't would you?" she finished, turning to me.

"No I would not," I admitted. "I'd spoken to her about not getting an egg if she didn't sing or at least sing some of the songs. She just gave me a haughty look. Also she kept kicking the boy in front of her and I had to tell her about that a few times too. Then the little madam said to me, 'I will get an egg. My mum will make you.' Well, that was it. No way on earth was she going to get an egg after that. She was like Antoinette, worse actually, and I was not going to back down to her. In fact if I remember rightly, didn't I eat the egg myself?"

"Yes you did, you walked off into the kitchen and we could see you slowly unwrap it and bite into it. I was furious with you too. Later when you explained it all to me, I could see your point, but at the time I was none too pleased. So now you all know why we had no sweets after singing and probably never will have again."

I wish I had a better memory. I would never have mentioned those sweets.

Tuesday 9th November

The good news is I'm early today as I had to hand deliver a birthday card to my niece and I wanted to catch her before she left for school. The bad news is, I noticed my car had a flat tyre. It must be a slow puncture as I'm sure it was okay yesterday. So I'm on my bike and cold and wet and out of breath. Never mind, I'm here now and I'll have time to phone the garage before we start. I'll have to ring the doorbell for someone to let me into the hall.

"Wendy! Thank goodness you're here, can you handle hamsters?" Hillary enquires breathlessly as she unlocks the door for me. Hamsters were the last things on my mind as I struggle with my bike into the hallway. My nose needs wiping, my eyes are watering, my coat is soaking wet, my hands are cold, and I need a wee.

"What?" I say, none too graciously.

"I said do you like hamsters? Can you handle them? We bought two yesterday for the children to watch and enjoy and when Julie opened the lid to their plastic tank to put in some fresh water, one of the little devils jumped out. I can't go in there. I can't stand the furry things, they make me shudder. Poor Julie is on the table in there, she said she could catch it but obviously she can't. Please say you'll do it. You're not frightened of them are you?" This last question was added, I feel, as an after thought. But I said with a sigh, "okay, okay. Let me go to the loo and then I'll sort it out."

As I walk into the main hall, I'm greeted with, "it's over there, look." Julie is indeed sitting on a table with her legs drawn up, looking rather sheepish.

"Hello Julie, are you comfy?" I ask with a smile on my face. "Where's the hamster food?"

"It doesn't need feeding, it needs catching," she screeches.

"I know. I know. Now calm down and tell me where the food is. I think it will be easier to catch him with some food. You know, entice him close enough to me so that I can grab him."

"Oh, yes, yes. It's over there by the tank and while you're there, can you put the top on properly so the other one doesn't escape? Oh, I feel such a fool. I really didn't think I was frightened of hamsters but when he ran up my arm and jumped, I just panicked. It all happened so fast and, and, and well, here I am," she finishes with a sigh.

"Don't worry. I'll catch him in a jiffy." I grab a handful of food and also pick up the rubbish bin, I don't know quite why, but it strikes me it may come in handy. I ask her, "do you know where the hamster is now?"

"He went over there towards the toy boxes," she answers pointing to her left.

After a careful look round I see the little fellow exploring one of the toy garages and obviously thoroughly enjoying his freedom. I feel mean having to catch him and put him back into that boring plastic tank. I put a small trail of food on the ramp leading to the top floor of the garage thinking it will be easier to catch him up there with no obstacles in the way. He happily munches his way to the top and straight into my hand, no problem what-so-ever. He seems happy to be handled and petted and I walk him back to his home. His friend rushes up to see him and he appears none the worse for his adventure.

"All clear, it's safe now. Panic over!" I call out.

"Is he all right?" Julie asks as she climbs off the table. "He jumped from the table to the floor, are his legs okay?"

"Well, he had no trouble running all over the floor, did he?" I say rather sarcastically. I don't mean to be unkind to her so I hastily add, "and he didn't squeak or complain when I was holding him, so I think he must be fine. Go and tell Hillary she can come in now."

"I'll put the kettle on, I really need a cup of coffee after all that," she says.

She needs a cuppa! It was me who was the hero of the hour. The rest of the day will seem quite dull by comparison. Oh, I must remember to phone the garage.

Thursday 11th November

"Morning, how are the hamsters today?" I call out to everyone and no one in particular.

"They need feeding and fresh water," was the reply I got from Hillary. "And I was hoping you would offer to do those two jobs for me on Tuesdays and Thursdays."

"Yes, that's no bother, but, Hillary, I've got to ask, why did you get hamsters if you dislike them so?"

"Well, as you know, it was suggested we have some pet and it's not really fair to have a rabbit indoors. I dislike rats and mice even more than I dislike hamsters. We couldn't really have a budgie with all the mess they create, and anyway I don't like to see birds shut up in cages. That doesn't leave much else because I'm certainly not having snakes or spiders. Dawn suggested hamsters and fortunately she likes them and she has offered to look after them on the days she is in here. She will take them home at weekends and in the holidays too. It's only a problem on the days she's not here. Please say you'll look after them then."

"Of course I'll do it when I come in. I'll feed them when the children arrive and then we can have a little talk about them. Is that okay?"

"As long as they stay in the tank, you can do what you like," was her grateful reply.

Once all the parents had left, I call a group of children to the tank and explain that they must not tap the side of the tank as it would upset the hamsters. I expect they have already been told this but it never hurts to say these things over and over. I also mention that they can watch the hamsters whenever they want to. I suggest we get a few toys for them to play with and the words were hardly out of my mouth when a few of the children are heading for our toy boxes. I have to call out to stop them and explain that our toys are not at all suitable. Hamsters love to hide in things and also they love to chew and nibble. I ask them collect some cardboard boxes and tubes from home and these can be put into the tank.

I ask if anyone has hamsters at home. It would appear none of them do. I go on to tell them some of the food hamsters like and fetch the carrot and dandelion leaves I have bought in. I carefully lift the lid off the tank and put the fresh food in. The hamsters rush over and, with whiskers twitching, soon start eating the carrot. Look at their cheeks, I tell the children, and soon the hamsters cheeks fill out like two little balloons. This made the youngsters laugh and they copy, puffing out their cheeks and laughing some more..

I ask if anyone would like to stroke the hamsters. Before I can get a reply Hillary is there like a shot. Possibly on her way to see what all the laughter is about. She says, "we're not covered on the insurance if a child gets bitten, so they can't stroke them!" I don't know if I believe that, as we seem to have to be covered for every eventuality even if there is no possible chance that we will need it. I think she's just scared one will escape again. But I don't say anything.

Fiona ambles in just then and comes over to look at the animals. She says, "I do like hamsters. We have two rats at home." She continues to tell us that her rats have the run of her bedroom during the day if she is at home. Then in the evenings

they often spend time in the front room scampering about and climbing onto everyone's laps. She's not afraid of them at all and, when I ask if she would help us with our hamsters she says she is happy to. That should make Hillary feel better knowing someone else is able to handle them and help with the cleaning and feeding.

"Hillary, did you hear that?" I call out." Fiona is willing to lend a hand with the hamsters. She's not afraid of them."

"Thank you, Fiona, that's a relief I can tell you," she says. "By the way, Wendy, yesterday I was looking through my file of Christmas work and as there are only five weeks to go before Christmas, I think we'd better decide what we're going to do and to make a start. I have already designed a card for the children to make this year. It's a stable scene and I want you to start today by cutting some card to size. Then encouraging the children to colour the top half black or dark blue for the night sky, and the bottom half yellow for the straw strewn floor."

She shows us a sample card she has made and it looks very nice. She carries on, "I would also like it if you would take home some templates of Mary, Joseph and baby Jesus in the crib, plus a small star. If you could draw round them and leave a border round them all. Then the children will then be able to colour them in and we can trim them up neatly before the children stick them onto the card."

"Why do you do it like that?" asks Fiona.

"It makes a neater picture. We can't expect these little ones to keep within the lines when they crayon, so doing it this way means we cut off the messy edges. It should look really nice when we put glitter on the star and in the sky," replies Hillary. "You'll also be pleased to know I have templates for four different sized stars, two different size of Christmas tree, a cardboard cracker and a small snowman shape. They will start us off nicely, we can use them on most things."

"If only that were all," I mutter. Then I say quietly to Fiona. "Those of us who have been with Hillary for a few years know this is only the start. She will also want as many Father Christmases, snowmen, and Christmas-tree picture combinations as possible and anything remotely Christmassy. We will be making pop ups, glitter ones, small one, large ones, mobile ones. Ones to take home and ones to decorate the hall. Plus ones to hang from the ceiling, to put on the tree, to cheer up the hallway and stick on the huge Christmas frieze. It's like Easter only much, much worse. Each year we try to stop her from getting too carried away with it all. It has never stopped her in the past but we do try. She just loves Christmas."

"I heard all that!" she laughingly calls to me. "Go and draw a festive hamster, we've never had one of those before."

We soon have children working away colouring their cards and I leave Fiona to keep an eye on them as I go to the library corner. I soon find a picture of a hamster and go back to the table and say to her with a grin. "I'm going to make Hillary a festive hamster and give it to her at home time."

She offers to draw a hamster shape onto some card for me and as Joe has just come over to do his colouring, I ask him if he would colour the hamster yellow for me, which he is happy to do.

"What's the hamster for?" he asks quite naturally.

"It's a surprise for Aunty Hillary." I tell him quietly.

The day is busy and as the children come to crayon their Christmas card, I ask them to help with the hamster picture too and explain it's a surprise for Aunty Hillary. Dilly has helped me by sticking some small stars on the top of the card and Sally insisted on a red Santa hat to be put on the hamster's head. There's a carrot for him to eat and some grass has been added. I manage to sneak out the glitter and had help sprinkling the whole picture with it.

By home time most of the children have been told about the hamster card and as they sit down waiting for their parents, I present the hamster picture to Hillary and we all have a good laugh.

When I go home, I leave with paper, card and templates knowing I shall be busy drawing and cutting out all weekend and that my front room carpet will be covered with lots of bits of paper come Sunday evening. Some evenings are just like that.

Tuesday 16th November

I'm on my bike again today. It's not raining thank goodness, but it's cold and frosty and crisp and sunny, and by the time I arrive my hands and feet are frozen, but my face is glowing. I have bought with me some bird seed and a few stale biscuits that I put on the bird table. I like seeing the little sparrows hopping about on the table.

Hillary asks me to work with Julie today and to continue with as many cards as we can. She gives me a pile of very, very large brown envelopes saying, "there's one for each child, for them to keep all of their Christmas work in. I have named them already and I would like you to draw columns on each envelope indicating the progress of each piece of work. You know the type of thing: To be started, Work in progress, Finished. Something along those lines."

This all sounds very organised, not at all like past years. She also hands me a list of the work she would like the children to do and asks me to copy it onto each envelope. It is quite a long list and I know it will only get longer.

Julie, Nicky and I soon have five victims, hrrum, children, sitting at the table with us. Some are colouring 'Mary' and others are colouring 'Joseph'. We have made an executive decision between us and decide Mary must be in blue but Joseph can be any colour the children like. As the children finish one piece of work we try to hang on to them and encourage them to colour something more. That way we even succeed in getting a few yellow stars finished.

I make a start writing on the envelopes and see that Hillary has found nine different pieces of work she wants the children to complete. Only nine! It'll be nearer fifteen in a couple of weeks, if I know her. She can find nine different ways of doing Father Christmas alone! This is just the beginning.

"Listen to this, Nicky. I'll read out what Hillary has in store for us. We start with a star mobile and a smiling Santa badge. We haven't done a Santa badge before, I wonder what that's like.

Then we have a glittering decoration for a Christmas tree and a Christmas cracker. Also there is a pop-up Father Christmas and a cardboard tree. A little Christmas finger puppet, a reindeer and sleigh, and last but not least, a frieze with trees, robins, snowmen and children playing. Plus the card we are working on, of course. What do you think of that then?"

"I can't wait to start," she replies enthusiastically.

"This is only your second Christmas isn't it?" I ask, knowing full well that it is. "Wait till you've been doing it for a few more years and then we'll see if you are still so keen. No, no don't get me wrong, I don't mean to sound as if I don't like it but it does get pretty busy what with all the other things as well."

"What other things?" she asks.

"Well, in the past we've had a trip to the pantomime and Christmas concerts, we've had singing for the parents, Christmas parties and Christmas dressing up days. Shall I go on?" I tease. "Let's call Hillary over and see what she has in store for us this year."

"I'm here. I was just walking by and heard some of what you just said," she says pulling up a seat. "I haven't finally decided yet but I think it will be a party for the children with the magic man, like we had last year. He was so good and all the children enjoyed it so much. We have already had singing this year, so that's out and we certainly won't be going to the pantomime again, that's for sure."

"Why not?" asks Nicky. "I think that the children would like that."

"That's what we thought, once," said Hillary with mock solemnity.

"This sounds interesting, do tell," says Nicky pleasantly.

Hillary looks at me and smiles and begins."The local dramatic society was advertising Jack and the Beanstalk as their pantomime and I phoned to see if it was suitable for our under fives. They said it was. We found out to our cost that it wasn't. It just went on and on and on. It was full of innuendo that, thank goodness, the children couldn't understand and was just so long winded. Our young children were just too young to sit still and quiet for that length of time. But it was funny in the interval, do you remember, Wendy?"

"I remember all right. The interval! I'll never forget the look of horror on that old man's face when Julie and I walked all the boys into the gents' toilets. He stopped mid-flow and rushed out all flushed and flustered. I wish I had control over my water works like that."

"Yes, so do I," laughs Hillary.

"We tried to apologize to him but he was gone like a shot," I continue. "Then we found the urinals were too high for the boys to reach anyway and decided we had to use the cubicle. Do you remember? It was locked, so we waited and waited and waited. Some of the boys began to fidget and squirm and we kept telling them it wouldn't be long. But still we waited. The occupant either had a dreadful medical condition or was just refusing to come out while we were there. At school, here, we aunties always use the boys' toilets, but of course we were in a public place and the chap was probably terrified, and justly so. We knew we didn't have a great deal of time so we ushered the boys into the ladies toilets, passing the manager, as we did so. His face was a picture too, watching us troop out of the gents. Do you remember, Julie?"

"Yes," she replies laughing at the memory. "I'm sure he would have said something if he hadn't been so shocked,"

"Luckily there were three toilets in the Ladies and our girls had all but finished in there so we soon sorted the boys out and had them back in their seats."

Julie adds a bit more to our reminiscing, "don't forget, as we came out of the ladies with all the boys, there was an elderly man talking to the manager and his face went scarlet as we passed them. I think he was the one in the cubical," she laughed some more then continued, "and Hillary was getting worried about us wondering why we were taking so long. We just had time to tell her about it all before the lights went down and the performance resumed. I remember that we spent most of the second half in fits of laughter and it had nothing to do with the performance on the stage."

We were all laughing at the memory and Hillary commented, "I don't expect we would be welcome there again even if we did want to go again. Oh! We have had some laughs over the years. Anyway, the reason I was passing was to ask you two if you would take home some more work to prepare. I'm afraid we will all be very busy from now till we break up." With that she rushes off and Nicky, Julie and I carry on.

"I told you we'd be busy didn't I?" I can't resist saying to Nicky.

At the end of the day all the large envelopes have lists and columns on them.

We have quite a few colourful Marys, Josephs and cribs on the table, ready for us to take home and trim up. We're all feeling very pleased with ourselves, until we see the mountain of extra work Hillary has found for us all to take home.

Thursday 18th November

"I'm glad you're here, I'll go now," was the greeting from Hillary as I walk in this morning.

"What's going on, Liz?" I ask as soon as I get my coat off.

"Oh, it's nothing to worry about. Hillary is off to buy some glue and glitter and one or two other things we need. She'll be back soon."

The very, very large brown envelopes are on the table ready and I can feel by the weight of them, that there have been some additions since Tuesday. I put in the items that I have prepared and notice a large piece of card in each one.

"What's this stiff card for?" I call to Liz.

"Ah, well. I was going to talk to you about that. I thought we could make some lanterns this year for a change. I saw the pattern in a magazine and they looked good."

I sigh, "you are as bad as Hillary. That makes ten things on the list now, and it's not even December yet. And that's not counting the cards we're doing."

"Arrrh. You love it really. We can make a start on the lanterns today and you'll see how nice they are," she says quite unperturbed.

"What did I tell you, Nicky? It just gets worse and worse from now on."

Actually the day flies by. The lanterns are easy and the children seem to enjoy doing them, especially sprinkling the glitter on them. As we have the glue out we also try to complete as many nativity cards as we can. We find ourselves repeating over and over that these items cannot be taken home yet and we tend to compensate by finding little bits of Christmassy work that they can take home. Just like in past years, little Father Christmas pictures, little fat snowmen and small fairies all add to the days workload. The list will just get longer and longer.

As soon as the lanterns have dried off a bit, we attach strings and hang them up around the hall. They really do look good, and when the parents collect their children at home time, we hear many complimentary comments about them. We ask the parents to bring in any cardboard tubes from home and also any bits of card and sparkling paper that they may not need, as we can use all sorts of bits and bobs at this time of the year.

It is raining hard as we leave and by the time I get home I'm drenched. Never mind, I tell myself, I'll have a nice hot bath and forget about school for five days. As the bath water is running the phone rings. Its Hillary asking if she can pop round, she has a favour to ask.

What can it be? What's she up to now? I bet it's something bad. I turn off the bath taps and put the kettle on while I wait. I'm just sipping my tea when she arrives.

"I won't come in," she says. "This'll only take a minute. While I was in town this morning I bought the Christmas gifts for the children. As you know they all receive a gift from Santa's sack on party day. And I was wondering." I notice a slight creeping tone enter her voice at this stage. "Would you mind helping to wrap some for me? I'm going to ask the others to help too. I just thought if we all do some it'll be easier?"

"Oh, is that all? No problem. Of course I'll help, bring some in," I happily say to her.

She collects a large box from her car and two rolls of Christmas wrapping paper and puts them in the hall. "Thank you," she calls out as she climbs back into her car.

Whilst soaking in my bath I wondered, why we always think the worst whenever someone says. "I have a favour to ask." Human nature I suppose.

Tuesday 23rd November

I feel awful again. My stomach aches. My head aches. The last thing I want is to go to school, and I'll have to call in at the supermarket on the way because I can't find where I have put my new pack of personal supplies. I know I have some. I must have put them somewhere safe, which means I'll probably never find them again.

"Sorry Leo you'll have to make do with the garden this morning," I say to the dog. I'm sure he doesn't mind as it is still wet outside from yesterday and it is very cold.

I'm late. As I enter the hall the children seem a little quieter than usual and I notice Nicky and Mandy have some children working already. Hillary is talking to a woman I have not seen before. This woman is holding the wrist of quite a large boy and is in the process of handing him over to Julie.

As I sit myself down at the jigsaw puzzle table, Julie cries out. I look up and see why. The boy is kicking her in the shins and has scratched her cheek.

"Wendy, can you take him for me?" She pleads. "He has already had a go at Hillary. And I need to put a plaster on my cheek."

I sit him at the table next to me and he promptly kicks me and thrusts his elbow in my side. Oh, what a delightful child! I don't think. And have you picked the wrong day to upset me?

"Don't do that," I say sternly to him.

"Why not?" He challenges.

"It's not nice."

"I don't care," he says and kicks me again.

"Don't do it," I say to him again."It's not nice and we don't put up with it here." Boy is he pushing his luck.

"Why not?" He says again.

"Because I say so," I reply shortly through gritted teeth.

I'm not going to get into a big debate about it because we're neither of us in the right mood at the moment. Just then he pinches the back of my right hand. How that hand didn't retaliate with a swift slap I'll never know. I grab hold of him, big as he is, and wedge him more firmly on my lap. Our legs can only just fit under the low table and I quickly cross my legs trapping his in between them. He can't kick me now. I also hold onto his hands, one in each of mine so that he cannot use them either. He squirms about and starts to yell.

"Now listen here. I don't put up with this type of behaviour," I tell him sternly. "So stop that noise, now. Are you hurt? Why are you making this noise? What is the matter? You're making yourself look so silly. Come on now, stop it."

I don't seem to be getting through to him at all. So I ignore the noise he's making and release one hand and try to play with a puzzle. He's not interested at all. In fact he swipes most of it onto the floor. He squirms some more and starts shouting and is making quite a spectacle of himself. I tighten my grip on him and tell him to stop and he bends forward and tries to bite the back of my hand. I raise him up and turn him to face me and he promptly spits in my face. That is the last straw. I am so mad I'm shaking inside with rage. I glare at him. I grit my teeth and snarl in his ear.

"If you ever do that again I will pull down your trousers and your pants, in front of everyone here, and I will spank your bare bottom."

I know I can't do this, but he doesn't. He is obviously stunned. He calms down and just sits looking at me, weighing me up. My words have had the desired effect. He shuts up. Hillary comes over. The sudden silence more worrying than all that noise. She asks, "are you okay?"

"Fine," I reply crisply. "Can we have some tissues and we want a little time on our own, please." I wipe my face and I don't say another word to him, I just bend down to retrieve the puzzle pieces from the floor and slowly make the simple puzzle. After I have finished it and have calmed down somewhat, I say to him "What is your name?" He glares at me. So I repeat the question and get the same reaction.

"I'm going to call you Tim."

"That's not my name."

"Probably not," I say to him.

"I don't like it."

"I don't like being kicked, Tim."

"I don't want to be called Tim."

"I don't want to be spat at," I counter.

"I don't like you."

"I can live with that," I return.

"My dad says that."

"Your dad sounds okay."

"He is. He's nice. He plays cars with me."

"Do you like cars?"

"Yes."

"Well, one of these puzzles has a big blue car on it, shall we make it together?" I ask.

After a couple of seconds he agrees.

We spent the next half hour making that puzzle and all the other jigsaws on the table and talking as if nothing had happened. When we have completed them all, I ask him if he wants to go to the toilet, and he answers yes. I ask him if he would like me to take him, and again he said yes.

"I will have to know your name if I am going to take you to the toilet." That made me chuckle to myself as it was absolute rubbish, but he said, "I'm Oliver."

"Okay Oliver, I'm Aunty Wendy. Hold my hand and we'll go."

When we come back into the hall I introduce him to Simon and Mark who are playing with the garage and he's happy to join in with them. If my stomach wasn't so painful I would sit on the floor and play with them but it is just not going to happen today. Maybe he was unpleasant earlier because he was frightened of being left with strangers, whatever it was he seems calmer now. He and Simon and Mark are happily pushing cars around on the paint that marks the basket ball court and pushing them into the garage. Then picking another car and doing it all over again.

At milk time I sit him at the end of the row nearest to me and explain all that is happening and how we reward 'good' children by giving them special jobs to do, like giving out the biscuits. He is the first child to be offered a biscuit and he ate it quickly and was beginning to get fidgety. I could see he would rather be doing something else but quietly told him if he could just sit still for a little bit longer he would have a drink of milk. We aunties fully understand it takes our new children time to adapt and we are used to them wanting to be off, so it's not a problem, but I must say every time Oliver's and my eyes met he made an effort to sit still.

As milk time came to an end I took Oliver over to the colouring table with me.

"Oliver, listen to me. Will you be able to be like the other big boys here and colour this in nicely?" With that I hand him a Father Christmas picture to colour, and I continue, "if you have any problems talk to me, okay?" He is really good at colouring and when he finishes it. I say, "that's really good. I'm going to put it on the wall for everyone to see. Would you like that?"

"Yes I would," he answers happily. He is so pleased and stands and looks at it for a while. I ask him if he would like to do some more colouring and he is so keen that I start him on a nativity Christmas card and he happily sits next to me till it is all completed.

I could see Hillary was bursting to talk to me but it was getting close to lunch time and we were busy. Not all of the children stay for lunch with us and when we let the few parents in who were collecting their children, I was pleased to see Oliver's mother amongst them. Oliver's mother went straight over to Hillary and had a few quick words with her and quickly left with Oliver. He turned and gave me a little wave.

As soon as she could Hillary was beside me asking, "what did you do to Oliver? What happened?" The others were crowding round too. I didn't know how much to admit too, after all snarling at a child is not something I'm proud of. As no one had actually seen what had happened, I casually said, "Oliver and I have reached an understanding and that is all I'm saying. I need a pain killer and a cup of tea, so lets get lunch under way."

As soon as I could I quickly put on my coat and left. P.M.T. took on a new meaning for me today. Pacify Monster Toddler.

Thursday 25th November

I'm still in two minds whether to tell Hillary just what did happen on Tuesday between Oliver and me. It's been worrying me and I have decided that as soon as I get the chance I will tell her everything.

She is waiting by the door for me when I get to school.

"We need to talk," she says and takes me into the small room. "I have had Oliver's mother on the phone and she wants to know what we did to him on Tuesday." My stomach sinks.

"I can explain," I start.

"Don't interrupt. I haven't finished," she says with a smile on her face. "His mother said he has changed a bit and actually did as he was told a few times without shouting at them. And they keep hearing about Aunty Wendy. Aunty Wendy said this and Aunty Wendy said that. Aunty Wendy put my picture on the wall. Aunty Wendy. Wendy. Wendy! What have you got to say now?" I can't speak for a while, I am dumbstruck and rather relieved.

She and I have a long talk about Oliver and she admits that he was a nightmare on Monday. The first day he'd come here. He had been spiteful and unpleasant all day and she had received some complaints from other parents about him. She also tells me that she had, had a long talk with his mother and had only agreed to take him on a trial basis. Apparently he has been banned from nearly every other group in the area and his poor mother was desperate. Hillary and I agree that he appears to be an intelligent boy but he certainly needs a firm hand.

"It seems that something you did struck a chord with the boy," and she quickly adds. "I don't think I need to know what it was."

Oliver was waiting for us when Hillary and I enter the hall. He walks up to me and asks very politely and enthusiastically, "what're we doing today, Aunty Wendy?"

"I don't know yet probably more Christmas work. How are you today, Oliver?" I ask him.

"Fine, can we play with the garage again?"

"First of all I need you to colour a few stars whilst I put your name and details of work on an envelope." I explain what all the work is and why I'm putting it all on the envelope.

"Can we play with the garage now?" He asks again.

"Yes, maybe. Have you said sorry to Aunty Hillary for being nasty to her?" The look on his face tells me he has not. We have a little talk about being unkind and saying sorry, but I can't persuade him to go over to say it. He goes to the garage and I enquire of Hillary, "what are we doing, today,?"

"Eve started the Christmas frieze yesterday, so you can make some trees or snowmen to go on it. Or, if you prefer, you can make a start on the pop-up father Christmases. Also keep checking in the envelopes and if you see any work that needs finishing off then just do it, okay? By the way, Eve will be coming in for a few extra days during December, to help us out. That should take the pressure off a bit."

Ro and I quickly discuss who is going to do what today and she elects to do some work on the frieze so I get to do the pop-ups.

"I've already cut out the Father Christmases," Ro tells me. "And there's a big bag of cardboard tubes in the inner cupboard and some ice lolly sticks in a beaker, on the shelf in there too."

Our inner cupboard is inside the main toy cupboard and we try to keep the craft work in there to keep it all together. We have boxes and bags of 'useful things'. We have a mountain of card in various shapes and colours. There are flattened cereal boxes, egg boxes and egg trays, loo roll tubes and kitchen roll tubes. We have cotton reels and cotton wool, knitting wool and buttons. We have silver paper, pretty paper, tissue paper. We have old magazines and calendars and birthday cards for cutting out. There are lolly sticks, candy floss sticks, yoghurt pots and plastic containers of every shape and colour. We have craft ideas cut out from magazines and simple recipes, newspaper, scrap paper, good paper, the list goes on and on. It's a veritable Pandora's Box in there.

Whilst I'm in amongst all this looking for the tubes, I come across a large bag of white fun-fur material and wonder what it's for? I eventually find the tubes and sticks and put them onto a table with some crayons and glue. Fiona comes over and asks if she can help me as she hasn't seen the pop-ups made before. She is changing a little. Her hair is always neat and tidy now and she doesn't always wear the shapeless tops she used to. She is a lot more chatty and a little bit more confident.

"They're quite straight forward," I explain to her. "In this instance the tubes are coloured black using the wax crayons, and this represents the chimney. Father Christmas is coloured red and is stuck onto a stick and put inside the chimney tube. The good news is, the children can take them home today."

When Hillary passes by I ask her about the white fun-fur I had seen in the cupboard.

"Oh, that. It was brought in by a mum, a few days ago, she thought it might be useful. Why? Have you had an idea?"

"No, not really, I just wondered what it was," I reply.

As Fiona and I work with some children I notice Oliver is playing with the large Duplo bricks and seems to be enjoying himself. Seeing him play with them has given me an idea. When I call him over to me to make his pop up Santa, I ask him,

"Do you like Duplo and Lego?"

"Yes, I do. I have lots of Lego at home. I like the pirates best."

I tell him, "I have some pictures of Lego men at home including some pirates and some spacemen." I had traced them, years ago, from a large poster and my son had enjoyed colouring them and I knew I could copy them again. I continue, "would you like a big picture of a Lego pirate to colour?"

"Yes I would," he answers gleefully.

"I'll bring one in for you but first I must ask you,"have you apologised to Aunty Hillary and Aunty Julie." He thinks about this for a while but doesn't move. I'm distracted by one of the other children who tells me he also likes Lego pirates and he obviously wants some Lego pictures too. So I tell myself I must call into the library and get some photocopied and bring them in next week.

A bit later on I see Oliver talking to Hillary and her eyes and mine meet over the heads of the children. She looks puzzled and then she smiles. He then walks over to Julie and she ends up smiling too. I can only guess he has apologised to them.

The children work well on the pop-ups and we soon have them all finished. I ask Ro if she wants us to do any work on the frieze and she sends over a bundle of bits to be worked on. I notice she has the hand puppets on her table and one on her hand. It looks like it is being used to encourage the children to sit and finish some work.

Julie is sitting near the playhouse which today is a busy shop. She is able to keep an eye on the shop and get some Christmas work done too. It is all hands to the deck toady and will be till we break up for the Christmas holidays. The morning rushes by and it is lunch time before we know it.

At home time, one of the dads comes over to me and says, "I can't see Hillary but perhaps you can you tell me if you can use any black cardboard? I've been working at a photography studio and have been told to dump this card. There's quite a lot of it and it may be of use to you."

"She's in the small room, hold on a minute." I rush in there and grab Hillary by the arm and we go and have a look. The card is in neat bundles and she says, "We'll take it, thank you." As we are unloading it from the car I can feel a glimmer of an idea forming and I ask if I can take one bundle and some of the white fun-fur home for the weekend.

Tuesday 30th November

I'm so pleased with myself this morning. I've spent the weekend cutting the fun-fur into snowman shapes and have made a fun picture. The black card is approximately A5 size, and I've stuck a white fun-fur snowman onto one piece. The contrast of white on black looks good and I've decorated the snowman with a green hat, a carrot nose, three red buttons and two black eyes and it looks great. I had enough material to cut out a few extra snowmen and what with all the white material left in the bag at school, I'm sure there will be enough for every child to make a picture to take home. In my scrap bag at home I found various pieces of material which I have cut out to represent hats, scarves, buttons, eyes and carrot shapes for noses and I've bundled all these together and brought them with me today.

I'm proudly showing Hillary my handiwork and it hits me that I, yes me, I have contributed to yet another item to be added to the envelopes to be completed for Christmas. After all the things I've said and thought about the amount of work we have to do, and here's me adding to it.

Hillary laughs at me. I think she's thinking the same thing. She likes the snowman picture and suggests Julie and I make a start on them straight away. It's 'my baby' and I'm more than pleased to start them and to see how the children cope with it. Oliver rushes over and wants to start his immediately and Dilly sits herself next to me expectantly. As Jennifer-Marie is near by Julie calls her over and her friend Arthur comes to see what's going on. Once they see the completed snowman picture they can't wait to start one of their own. We have four keen and able children and we're off.

We soon discover we need a lot of glue as the fabric seems to absorb most of it but once the snowmen are securely on the card. Then the fun really starts. We have to limit the amount of extra bits the children put on the snowmen because I'm not sure there is enough cut out for them all to have hats, scarves, eyes, noses, mouths and buttons. It is fun watching the children spending time selecting just what they want. This makes each picture quite unique. Our first four completed pictures are soon put up on the wall for all to see, and once the other children see them they're clamouring to do theirs. So eager are they that some stand by the table watching and are just waiting for a chair to become vacant.

The time till milk break flies by and when Julie and I stand up we are covered in bits of white fur. I suppose we should have worn aprons, but it's too late now. I had got into a frightful mess at home so I should have remembered.

As we get up after our drinks there is a rush to our table. Some of the more resourceful children pull up extra chairs resulting in a few long faces as we have to turn them away. We can only cope with four children at a time. Hillary takes a few photographs of the work we are doing, for the file. Then she pushes another table next to ours and joins in with us. It is such a fun activity and we are laughing and enjoying ourselves as much as the children. I also notice Nicky and Mandy keep finding reasons to walk past us and glance at what we're doing.

By lunchtime we're all covered in white fluff, which will not brush off, and the floor is a mess and makes me sneeze when I sweep up. I should have expected that as well, as I'd sneezed most of the weekend when cutting out the material. And my carpet still looks as if it has had snow on it in places, even though I have vacuumed it a couple of times.

It's all worth it though, as we have had a really successful morning. Everyone has enjoyed making those pictures, including the adults, and all the children have something nice to take home. We tidy away as best we can and we leave my specimen snowman picture on the wall so that when the Wednesday children come in, in the morning, they will be able to see what they will be making. It has proved to be a very popular idea and I had thought of it. Yes me!

Thursday 1st December

Well, here we are in December. I'm looking at the children's envelopes and see that we still have seven pieces of work to start and only three weeks to do them in.

After calling good morning to me Hillary says,"you may find a few more of your snowmen pictures need doing, but there won't be many as everyone has been so keen to do them."

I check in the very, very large brown envelopes and there's just one more I can do today, little Amy's. I collect everything I need and call Amy over to me. She's excited to be making her snowman and we soon have have hers finished. She asks if it can go on the wall, so I quickly pin it next to my original one.

I clear away and go and sit down with Nicky who has made a start on the mobiles which consist of five stars dangling from different lengths of wool. The children are to colour the Christmas stars any colour they like and then glitter is sprinkled on to them. Then we aunties punch a hole in the stars and string them together. The finished effect is quite nice as they twist and turn in the air. It is rather time consuming and time is something we don't have a lot of.

When Oliver comes over to start his mobile it reminds me I have the Lego pirate and Lego spacemen pictures in my bag. I have a quick word with Hillary about them and she is happy for the any of the children to take a Lego picture home with them when they leave.

Hillary and Ro are making smiling Santa badges with the children and we're passing children from table to table in an attempt to complete as much work as possible.

Liz has found enough paper to make envelopes for the Christmas cards and she has shown Fiona how to make them. She's also helping the children to write their names and put kisses in their completed Christmas cards.

We're a hive of happy activity. Then the doorbell rings. Hillary goes to answer it and comes into the room with a lady carrying a briefcase. Hillary is not looking too pleased. She claps her hands to get our attention and announces that this lady, Mrs. Perry, is from Ro.S.P.A, (The Royal Society for the Prevention of Accidents.) and she has come to talk to us all about accidents.

If I know Hillary, that look on her face is saying, why now? Why, when we're so busy? As the time is getting on towards ten o'clock she invites Mrs Perry to join us at our break. Mrs. Perry says she's happy to have a coffee with us as she's only seeing us today, then she's finished for the day. (She calls that working?) She asks if we have an easel as she has a poster to illustrate her talk and wants to display it.

Hillary asks Ro and Liz to rush the children down to the toilets and whilst they are gone, Julie, Fiona and I put the chairs into a horseshoe shape and get the easel out of the cupboard.

We try to be as quick as we can be with the milk and biscuits routine and afterwards I go into the kitchen to wash up quietly while Mrs. Perry gives her talk to the children. I keep looking through the hatch doors and see the children are sitting nicely. They're listening to her and answering her questions when they can. I also hear a 'Holding hands with an adult' story being emphasised and also a lot of 'clunk click' words being shouted. The children appear to be enjoying her approach to the safety subjects.

Hillary is discreetly taking photographs for the folders. I notice she is also glancing at her watch and raising her eyes to the heavens. Mrs. Perry finally finishes by giving pictures to the children to take home and colour, and to talk about with their parents.

Hillary sees her out and when she comes back she exclaims, "It's almost eleven forty-five! Where has the time gone? The children have not had much time to do work or to play and there's no point in trying to do any work now as it's so close to lunchtime."

She suggests that we all play some musical games with the youngsters for a while as they have been sitting for a long time. We manage a couple of goes of 'Farmer's in his Den' and 'Row, Row, Row the Boat' and then it is time to start the lunch time routine.

Thank goodness they have the picture from Mrs. Perry to take home with them today. And the Lego pictures.

Little Amy reminds me that she has her snowman picture on the wall, which I retrieve for her. She holds on to it tightly and is talking about it to her mummy, as they walk out together.

Tuesday 6th December

This is like an action replay of Thursday for me, as I'm sitting looking at the very, very large brown envelopes again and doubting if we'll ever finish the work in time for Christmas. Admittedly some items have been crossed off but we still have a lot to do including finishing the Santa badges and the five star mobiles. Then there are the reindeer and sleigh, the finger puppets, the crackers and the frieze to complete and the tree decorations. These have taken a jump up the priority ladder as we now have a Christmas tree standing naked in the corner of the hall.

Julie and Nicky are busy at one table with the Santa badges, Mandy has commandeered another table onto which she is putting crayons and the small Christmas trees and snowmen shapes. Fiona and I have the stars under way again. And we're all trying to get the children to colour in some tree decorations. The children are going from table to table as we encourage them to complete as much as they can. There's paint and glue and crayons and glitter on all the tables and every spare space has work lying out to dry.

There's an assortment of toys on the work tables too as the children just find one they want to play with and we call them over to do some work. If they leave the toy on the floor or in its box, they then have to spend precious time finding it again, and by that time we have probably called them again to do more work. So they've started to bring the toys with them. This reduces the available space for work at the tables but we can hardly blame them for doing it. What is so sweet is that some of the children, those who are lucky enough to get to play for a few moments, see we adults are busy and go off and make us cups of tea. I think it is quiet nice and I'm always happy to stop for a cuppa even if it is only a pretend one.

Nicky says they only have a few badges to finish and Mandy calls out, "can I have Julie to help me then, as I want to try to finish the frieze today." Julie's happy to oblige and gathers a few children to take with her.

Hillary pulls a table over to ours and has Alison and Oliver next to her colouring tree decorations. The tree decorations are all different Christmas shapes and they're not too big, so are quickly completed. We aunties cut a small length of pretty string and tape it to the decoration. Then the children can take their decoration and hang it onto the tree. They enjoy going over to the tree and hanging their decorations on it, and if they're lucky enough they even get to play for a while too, having escaped to the other side of the hall.

Hillary has a notepad beside her and she says, "we need to do a list of food-stuffs for the Christmas party or else we'll end up like last year, with loads of sausage rolls and mince pies and not much else. What sandwich fillings shall we suggest?"

Quick as a flash I answer, "nothing smelly." I realise Fiona is near and quickly add, "how about cheese sandwiches and maybe some strawberry jam? They're always popular with children."

"How about some fruit this year too?" calls out Mandy. "We could have satsumas and raisins and maybe even dried banana. And don't forget to add drinks like squash and juice, we don't want all fizzy stuff."

We call out our suggestions and come milk time she has a long list. She writes it all out on card with spaces for the parents to tick off what they would like to contribute. Milk time is as quick as we can make it and we're soon back to work.

"Wendy, I've finished all the badges," Nicky calls over to me. "Can you cross them off the envelope. What do you want me to do now Hillary?" she adds.

Hillary is putting her list on the wall and from memory says, "there's the sleigh and reindeers to start. We need a fairy for the tree and the tree also needs some more decorations. And I'm sure Wendy can tell you if there is work to finish in the envelopes."

"We still have eleven mobiles to finish and it might be sensible to finish them before starting something new," I mention. So Nicky comes to our table, taking Hillary's place and we all try to do as many stars and tree decorations as we can.

"Joe, would you like to come over to me again?" I call out to him as he is passing. Over he comes with his little mate, Troy.

"We did our tree ones," says Troy. As if that would stop us grabbing them again.

"Yes I know, now I want you to do a mobile. Are you feeling better now Joe? We missed you last week."

"Yes, I had a bad throat and a cough and I had to go to bed a lot," he answers.

"Joe, come and sit down next to me," I say, pulling out the chair for him. "Troy, do you want to go and sit next to Aunty Nicky?" Joe picks up a crayon and begins colouring, no trouble at all. Nicky makes a space for Troy and we soon have a full table of workers again.

Julie says, "I need to borrow Joe for a while as he hasn't signed his Christmas card."

"Come to think of it, I don't remember doing a badge with him?" says Nicky. "Have a look at his big brown envelope for me, Wendy"

"You're right, he needs to do his furry snowman, his badge, and he also missed doing the pop-up Santa too. Having that nasty cold has meant he's way behind everyone else. When Julie's finished with him we'll have to hang on to him."

"I need him too," calls Mandy. "He's done nothing for my frieze."

After Joe has signed his card Julie passes him over to Mandy where he colours a small Christmas tree. I have collected everything he needs to make his snowman and call him back over to me again. He seems to enjoy making the snowman picture and is very pleased when I pin it on the wall for all to see. Before he could go and play Nicky calls him to make his Santa badge with her.

Joe coloured and glued and glittered, and coloured and glued some more.

"Can I go and play now?" he asks.

"Not just yet. Can we try to finish this mobile first."

"Troy's playing," he says petulantly.

"Yes I know but he has finished his work. Just colour this a bit more."

"This isn't much fun," he mumbles.

"Fun! Who said it would be fun? This is Christmas!"

Thursday 8th December

Ro is hanging the finished frieze on the wall and I notice one or two other paintings and pictures have been hung up too. I give her a hand as I pass near to her and we both step back to admire it. I see how robins, children, toboggans and the odd snow covered house have appeared on it. More extras, I think to myself, although I'm not surprised as it happens every year. But the frieze does look very, very good I have to admit, and really makes the wall look cheerful and festive. The children like to look at it too and find their pieces of work, be it a snowman or a tree, and point them out to their friends.

"Reindeer's and sleighs take priority today," says Hillary. "We managed to start quite a few yesterday and we must finish as many as we can today. I want the sleighs painted red or green and the reindeers crayoned brown."

I sit down at the prepared table and say to Hillary, "thank goodness we only have two reindeer to colour and not all eight."

Dilly is settling herself down beside me as I say this and she asks, "do all the reindeer's have names Aunty Wendy? I only know Rudolf."

"Now there's a question. I know there was Donner and Blitzen but I can't think of any others. Can you Hillary?"

"There was a Prancer as well. Hey Liz," she calls. "Do you know any more reindeer names?"

"Not off hand but I'll let you know if one comes to mind."

Oliver and Amy come over and want to sit with us too.

"What are those?" He asks pointing to a little plastic dish with small pieces of Christmas wrapping paper in.

"Those are to represent parcels and we're going to stick them onto the sleighs once they have been painted," replies Hillary. "And those shiny red dots lying in that saucer are noses for the reindeer." Then looking at us adults she reminds us that we really must remember to name all the individual pieces of work. No matter how hard we try to keep all the bits together on the table, some things are getting pushed aside or getting knocked onto the floor. And it takes so much time trying to find out who did what."

I see we have some of the Christmas tree pictures on the table too. There's also the glitter out again and some cotton wool balls to be shredded for snow, to be added anywhere we can think to put it, and a packet of gummed shapes to decorate the tree pictures with.

There are also some unfinished Christmas cards on another table, and tree decorations, all waiting to be completed, another busy day by the look of things.

There's not an awful lot of room on the tables but we cope and the children are getting used to the work, work, work idea (a case of having to, really).

The first of the sleighs are drying on a nearby ledge and we keep the children with us to colour their reindeer. Then if we can hang on to them, we persuade them to colour and decorate their Christmas trees Once the trees are complete we put them on the wall with all the other Christmas work. All of which is making the hall look very festive. If we also manage to get some tree decorations completed, they're put straight onto our tree, which is looking better by the day. All is going well.

Hillary has the camera out and is taking photographs of everything.

Poor Troy has a nasty cold, possibly picked up from his friend Joe, and he's coughing and sneezing a lot. He probably shouldn't be here but both his parents work full time and as there are so many bugs about at this time of the year most of us are sniffling anyway. He doesn't have a temperature and seems happy enough in himself. He plays and works well and at least it's warm in here and he doesn't seem unduly worried about his cold. He comes and sits down at the table with us and starts to colour his reindeer. He needs his nose wiping and I just finish this task when he sneezes. And what a sneeze! The cotton wool pieces go everywhere. His sneeze has blown paper parcels and small red noses and gummed shapes all over the place. The majority of them are blown into Liz's lap and some are clinging to the front of her jumper. There are even some in her hair and a few on her face. She looks really comical. Hillary shouts out in a flurry."Don't anybody move, I must have a photograph of this!"

Troy looks as if he's about to burst into tears and I put my arm round his shoulders and give him a small hug, and then I start laughing. I couldn't help myself.

Liz is so stunned she can't move. The children around the table don't know quite how to react for a second but are soon laughing too. Then everyone round the table is laughing including Liz. The other Aunties and the children playing in the room come over to see what's going on and it soon seems as if everyone in the hall is laughing. After the tension of the last few weeks it's a wonderful release. We decide to stop for milk and coffee and whilst the chairs are being arranged I help Liz pick bits of cotton wool and paper off her jumper and out of her hair, and try to get the usable ones back into the correct containers.

After drinks, and whilst we are still sitting, we sing a few Christmas songs.

I ask Hillary mischievously, "how long will it be before you can develop that film? I'm sure we're all eager to see this photographic evidence. Maybe we could get it enlarged, I'm sure Liz would like that," I add chuckling.

"No I wouldn't." We hear her call out.

The second half of the morning rushes by in a happy and constructive way and we complete a lot of work and all go home well pleased with ourselves but we still haven't thought of any more reindeer names.

Tuesday 13th December

As I walk into the hall today I see that Hillary has found last year's Christmas post-box and by the look of the parents and children queuing by it, it is being well used again this year. It looks a bit tatty but it is still just about fit for purpose.

The room is looking more and more colourful and Christmassy and I notice some parents are being pulled round by their children to look at their pieces of work dotted about the hall.

I find my boxful of large brown envelopes and it takes me a while to find the ones belonging to today's children, and when I do, I discover yet another new addition.

"What are these doilies doing in here?" I hear my exasperated tone say to the room.

"Good morning, Wendy," says Hillary. "Those are for making angels and before you say anything, some of the children have nearly finished all their work and will need a little something to do. It’s just a little extra and only if we really need them. I just thought...”

“I know what you thought,” I interrupt. “I’ve been here long enough to know just what you thought.” I finish off good naturedly.

I join Mandy at one of the work tables and we get stuck in again. (no pun intended) The usual glue, glitter, cotton wool, crayons, and bits of paper are arrayed ready for use. We all have our heads down working hard, encouraging and cajoling the children to glue this, colour that, sprinkle glitter, and lick shapes.

“Lick them, don't chew them.” I frequently have to remind them.

We all want them to complete their work and we all seem to be saying similar things. 'Hurry up', 'Do this', 'Do that', 'No, you can’t go to play till you’ve finished', 'Concentrate!', 'Come on now', 'Yes, you can go soon', 'Just do this bit', 'Where’s the next child?' On and on it goes.

Milk time comes and goes. We’re so pushed for time now so milk time is as quick as we can make it. We need to give ourselves maximum time to complete as much work as possible. Nicky is watching the colouring whilst cutting out shapes in the doilies and she nudges me saying quietly, “look at Eve.”

I look up and see Eve has a group of about seven or eight children all seated round the blue reading mat. We’re too far away to hear what is going on but the children are engrossed.

“What is she doing?” I say with a look of amusement.

“I don’t know.”

To most of us that blue mat is for sitting on and looking at the books. But we have known Eve transform it into a trampoline, a duck pond, a pirate ship, a magic garden, a ballet stage, well, no end of things really.

“Look! She’s got some of the children walking in a line around the edge of the mat, holding hands but with their heads bowed down. What can that be?” We keep working but watching her too. It’s fascinating.

“Look at that,” says Nicky again. “There’s a child walking across the mat diagonally, very slowly and with her arms outstretched. What is she doing?”

“Julie, Hillary,” I call quietly.” Look over at Eve. Can you work out what she’s doing? What has that mat been transformed into now?”

She seems to have two boys bending and stretching now and when they sit down, four youngsters get up and start skipping round the edge of the mat with Oliver standing in the middle watching them. We’re all mystified and can’t think what she’s thought up.

We work till the last moment and rush about trying to pack away and be ready on time, but knowing we will be late again. It’s not until all the children have left and we’re putting on our coats that we get the chance to ask Eve what she was doing.

“Doing? Doing when?” She asks puzzled.

“You had children round the mat and we want to know what you were doing,” inquires Nicky.

“Oh that,” she said, as if it were nothing. “I thought they needed a short break from all the intense work they were doing, so we were at the circus being trapeze artists, prancing horses, strongmen, elephants. In fact everything that was on the carnival float. Oh by the way, do you still want the reindeer names? I’ve got them here, I've been jotting them down as I remember them.” She rummages in her pocket and pulls out a piece of paper and reads,“they are Rudolf, Donner, Blitzen, Cupid, Prancer, Comet, Dancer, Dasher and Vixen. Bye now, I’ve got to rush.”

And with that she left. She’s a rare gem, that one.

Thursday 15th December

“There’s a lot to be done today,” says Hillary to all of us once the mums have left. As if there isn’t every other day, I find myself thinking.

“We must sort out all the Christmas cards from the post box and we must send home as much finished work as possible. I’ve brought in some carrier bags that we can name and put the children’s work into. The party is on Tuesday and we must have the work sent home by then. The scout master has said we must clear all the work from the walls and from the hallways before we leave for the Christmas break. So we must do as much of that today as we can. But I think we should leave the frieze. It will be a little bit of Christmas decoration to cheer up the walls and it won't take long to remove after the party. Every child has done some work on it and there may be some parents who will want to look at it. Any questions?"

"Yes," says Liz. "Where is the Mother Christmas costume? Mandy will need to take it home and wash it."

"What does she want that for?" I ask curiously.

"Ah! Yes, I was going to mention that in a minute," says Hillary. "We were talking yesterday and decided that we should all wear fancy dress for the party. Something Christmassy, just for a bit of fun. What do you think?"

"What, all the children?" I cry with disbelief, my mind filling with the horrors of having to find, wash, iron, alter or make so many outfits.

"No, no of course not, just us aunties and any helpers who may want to," she answers with amusement.

"That's a relief," I sigh. "Yes I'm up for it, although there's not much time to make anything too fancy. Has anyone decided what they're going to wear?"

"Come over to my desk," says Hillary. "I've got it all written down somewhere." Hillary's desk is a misnomer. It's really just another table covered in papers, money, carrier bags, odd toys, broken pencils, puzzle pieces, lists, diary, register, files, lunch-boxes, and any odd item we are handed during the day. It all gets put on there to be sorted when we get a moment. (Ha ha ha!)

"Look at that food chart," she hands it to me as she searches for the correct piece of paper. And she carries on happily, "the parents have been so keen to help they have even added on some extra items. We have a good bunch of parents this year. Oh, by the way, Mr. Holby is coming again to be our Father Christmas. He loves doing it. When I phoned him to ask if he could, he said yes he was looking forward to it. He added he was a bit worried we did not want him, as he had not heard from us earlier.

Here it is, here's the list. Now, Dawn is being the Christmas fairy. Mandy is the right size to fit into the Mrs. Christmas costume. Julie is going to be a cuddly teddy bear. One of the mums is coming as an elf and Nora says she has an advent calendar skirt."

"What's that?" I inquire.

"I had to get her to explain that one to me too. Apparently it's a skirt with twenty four net pockets and a gift in each pocket. Rather novel that, I can't wait to see it."

"I've never heard of that before but it sounds good," I agree.

She continues, "I'm hoping I can alter the once Easter-rabbit cum carnival-performing-dog-costume into a snowman. I'm sure with its ears off and some padding it will do nicely. It will be a bit short but I can put black boots on. What do you think?"

"That bit of fabric has been altered to so many things over the years we've certainly had our money's worth with it. Yes I think it'll be good and I've got a wonderful red hat that you can have," I reply.

"That's settled then, I'm defiantly going to be a snowman at the party," she answers happily, and continues, "some people don't like to dress up so I've suggested to them that perhaps they would be able to put a bit of tinsel on their heads or round their necks Or perhaps wear a reindeer headband or flashing earrings, or something a bit Christmas related just to get into the spirit of the day. So now you know. You can do as much or as little as you wish," she finishes with a grin.

Whilst we've been talking Ro and Nicky have been busy near the post box. There are little mounds of Christmas cards on the floor radiating out from the post box. There are piles of work on the floor near the window and there is a heap of carrier bags waiting to be filled.

There is a table laid out with the, now usual, glue, glitter, crayons and cotton wool in readiness to finish any pieces of work. I see Eve has a small pile of items she is trying to get the children to work on. I go to the large brown envelopes and look through them in the hope the majority are empty at last. Unfortunately there's still some work in a few of them. Liz and I join Eve and we put all the unfinished work out on the table and grab unsuspecting children as they go by and try to get as much work from them as we can.

"Can you hear crying?" I ask Liz as I turn to see where it's coming from. Dilly is walking towards us with a very unhappy Jennifer-Marie.

"Aunty Wendy," Dilly begins, "Jennifer-Marie's crying because it's her mummy's birthday and she hasn't got her a card or anything. But I told her not to worry as you will help her make one."

In the midst of all this mess and mayhem I've to stop and make a birthday card because my little friend Dilly has such faith in my abilities. Bless her. Liz, I notice, suddenly needs to keep her hand over her mouth and is coughing unconvincingly. Not trying to smother a smirk is she?

I soon have Jennifer-Marie's tears dried away and a clean sheet of card in front of us. I could only find yellow card, we seem to have used everything else. I'm wracking my brains trying to think of something quick, easy and cheerful. I know it is no use suggesting flowers as I can't draw them convincingly and neither can I disguise them as I couldn't see any tissue paper.

"What does mummy like?" I ask a slightly happier Jennifer-Marie.

After a second or two she says, "I don't know." And her bottom lip starts to quiver a little. Dilly pipes up, "my mummy likes animals." Thank you Dilly, that's given me an idea. I rush into the cupboard and find the container with all of the pictures salvaged from calendars and magazines. I suggest to Jennifer-Marie she finds some animals she thinks mummy would like and we can make a picture. She selects some she likes and we soon have an animal collage glued onto the card. The cats, dogs and budgerigars, and the little mouse she has found, all look very cute but I'm not sure about the large snail she has positioned right in the middle. I write Happy Birthday inside the card and she writes her name and puts lots of crosses at the bottom to represent kisses. It hasn't taken too long and she and Dilly happily go back to play.

The day has whizzed by again and all the children leave with a carrier bag full of their Christmas work and Christmas cards.

"Have you thought of a fancy dress costume yet?" Hillary asks me as we're putting on our coats.

"Oh gosh, I've clean forgotten that. I'll think of something. See you Tuesday, bye everyone, bye."

Tuesday 20th December

Party day! 'Have I got everything I need to take with me today?' I ask myself as I struggle downstairs with my party costume. Hillary asked me to bring in a few things and I've been putting items on my hall table as I remember them. Black rubbish sacks, balloons and pump, the children's parcels for Santa's sack, camera, gifts and cards for my friends. Milk! I must get that extra pint from the fridge.

I've just tried on my outfit upstairs in the bedroom and I'm quite pleased with my effort. I have put it by the door ready for loading into the car. I think I've got everything. On with my mackintosh and off I go.

Once at school I unload all my stuff, milk and rubbish sacks into the kitchen. The gifts for Santa's sack and my outfit into the small hall with all the other costumes. All the rest of the items I take into the main hall with me.

Even though we didn't have to get here till ten o'clock, I still managed to be a bit late. Most of the other aunties are here already and Hillary calls out, "good morning, Wendy. I see you've remembered your camera. Nicky is just phoning her husband to ask him to bring hers in. I told her she would forget her head if it wasn't attached."

I'm agreeing with her and about to make a rude comment, but as I take off my mackintosh I make an awful discovery.

"Oh no!" I screech.

"What on earth is the matter?" asks a concerned Hillary,

"I've forgotten my skirt!"I blurt out. "Under my fancy dress outfit I just wear a black jumper and thick black woollen tights. I was trying it on just before leaving and, with everything else on my mind, I've forgotten to put my skirt on."

Hillary is relieved that is all it is and can't help but laugh. Soon all the others, and me as well, are having a laugh at my stupidity and when Nicky comes back and asks what we are laughing at, Hillary tells her and it sets us all off again.

"At least I only forgot my camera!" she quips good humouredly.

There's so much to do and there really isn't time for me to go home, so I announce that I'll stay in the kitchen out of full sight, and work in there until it is time to change, if that's okay with everybody. And I add, "thank goodness, we're all girls together"

Soon all the tables are put in position. They have festive plastic cloths, paper plates and crackers quickly arranged on them. In the kitchen, I'm able to plate up the food that's been brought in already. Some of it from the aunties, and a selection of packet stuff that some of yesterday's parents bought in. These I position on the hatch and they're taken over to the tables. We have crisps and savouries, biscuits, raisins and currants, dried banana slices, satsumas, and grapes. Someone has bought in a large bag of dolly mixture sweets. Looking through the cupboards I find a stack of small dishes and pour the sweets into them. The table looks very inviting and colourful.

I soon get the kitchen organised with jugs full of cold drinks and beakers all together. The tea, coffee and cups are in another corner by the urn. There are trays in a pile and plates ready for more food. I know sandwiches are coming and also small sausages. I hope there are some small chocolate cakes coming. Those I had at the singing day were so nice.

When we've done all we can, I mention that I've brought in some balloons and a pump, thinking they would help cheer up the walls now they're so bare.

"Let's be having them then," says Hillary happily. It doesn't take long before they're blown up, and we're tying wool on them and bunching them together when the doorbell goes.

"That'll be my Rob," says Nicky. "I'll go and get my camera from him."

I can hear her asking him if he has time to come in and hang up the balloons for us. Oh no. Please be too busy Rob, I pray. I don't want him to see me like this.

"Yes that's fine," I hear him say good naturedly.

"Good, thank you," responds an enthusiastic Nicky. "I'll introduce you to everyone. You haven't seen them since the wedding and you've probably forgotten their names,"

Must you? Must you do it now? I grab two tea towels from the hatch and improvise a skirt by tucking them into the waistband of my pants, much to the amusement of the others. I just finish as Nicky pushes open the door and introduces Rob. I feel a right prawn. I'm being introduced to this young handsome chap and I'm wearing one red checked tea towel and one 'Views of Devon' tea towel. He'll not forget me.

After the introductions, he starts hanging up the balloons and we go off to put our outfits on. It's a bit of a squash in the small hall so I take myself into the disabled persons' toilet cubicle to change. At least it will have been used now after all these years. I'm dressing up as a present, a Christmas parcel. My outfit is a large cardboard box, which I have wrapped in Christmas paper. I step the box and pull it up to my ribs and then it also covers my bottom and thighs. I hold it in place with tinsel 'braces' over my shoulders. I have a large red bow in my hair to complete the ensemble. Well, it was the best I could come up with, with such little notice. I'm quite pleased with it as it's silly and different, and I think the children will like it.

We all assemble back in the main hall and admire each other's costumes and take a few photographs of each other. Rob takes a group photograph of us and we just finish when the doorbell rings again.

"Who can that be?" Asks Hillary looking at her watch. "Gosh, it's later than I thought, it must be Mr. Chips." Off she goes to answer the door.

Rob gives Nicky a quick embarrassed kiss and says he'll go now and follows Hillary out of the hall.

"Who's Mr. Chips?" I ask.

Liz is by the hall door and she says,"It's the magic man. I didn't know that was his name either, as we only ever refer to him as the magic man."

Just then he comes into the hall and calls a greeting to us all. He then takes his

case of equipment to a space Hillary indicates to him behind some of our screens.

"There are a lot of eager children outside," he tells us. So Hillary asks Dawn to man the main door and let the children in.

The children are to eat first, so we begin by seating them at the tables. I try to go back into the kitchen to carry on preparing the food which is coming in. But, I can't get through the door! I'm too wide in my box! Dawn finds this highly amusing and offers to go in my place if I take her place by the door and welcome in the party-goers. I pass bags of food and drinks into the kitchen to Dawn and to Mandy, who has joined her in there as it is getting rather busy.

I can just manage to help the children take off their coats and hang them up but when it comes to putting on party shoes, I'm useless. I can't see past this box. If I turn sideways I can see but then I can't reach. It's all very amusing to the parents and the children. I can't leave my post so I ask one of the parents to find Eve and ask her to come out to me. I explain my predicament to her and she offers to swap jobs as I can't perform this one properly.

I go into the main hall which is filling up quickly with excited and happy children. I pick up a tray of food from the hatch and carry it over to a table but I can't bend over very far. Unloading the plates from the tray onto the table is a bit hit and miss. When one selection of sandwiches slides straight off the plate directly onto the table. Hillary rushes over to take the rest from me, laughing at my awkwardness.

This is getting ridiculous.

"Aunty Wendy, will you take me to the toilet, please?"

"Oh Dilly, you do look lovely. Of course I'll take you, come on." Off we go hand in hand and she tells me she's wearing a new dress.

When we get to the toilets I find I can't get through that door either. Luckily Dilly is very able and sensible and she just gets on with things. I won't be able to do the loo runs either, I think to myself. When it comes to washing her hands I take Dilly to the roomier disabled persons' loo. Used twice in one day! We hurry back into the hall and she finds her chair and sits down.

The party food is being enjoyed and rapidly disappearing. Aunties, helpers and children alike are tucking in and having fun. I can't reach the food on the tables and have to keep asking someone to pass things to me or going over to the hatch and hoping there is still something there. I'm beginning to think being a parcel is not such a clever idea. Mind you, we all have a lot of laughs about it and the children seem to like it. About the only thing I can do is to pull the crackers with the children, assuming they pass the cracker to me.

Once the children have finished eating we take them down to the toilets, that's the royal we and excludes me. I do try to help clear the tables but I can't see what I'm doing and I have to twist into odd positions to reach anything and am more a hindrance than a help.

Earlier the screens had been put across part of the room so Mr Chips could set up his tables and things without the children seeing what was going on. Now it is time to remove them and I'm pleased to say that I am able to help with that. After they have been rolled away and the children return from the toilets, they are instructed to sit nicely on the floor. Hillary tells me to go and sit with them. Sit? I wish I could. I can't bend enough to get onto the floor and the chairs are too low too. So I perch on the edge of a table and hope no one notices. Sitting on tables is definitely against the rules in our nursery school.

The show starts and the children quieten down. Mr. Chips has been to us before and has adapted his performance for our young audience. He soon has them in the palm of his hand, in a manner of speaking. They love his show, they watch, they shout, and they squeal with delight when he produces a rabbit from nowhere. They just love it. They laugh, they clap, they shuffle forward, they point and they cheer and it's as much fun watching them as it is to watch the show.

Mr. Chips does simple magic and asks for helpers to assist him. He tries to involve as many children as he can and there's never a shortage of willing volunteers. He also models animals from balloons, deliberately allowing the balloons to deflate before he has time to tie it and allowing them to whiz around the room and managing to look fed up when it happens. The children yell for more, they're captivated by it all.

During his forty five minute show we quietly usher the parents into the hall as they arrive and seat them on rows of chairs positioned behind the children. Most of the children don't even know this has happened so enthralled are they by the show. Towards the end of his routine he tries to calm things down a little. He manages to get the children quiet by holding a conversation with his magic rabbit. And it is his magic rabbit that first hears Santa's sleigh bell.

"Shush, listen," calls out Mr. Chips. Then to his rabbit he asks with surprise in his voice. "You can hear something? What can you hear?" Then he says out loud to everyone, "can you hear a bell ringing?"

There is definitely a bell ringing nearby. Aunty Hillary gets up and indicates for the children to be quiet. She makes her way to the door. You could hear a pin drop.

She comes back after a minute or two and announces, "Father Christmas has arrived and is outside. He will come in to see you all in a short while."

The noise level goes up a notch and the talking and the fidgeting increases. Hillary calms them all down a bit and she tells them. "He will only come in if you are good. I did see he has a large sack of parcels with him. He has asked me to say that he has a gift for each of you."

The children are so excited.

Hillary keeps her voice calm and continues, "he also said he hasn't got much time as there are lots of other children he must see. He would like it if once you have your gift you find your parents and then go home and have a little rest, as you have all had such an exciting and busy day."

She then disappears into the small hall and brings out a special chair for Father Christmas to sit on. There's a different type of excitement filling the air now, expectation and joy. The other aunties position themselves in amongst the children to try to keep some kind of order and also because over the years we have witnessed differing reactions to Santa. Some children are shy of him and others are frightened and of course others are just eager to get to him. Me, I just stay perched on the table edge.

Mr. Holby walks into the room. He has been our Santa for years now and he 'Ho, Ho, Ho's' his way over to the chair, waving and smiling at everyone. The children are excited and start calling out.

"Hello everybody, hello. Happy Christmas," he booms out jovially. "I've got lots of parcels here. If you'll all quieten down a bit, I'll start to give them out."

He takes the top parcel from the sack and asks, "is Arthur here?"

Arthur is up on his feet in a flash and he boldly marches up to Santa saying, "I'm Arfur." Many of the parents like to photograph the moment that their child is next to Santa. Mr. Holby looks up quickly and if he spots a camera pointing his way he will positions the child in the right place for a good picture. He does this almost effortlessly and it is so appreciated by the parents. It takes a while to work his way through all the seventy odd children and he tries to give each child a little of his time but without holding up the proceedings too much. He's a marvel and so good with the children. If a child is a little shy, one of the aunties tries to help, and between us all, the process is accomplished. Once a child has a gift we encourage the parents to take them home. This helps clear the room and also eases the congestion in the cloakroom.

I move over to stand by the hall door and only allow the children out if they have their parent or an adult with them.

I see Dilly talking to all of the aunties and as she and her mum come towards me, I see she is clutching her unopened gift. She says, "goodbye Aunty Wendy and Happy Christmas." She has been a delightful child to know.

Oliver too, comes over to say goodbye to us. The change in him has been remarkable. His mother recently told Hillary that half his problems were to do with food additives. His starting here and being able to stay here had helped him too. He has made some little friends and has settled in nicely. The routine of coming here and being happy and the health worker suggesting a change of diet has all helped to make a calmer, happier Oliver and a calmer and happier home for everyone. Everyone has benefited and now that they were watching his diet closely, he is a different boy altogether.

Hillary talks to Oliver's mother explaining how we all tried to discourage him from eating some of he foods she had told us he reacts too, but maybe a few were eaten. Her reply was, "as long as he has had an enjoyable afternoon, we really don't mind. And thank you all for being so kind and patient with him."

That was so nice.

The hall is noticeably quieter now and there are only a few more children left to see Santa, one of which is Joe. At last his name is called and his mother takes a couple of photographs of him and Santa. Then he walks over to me and says, "I have asked Aunty Hillary if I can have a photograph of all the aunties, so can you come now?"

As there are so few people left in the hall, I close the door and join the others. We all jostle together, with Joe in the front of us. That should be a good photograph for the album.

At last every child and parent has gone. Hillary puts the kettle on and announces that we all deserve a cup of tea before we go. We put away the tables, stack the chairs, sweep the floor and put all the rubbish in the bin outside. That is the 'royal we' again. Everyone is working hard except me. I did manage to help to get the frieze off the wall, so I did help a little bit. Being a parcel wasn't such a bad idea after all.

I notice I have only three more pictures to take to use up the film in my camera, so after we've had our tea, I take a couple more photos while we are still in our costumes. We wish each other Happy Christmas and exchange gifts and cards and are all ready to call it a day.

I go into the disabled person's loo, for a third time in one day, and remove my box and put on my mackintosh ready to go.

I return to the main hall to say goodbye and call out, "Happy Christmas everyone and see you next year."

Did I really say that? I can't believe I said that. Am I really going to put myself through all this again next year?

END OF TERM

Printed in Poland
by Amazon Fulfillment
Poland Sp. z o.o., Wrocław